# THE SIXTH MAN
# AND OTHER STORIES

*Recent Titles by the Author from Severn House*

DOUBLE JEOPARDY
FORGET IT
KING'S FRIENDS
THE LAST ENEMY
HEAR ME TALKING TO YOU
TIP TOP

# THE SIXTH MAN
# AND OTHER STORIES

## Bill James

This first world edition published in Great Britain 2006 by
SEVERN HOUSE PUBLISHERS LTD of
9–15 High Street, Sutton, Surrey SM1 1DF.
This first world edition published in the USA 2006 by
SEVERN HOUSE PUBLISHERS INC of
595 Madison Avenue, New York, N.Y. 10022.

British Library Cataloguing in Publication Data

James, Bill, 1929-
    The sixth man and other stories. - (The Harpur & Iles series)
    1.  Harpur, Colin (Fictitious character) - Fiction
    2.  Iles, Desmond (Fictitious character) - Fiction
    3.  Police - Great Britain - Fiction
    4.  Detective and mystery stories, English
    I.  Title
    823.9'14 [F]

    ISBN-13: 978-0-7278-6438-3  (cased)
    ISBN-10: 0-7278-6438-6      (cased)
    ISBN-13: 978-0-7278-9181-5  (paper)
    ISBN-10: 0-7278-9181-2      (paper)

Except where actual historical events and characters are being described
for the storyline of this novel, all situations in this
publication are fictitious and any resemblance to living persons
is purely coincidental.

*All Severn House titles are printed on acid-free paper.*

Typeset by Palimpsest Book Production Ltd.,
Polmont, Stirlingshire, Scotland.
Printed and bound in Great Britain by
MPG Books Ltd., Bodmin, Cornwall.

# Contents

## Publication History

'Going Straight': original

'The Sixth Man': original

'Elsewhere': *Crime In The City*, collection compiled by Martin Edwards for the Crime Writers' Association, Do Not Press, 2002; *Ellery Queen Mystery Magazine*, August 2003

'For Information Only': *Winter's Crimes 24*, edited by Maria Rejt, Macmillan, 1992, *EQMM*, September 1994

'War Crime': *Ellery Queen Mystery Magazine*, April 1994; *Midwinter Mysteries 4*, edited by Hilary Hale, Little Brown, 1994

'Free Enterprise': original

'Body Language': *Winter's Crimes 23*, edited by Maria Rejt, Macmillan, 1991; *EQMM*, January 1995

'Rendezvous One': adapted from *The Girl With The Long Back* by Bill James, Constable 2003

'Fancy': *Culprit*, edited by Liza Cody, Michael Z. Lewin and Peter Lovesey for the Crime Writers' Association, Chatto, 1994

'Big City': *16 Stories By Famous Authors*, compiled by Jason Cheriton, Chancellor Press, 1995; *Big Issue*, August 2000; *Ellery Queen Mystery Magazine*, April 2002; *Best British Mysteries*, edited by Maxim Jakubowski, Allison and Busby, 2003; *Big Book of Cardiff*, Seren-Books, 2005

'Like an Arrangement': *Men From Boys*, edited by John Harvey, Heinemann, 2003. Adapted from *The Girl With The Long Back* by Bill James, Constable 2003

'At Home': extended from an idea in *Making Stuff Up* by Bill James, Severn House 2006

'A Bit of Eternity': original

'Night Light': original

'Emergency Services': original

# Going Straight

I wear head-waiter's tails by choice:
these orderly, lickspittle years.
Most mornings I take breakfast late
and read the *Mail*. Last night came lordly
praise with routine, folded note
aggrandisement in tens, and hand to hand;
'Oh, thank you, sir.'

Blurred happiness can be arranged
some afternoons. Those mid-life taints
of fright and safety-first slide off.
Pub lunchtime vodkas work the trick,
plus snorts of something fine at home;
a man-sized, healing coma for a time;
then flunkydom.

'No other maître-d takes care
of us as well as you, Jerome.'
'Oh, thank you, sir.' Fresh pocketable
sweeteners flow my kow-tow way
A time ago, I'd do their mansions—
burglarize with tact when they dined out,
no bulky stuff.

I wear head-waiter's tails by choice:
my rectified, lickspittle years.
And after – sleeping prim till late—
I dream-do crimes. Work nights bring lordly
praise and nothing like enough
aggrandisement: we're stung for tax on tips;
'Oh, thank you, sir.'

# The Sixth Man

The thing about Assistant Chief Constable Desmond Iles, as many knew by now, was that at funerals he could get really a bit out of proportion. This one coming up today after the crossfire killing: dicey, dicey, dicey, Harpur thought. It had big overtones and Iles loved overtones, danced and dreamed to them. Consider: a middle-aged, born-again factory worker, out ardently slipping salvation gospel tracts through people's letter boxes on his afternoon off, gets somehow in the way of a motorized turf battle between drugs firms and picks up two .38 bullets in the back. And a spread of spent bullets around, as well as those that hit him. Iles would scent chaos: this victim, born-again but dead. Did it *look* like salvation? Harpur himself scented chaos. Iles would love to sound off to folk in funeral pews a bit about chaos, and more than a bit.

As an additional element, sure to disturb the Assistant Chief, this shooting took place very close to the spot where a young, cheery, ethnic girl, rather favoured by him, had her beat, and he would fret in a very Iles style of fretting about the danger she, also, might have been in. Iles used to meet her down there on waste ground now and then, in change-every-time, by-the-hour hire cars, for anonymity. Part of Harpur's job was to know about anonymities.

At certain funerals following criminal violence, a police presence might be necessary as a public relations duty. It indicated concern and sympathy. Harpur always hated going with the ACC, whether the service happened at a church or chapel or the crematorium direct, but felt he must be handy in case some kind of restraint were needed against Iles so as to preserve reasonable calm. After all, Harpur considered it more or less obvious that funerals should have dignity, decorum. They could be ticklish events for him. Although only a Detective Chief Superintendent, he might be required to curb and lull a superior officer while eyed aghast by the congregation and minister, possibly in parts of a church that would reasonably be considered special, such as the pulpit.

Actually, 'such as the pulpit' would not really do in describing these crises. If Harpur had to reach him, and apply a degree of quietening, repressive force, it would nearly *always* be because Iles had decided to bulk out the proceedings with a personal, extra sermon, and had somehow taken over the pulpit – or its equivalent in fundamentalist meeting halls. Then, at least until Harpur's intervention with muscle and/or pleas for sense, the Assistant Chief could not be persuaded out and/or silenced. Now and then at tragic funerals he would weep thoroughly; weep blatantly and noisily before he gave an address. Today's was unquestionably a tragic funeral. There'd been bloodied tracts on the pavement. Sometimes during these episodes, Iles would slander the Home Secretary for the national state of things leading to the death, or the Prime Minister, or the Trinity, or his mother and aunts, or school attendance officers, or all of the above, or permutations. Often he slandered himself and, of course, Harpur. Generally, these onslaughts came over impressively via a pulpit microphone and amplifying system. Failing these, Iles bayed.

Naturally, he would try to fight off Harpur, or anyone else who turned physical in an attempt to suppress him: say, a vicar, if he/she thought Iles's behaviour had become too wild. The ACC was not big, but possessed craftiness and knew head-butting well from way back in his career. Always, it had seemed especially unkempt to Harpur for someone to head-butt in a place of worship, whether he, Harpur, was on the end of it, or somebody else. Against anyone who opposed or attacked him, Iles could summon an abnormal weight of momentary but true loathing, especially against Harpur, on account not just of immediate irritation, but that past chapter with the ACC's wife. These reserves of hatred seemed to help increase Iles's hideous strength and, more often than not, gave his lips true froth during tussles. He usually went to funerals in full dress uniform, and that made him additionally ferocious, unhinged and malevolent, as though

3

convinced he should live up to the high-grade cloth, Queen's Police Medal ribbon, superb black lace-ups and insignia of his rank.

This funeral, then, Harpur considered could be one of the worst: one of the worst, that is, from the Iles aspect. Harpur guessed that, to describe the death, Iles would have been rehearsing some of his favourite terms, such as 'symbolic', 'ironic' and 'encapsulates', for any pastoral chat he might choose to offer. If he turned to abuse of one or several or all of his targets, the words might be 'slimy', 'smug', 'somnolent', 'supine'. Yesterday, Harpur suggested to him – hopelessly – that it would be wise, in view of the extraordinary tensions, to send someone of lower rank to represent them – for instance, Chief Inspector Francis Garland. 'How about thinking of it for once from *my* angle, sir,' Harpur had said.

'Which angle would that be, then, Col?'

'Well, it could be stressful. If you become – I mean, I might have to do another grapple, and—'

'My soul's involved here, Harpur,' Iles replied.

'That's what I'm getting at, sir.'

'What?'

'The buzz will be around.'

'Which buzz is that, then, Col?'

'Re your soul, sir,' Harpur said. 'People will tell one another: "This funeral: another Mr Iles soul session."'

'I do try not to make too much of it – my soul. Showiness one abhors. Performances one detests.'

'But people already know you can be very souly, sir. You're famed for it. Probably it's on your Personnel dossier. "Deeply souly." People will realise you're likely to become uncontrollably moved . . . well . . . even berserked by the funeral, so we'll get an enormous crowd there, sightseers, not just mourners, gawking in case you put on one of your perf . . . in case your soul takes over again in that tremendous way it has. The shouting, the arc of armpit sweat, the alliteration.'

'I must go,' Iles replied. '*We* must go.' They had talked in the ACC's suite at headquarters. Harpur occupied a leather armchair. Iles paced. He liked to concentrate on nimbleness. There was a long wall-mirror near the door for him to check his appearance in civvies or uniform before going out. Harpur noticed Iles kept his eyes away from that now, though, which must signal he had bad feelings again about how his Adam's apple looked. The ACC regarded his Adam's apple as part of a skilfully focused, foul genetic joke against him. He had on one of his navy blazers, plus narrow-cut, dark grey flannel trousers to do his legs justice, and what might be a rugby club tie. He said: 'This funeral demands me, Col. My presence. Well, our.'

'I—'

'Unignorable, Col. This death, this pyre – unignorable.'

'I—'

'Oh, you'll reply, "It was merely someone accidentally peppered in a gang spat."'

'Well, no, I don't think I would ever . . . I see nothing "merely" about any death, sir. It's just that, perhaps as far as the funeral goes, we—'

'People, Col. You mentioned *people*.'

'Is that OK?'

'People in relation to my soul.'

'Very much so.'

'They're an interesting entity, Harpur.'

'Who?'

'People.'

'Absolutely sir, but—'

'Yes, it's a fact, Col. Out there, where they immemorially are, people do seem fascinated by me.'

'Patent, sir.'

'Many would like an, as it were, glance *into* my soul.'

'I've heard more than one express this longing,' Harpur said.

'How many more?'

'Or a desire to know you in what they call "the round". They wonder what you're like "in the round".'

'It's something I by no means understand.'

'What, sir?' Harpur replied.

'This . . . well, yes, I don't think this exaggerates . . . this fascination.'

'That's because of your astonishing flair for self-effacement and—'

5

'Much less do I actually *seek* their fascination, Col.'

'Few would accuse you of that, sir.'

'Which fucking few, Harpur?' The ACC stared from this third-floor window down on to passers-by in the street, as though some of that disgusting few might be there, conspiring. In a while he turned back: 'Let me ask: what was that poor sod doing when wiped out, Col?'

'This has been thoroughly covered in the reports, sir.'

'I know, I know. You see it's symbolic, do you, Harpur?'

'Symbolic?'

'You spot the irony?'

'Irony, sir?'

'These are terms that always confuse your struggling little mind, don't they? But I certainly absolve you of blame for this. I think of that bloody nothing school you went to.'

'Someone was shot,' Harpur replied.

'Let me ask again: what was this poor sod doing when wiped out?'

'Religious tract deliveries on Valencia Esplanade and in the side streets.'

'Exactly, Col. And that is surely why we must be at the funeral. This death – I have described it as symbolic. Yes, I think so. This death – I have described it as ironic, painfully ironic. Yes, I think so. Doesn't it tell of our times, Harpur? Yes, tell of our dismal, sickening times. A man, Walter Rainsford Lonton, devotedly, pro-actively taking religion to householders, blasted suddenly by thugs. Anarchy? Hellishness? Barbarism triumphant? Forgive me, do, Col, but here's another one you may have heard me use before and been baffled by – "encapsulates?" It's a word. You'll find it in the dictionary. For me, this shooting *encapsulates* appalling social decline, moral decline. It's happening every-where, Harpur, accelerating.'

Symbolic. Ironic. Encapsulates. Yes, Harpur feared these perennial insights would almost certainly pop up if Iles went into his standard mode at the funeral and splurged some bounteous, thudding, possibly actionable, bum oratory. Iles liked fixing a worldwide significance to limited local inci-dents and crises. It could be a tic taken from the former Chief Constable, Mark Lane, who'd always feared universal disintegration might begin on his patch from some seemingly limited local incident and crisis. A doorstepping, part-time missionary holed by two .38 bullets in the back would constitute such a seemingly limited local incident and crisis. Iles saw endless ramifications. Perhaps all officers who made it to Staff College had this habit of bumper-size thinking banged into them. Iles used to mock Mark Lane for his dreads. Now, though, the ACC seemed to echo them.

'But then again, I don't suppose you suffer much anxiety about social decline, moral decline, Harpur,' Iles said. His voice shifted upwards towards an agony scream or screech-owl cry. Harpur took a few steps across the room and checked the door had been properly closed. This was routine when Iles seemed on his way to a reminiscence interlude. Headquarters staff would hang about the corridor outside Iles's suite if they knew he was talking privately to Harpur, in case they could eavesdrop one of the Assistant Chief's fits. Iles said: 'Social decline, moral decline – they couldn't have mattered much to you when giving one to my wife in bedbug hotels, vehicles – including possibly even official police vehicles – and, I wouldn't be surprised, on industrial canal tow-paths.'

'How's your nice leggy friend down Valencia Esplanade, sir?' Harpur replied.

'Honorée? Troubled. A kind of superstition has crept in. Fears the Esplanade area's jinxed. She likes to work other sites since the shooting.'

'We think we've got several decent leads on the people involved, sir,' Harpur replied. 'Some locals, some not.'

'My faith in you is total, Col.' the Assistant Chief said.

'Thank you, sir.'

'As to the job, I mean, Harpur.'

In fact, Iles behaved with great and sustained sweetness at the funeral. For Harpur, the proceedings turned out significant, not on account of any outbursts by the ACC, but because suddenly, from behind, someone, a male, muttered, very close to Harpur's ear, 'I guessed you and Ilesy would be here, so took a chance. Number Three. Ten tonight.'

This was at the very end. The coffin had left for the crem and a general shifting about among the congregation began

7

as people edged from their seats towards the aisles, making for the door. The place was as crowded as Harpur had expected, so this dispersal took a while. Harpur did not turn to see the man who'd whispered. Unnecessary. And it might have been unwise. Of course, he recognized the voice. Although it stayed low, and had to compete with an organ finale, Harpur knew who'd spoken to him in the throng. And, of course, he understood the message.

Iles had, indeed, given an address, but by invitation, and he made it short and heartfelt. Today, in Harpur's opinion, the Assistant Chief could be regarded by almost anyone fair-minded as virtually decent and stable, even an asset, regardless of previous form at such functions. Iles referred to the 'terrible symbolic impact' and 'grim, searing irony' of Lonton's death. But he ditched 'encapsulates'. This, after all, was a Gospel Hall service, and the congregation mainly ordinary people whose education might have been as ramshackle as Harpur's. Iles, gazing out upon them, taking their tone, probably realized that 'encapsulates' would sound fruity here. Iles could be surprisingly sensitive if you had time to wait.

Gospel Halls ran without clergy or ministers, and the funeral was conducted by a gruff, middle-aged man in a black jacket and silver pinstriped trousers. After he had preached from the platform about Lonton and his certainty of heaven, he asked if anyone else wished to say something. Iles hesitated. It astonished Harpur, but he detected a definite, as if modest, reluctance: perhaps Iles recognized the salt-of-the-earth qualities in this congregation and would not impose on it any of his mad monkeying and egomaniac slobber: witness, later, that editing out of 'encapsulates'. The simplicity, plainness, unpretentiousness of Gospel Halls might be new to him. Not to Harpur: he'd been sent to Sunday School at one as a child. He remembered emulsion-painted walls similar to these, adorned only with large-letter Bible verses.

The ACC went forward eventually and climbed on to the platform. He'd brought with him a couple of Lonton's tracts, mud-stained from the pavement and blood-flecked. Iles held them up for a time, and then read aloud the text from their front page: 'It is appointed unto men once to die and after this the judgement.' Iles nodded. 'Harpur will do what he can about the judgement.' Afterwards, the Assistant Chief remained up near the top end of the Hall until everything finished, and then talked there for a while with some of the family.

Back home, Harpur found his two daughters had watched television news coverage of the cortège. 'Some of them at school say police can't keep the streets safe any longer,' Hazel told him.

'Who at school?' Harpur replied.

'You want names? You want me to fink?'

'I mean, pupils or staff?' Harpur said.

'Which would worry you more?' Hazel replied.

'Neither. They'd both be wrong,' he said.

'My friends say it,' Hazel replied.

'Staff as well, I expect,' Harpur said.

'I hate it when people say rotten things about you, Dad,' Jill told him.

'I've heard worse,' Harpur replied.

'Dad, listen, I think you ought to pack something,' Jill said.

'We don't talk like that,' Harpur said.

'Like what?' Jill asked.

'"Pack something", of course,' Hazel said. 'Do you know how dim you sound, a thirteen-year-old, with words pinched from cop dramas – corny, ancient, reshown TV cop dramas?'

'I think dad should have a gun,' Jill said. 'OK? What do the all-wise and wonderful fifteen-year-old and her all-wise and wonderful friends feel about that, then?'

'*Have* you lost control of the streets, Dad? Valencia Esplanade is "No Go?"' Hazel asked.

'Of course he hasn't lost control of the streets,' Jill bellowed at her, half about to cry. 'Or he wouldn't if he packed something. It's obvious. I think he should look after himself. You should look after yourself, Dad. People blasting from cars. What could you do? What could this poor Holy Joe do? He'd got some bits of paper. What's the use of them?'

'You sound like the US gun lobby: bang-bangs for everyone,' Hazel said.

'Not for everybody. For Dad.'

'I have to go out later,' Harpur replied. 'I might be late. Lock up properly and turn in.' He single-parented since Megan's terrible death[*], and found it a strain sometimes.

'Go out where?' Hazel said.

'Work,' Harpur replied.

'Is it?' Hazel asked.

'Yes,' Harpur said.

'Of course it is,' Jill said.

'What work?' Hazel asked.

She liked to keep track of his morals. 'Routine,' Harpur said.

'Is this a one-to-one with a grass, for example?' Jill said.

'Routine,' Harpur replied.

'You ought to pack something,' Jill said.

'And we don't call them grasses,' Harpur said. Of course, everyone *did* call them grasses, but the term seemed wrong from a child. 'Informants, Jill.'

'What's the difference?' she asked. 'Informants grass, don't they, the same as grasses grass? Wasn't there a song – "Why Do You Whisper Green Grass?"'

'No police force could run without informants,' Harpur said. 'They are valuable and often brave people.'

'I didn't say they weren't, did I? I only said they grass.'

'"Grass" makes them sound contemptible,' Harpur said.

'So?' Jill replied.

And, yes, it *was* for a one-to-one with an informant that Harpur left them at about 9.30 p.m., perhaps the greatest grass Harpur had ever met. Perhaps the greatest grass any detective had ever met. When Harpur did meet him, it had to be in reliable secrecy. Grasses could lose limbs for grassing, could get killed for grassing. Among villains, grassing rated as easily the greatest villainy, maybe the *only* villainy. Harpur made for an old concrete block house on the foreshore, built during the war to help throw the Germans back into the sea if they ever tried it on, and still standing. Harpur reached it just before ten o'clock. Jack Lamb was already there. Lamb seemed to like this spot best of their carefully varied rendezvous points, their Number Three, as he'd called it at the funeral.

---

[*] *Roses, Roses.*

It was dark, and darker inside the windowless block house. An occasional flash of moon poked through a loophole when the clouds cleared for a few minutes. Jack had on what might be a cavalry officer's 'bum-freezer' greatcoat, designed for when cavalry meant horses, not tanks, and cut deliberately short, like a riding jacket. Jack stood six foot five and weighed over two hundred and fifty pounds, so there was a lot of bum to freeze. He also wore a green Commando beret, with some large badge on it, which Harpur could not identify in the darkness. Whenever they came to Three, Lamb liked to wear army surplus clobber, in keeping. In each hand tonight he carried a brown briefcase, perhaps also once military. These cases looked well-filled, as if he would soon be off to brief Eisenhower for D-Day. Jack put both on the filthy concrete floor, opened them and brought out six automatic pistols, which he laid alongside one another on the leather. Harpur thought they might be 9 mm Walthers.

'As to the Walter Rainsford Lonton aftermath, you'll need these, Col,' he said. 'You've got to pack something.'

'I keep getting told that.'

'Because it's right. Who by?'

'It's well intentioned,' Harpur replied.

'Of course it's well intentioned. Tooling up – vital at this stage.'

'That right, Jack? Which stage?'

'You've got to recruit a little private army – you and if poss five others.'

'That right, Jack?'

'I don't want a big mob of police.'

'Where don't you want a big mob of police?' Harpur said.

'Just you and a nice, capable, small team. And in such clandestine circumstances, you won't be able to draw official police weapons, will you?'

'Hardly.'

'So, I supply. They're all loaded, of course.'

'Of course.'

'Fifteen-round magazine,' Lamb said. 'Good firepower.'

'Yes, I know.'

'At one time, the police used Walthers, I think.'

'Some are still around,' Harpur replied.

11

'Reliable. Stoppers.'

Lamb, like some other informants, *most* other informants, went in for an amount of mystification when they presented their stuff. They let the material out slowly, perhaps to make it seem more, and so qualify for bigger cash; perhaps just as a playful, theatrical exercise by creating suspense and curiosity. With Jack, it would be the second. He did not have to worry about money. But he did enjoy acknowledgement and admiration. By puzzling Harpur and then gradually making things clear for him, Jack must feel he'd come over as abnormally bright and kindly. And it was true, he *was* abnormally bright, despite the beret. Even kindly.

Jack Lamb now did as he usually did and crouched for a while at one of the rifle apertures, gazing at what he could see of the sea, ready to take on anything Mr Hitler could chuck at him.

'What Lonton aftermath?' Harpur said.

'You know what happened there, do you?' Jack said. He abandoned his sentinel stint and came and stood over the pistols.

'He took two stray bullets,' Harpur said. 'Walter Rainsford Lonton had God on his side, most likely, but not luck.'

'Somebody in one of the cars mistook him and panicked.'

'Mistook him for what?'

'There were two cars,' Lamb replied.

'That we know. Four people.'

'It was to be a simple but ample deal. One car brought packets of substance – a lot of packets. The other brought cash, a lot of cash. There should have been a swap. Yes, simple, but also, as you'd expect, very nervy, very excitable. These are people who live with two-timing and rough tricks.'

Ritualistically and uselessly, Harpur would always ask Jack where his information came from. Ritualistically Jack, like any other purposeful whisperer, always ignored this. Sources stayed secret, or next time there would be no sources. There might be no Jack, either, if he ever disclosed too much, or anything, about those who disclosed to him. When Jack told you something you'd better believe it, and you'd better be content with that. 'Who've you been in touch with, Jack?'

'On the day, one of them in one of the cars, or perhaps

more than one and in both cars, sees Lonton flitting between houses and assumes he's some sort of look-out and is alerting hit squads standing by behind a couple of front doors to dash out at the crux moment and hijack everything – substance and cash. Anyway, somebody opens fire on Lonton . . .'

'So *not* accidental, not just trapped in crossfire?' Harpur said.

'They open fire deliberately on him, and would have on anyone else who appeared from the houses, if anyone had, which, as we know, nobody did, because Lonton was a total innocent. The noise of firing convinces some of the others they're being attacked – that an attempted snatch of the substances or cash is under way – so, of course, they retaliate. But as far as I've discovered, neither car has injuries.'

'I don't know,' Harpur said.

'Both cars finally pull away. Only Lonton is left.'

'So who, Jack? In the cars.'

'No names, or you'll go and pick them up now and charges might not stick. I want them done as they are doing what they do. They'll come back. They won't let a botch muck up their trade, not trade of this scale.'

'I—'

'Look, Col, I only give tip-offs when I think people have acted with real vileness and disregard. I'm not a mouth for mouthing's sake.'

'Absolutely.' Harpur had listened often to Jack's gospel of grassing. It was important for Lamb to feel all right about what he did. No money went to him for his help, but neither did Harpur ever ask too much about the rich art business Jack ran. That's how the arrangement worked, and overall it worked well.

'I consider it monstrous to knock over an amateur apostle on his divine rounds,' Jack said. 'All right, an error, but people so jumpy shouldn't be out with guns. So jumpy they can't even hit one other.'

'They hit Lonton.'

'I wonder how many shots it took. Did you recover other bullets?

'A quantity,' Harpur said.

'A ton?'

'We're still searching.'

'This kind of cruel, blast-off craziness – I see it as a symptom of something rotten nationally, Col. And it deteriorates.'

'Mr Iles says that.'

'There you are, then.'

'He can get things right sometimes,' Harpur replied.

'Yes, they'll come back,' Jack said.

'The buyers and sellers?'

'That's part of their brazenness, part of the general rottenness. This is commerce, Col. This is gorgeous livelihoods, Col. A bit of a shoot-out, a mistaken shoot-out, can't be allowed to stop the free flow of merchandise – dirty merchandise, but merchandise. Yes, they'll come back, not to that particular bit of ground, obviously. But I can point you the right way.'

'How the hell do you know this, Jack?'

'You, plus trusted pals – pals able to handle a Walther – will be waiting. Not a full-scale swarm operation, please. Now, *please*. Leaks can happen when too many are in the know. The business would be called off. And they'd guess how police came to find out about the new plans, the new site. How? Me. Too perilous, Col. You and your picked group can certainly manage them.'

'How many?'

'Probably four again, two in each car. You'll outnumber. You'll have surprise.'

'I hope.'

'A big BMW. A big Volvo. These are a switch from previously. They're not going to risk the same transport, are they, especially as their previous cars might be damaged? But I've got registration numbers for you. Can you call on some good, discreet boys?' He put an encouraging, huge palm on Harpur's shoulder: 'But of course you can, Col.'

'Francis Garland as a start. Yes, I'll be all right.'

'And as long as you scoop them all up—'

'—it won't matter if they work out who sold them,' Harpur said.

'I don't like "sold".'

'Sorry. Let's amend: It won't matter if they work out who *scuppered* them,' Harpur replied.

14

'Because they won't be around to do anything about it.'

'You want the Walthers back afterwards?' Harpur asked.

'Not if they've been used. Police can prove all sorts from a used gun. But you probably know that already.'

As it would turn out, only one of the Walthers was eventually used, and, a little later than eventually, Harpur committed that to the river. He returned the rest to Jack at a subsequent short and joyful debriefing session at Number Three.

Harpur had found he could recruit four helpers, including Garland, not five. The pool to draw on was small. He wanted good marksmen ready to believe they'd be passably safe, regardless: passably safe, regardless, from the crews they had to stalk; and passably safe, regardless, from superior ranks after running an uncleared shooting romp. Harpur considered that to convince four in the circumstances might be good going. Luckily, so luckily, one of them was Garland's sergeant, Vic Callinicos, an esteemed marvel with handguns. In the swoop, when it came he fired ahead twice from out of the passenger window of a Citroën moving fast over uneven ground after shots aimed at them from the Volvo and the BMW. Their shots missed. Vic's didn't.

Harpur's interception platoon were in the Citroën and a Ford, both unmarked. They'd waited and watched in the dark, unnoticeable among a string of parked cars on the road bordering a public open sports field. This had been specified by Lamb at the block house as the new transaction site. A Vauxhall and a Peugeot already stood at one end of the field, probably immaterial. Harpur thought they could be love buggies: a soccer ground in the day, nooky at night. Jack had said to expect the target cars between ten thirty p.m. and eleven. At ten fifty, the Volvo, its registration spot-on, arrived and waited. It was at a distance, but near enough for them to hear that the driver kept its engine running. At two minutes to eleven the BMW came to a stop by the Volvo.

In the Citroën, Harpur said, 'We go now.' He drove, with Vic Callinicos alongside him. Harpur took the car up over the kerb and pavement and on to the grass. The Ford with Garland in charge followed. They had fix-on blue lamps and got them going at once. Garland also carried a loudspeaker in the Ford and began yelling: 'Armed Police, Armed Police, get out with your hands up.' Despite this din and the cars' engine roar, Harpur heard shots from the BMW and Volvo, and heard Vic Callinicos's reply. He saw the driver of the BMW pitch forward against the windscreen and the man in the Volvo passenger seat lurch to his right. In a minute the Citroën had reached the BMW and Harpur braked and jumped out. He had a Walther in each jacket pocket and produced one of them now, and started howling the 'Armed Police' advertisement himself. You could valve off some of the fear that way. He was on the driver's side of the BMW, its window down. With his free hand, he was about to pull the door open when the man in the passenger seat leaned across behind the body of the driver and blurted: 'All right, all right. Here,' and threw a Browning pistol out through the window. When Harpur did open the door, the driver's body tumbled on to the field and covered the Browning. Harpur got a grip on the front passenger's arm and dragged him out. Harpur did not recognize either of them: a supply firm from away, most likely. The packages were very neatly laid out right the way across the back seat. As Jack had said, a lot.

At the Volvo, too, resistance stalled, though the engine kept going. Vic could not only shoot, he could identify the right ones to shoot to neutralize an enemy. When Harpur went to that car, he found he did know these men, the alive and the dead: Karl Dane, arrested, and Joshua Tive-Amory, both local, both very small small-timers until now. So, perhaps Lamb's and Iles's joint theory of a fast-widening threat stood up. Garland handcuffed the two survivors to the BMW steering wheel while a money search of their clothes and the Volvo went on. Dane said: 'Who the fuck sold us then, Mr Harpur?'

'*Sold* you?' Harpur said.

'You had us surrounded, didn't you. Four fucking cars here to swamp us. Major planning. Who sold us?'

'Just two, the Ford and the Citroën,' Harpur said. 'All we needed for such a soft job. The other two cars are not ours. A bit of rudimentary guesswork told us you'd be back.'

'I don't believe it,' Dane said.

'You'd better believe it,' Harpur replied. And he decided,

then, that he ought to make sure the people in those original two parked cars were all right. Salvoes had flown tonight,
who knew where? The Vauxhall moved off fast as Harpur
approached. Somebody, or some pair, or even some trio,
hetero perhaps, homo perhaps, mixed perhaps, didn't wish
to get sucked into this scene. He memorized the registration
all the same, in case they'd do as witnesses.

In the back seat of the second, the Peugeot, he now recognized Iles and his friend Honorée, efficiently getting themselves back into presentable shape. Iles lowered a window
and said: 'Perhaps I mentioned previously, Col, that Honorée
wanted a change of location following the Lonton business.
Well, I'm not sure this *is* better, after all, are you? I think
we took a shot through the driver's door and into the upholstery. One might have been sitting there, you know, Harpur.'

'Probably you're a back seat person in fields, sir.'

'How about you give me the Walther, Harpur?' Iles replied.
'It will look to the rest of them as if I'd been duly notified
of this operation – and I should, should, and *should*, have
been duly notified of this operation, holding the position, as
you'll recall, of Assistant Chief (Operations) – and so, having,
we'll imagine, been notified of it, decided to contribute in
a personal, armed capacity. That would make the illicitness
of this more or less all right, I feel. And the car hirer can
then charge headquarters for the bullet trouble to his car.'

'The illicitness of what, sir?' Harpur replied. 'You mean
you and Honorée having a—'

'Let's go and chat to the baddies and their captors, shall
we, Col?' Iles left the car and he and Harpur walked towards
the BMW and the Volvo. Iles paused, and Harpur paused
with him. The ACC said: 'Sly and eternal thicko, when I
call it illicit, I mean, of course, you running a damn secret,
unapproved, cordite campaign in which I might have got my
balls shot off. But fortunately, now this has become an official police victory, with the Assistant Chief a participant. I
think we can swing that. It's why I wanted your Walther.
Authenticity. But, all right, if you object, I'll—'

'I have a spare Walther, sir.'

'There we are then,' Iles replied.

Harpur gave him the pistol intended by Jack for the sixth

17

man. Iles would do as the sixth man. 'It has to be handed back later.'

'Handed back to whom?' Iles said.

'Will Honorée disappear while we're over here, sir, with the task force, prisoners and deads? That the idea? She can sneak away to the road and a cab?'

'Disappear? Of course she won't disappear, Col. This is a fine and precious girl. This is plainly a girl I brought with me as cover. If you're masquerading as an *amour* car for the purpose of ambush, you need to have a girl with you, don't you, Harpur? She's like a theatrical prop, isn't she? It's called verisimilitude. You'll find that one in the dictionary, too.'

'I hadn't thought of cover as an explanation for her, sir.'

'Don't get despondent. I can think for both of us, Col. It's a habit.'

'I haven't had time to congratulate you on the funeral, sir. You were very measured, if I may say.'

'I think you may. I appreciated the setting. I loved that wall text.'

'Which?'

'The main one,' Iles replied.

'"Without shedding of blood is no remission,"' Harpur said.

# Elsewhere

At the time, Graham Campion certainly did not realize he had strayed into a murder. All he experienced – or all Graham *thought* he experienced – was a sad voice answering the early morning phone call he'd made in search of comfort. That kind of call he often made lately.

Naturally, slaughter is out there always in the city – in all cities: London, Los Angeles, Leeds; Miami, Marseilles, Marrakesh. For most people, it remains remote and generally unencountered, thank God, not part of our daily . . . well, intercourse. Yet most of us have heard how a killing can abruptly shatter what previously had been the peaceful, carefully ordered, even joyous lives of a family or group. Graham had always appreciated crime as the subject of novels and stories, but thought few such tales caught this constant, huge variability of things in our actual world: the jolting, savage moves from normality to violence and from near-farce to full tragedy.

Listening to the dawn voice on his telephone, Graham could not know that one of these terrible shifts had happened again. Afterwards, when newspapers reported the street stabbing, and Graham recognized some names, he did begin to think a bit, though even now he is not totally sure. And it would be unwise to ask for explanations, wouldn't it?

Graham had a lover named Alison who lived in St John's Wood, on the other side of London in a considerable avenue, and who telephoned him very late most nights at his flat in Brixton, a distance away socially and otherwise, though, of course, part of the same city. Obviously, *he* could not ring *her* because she was married and her husband might get suspicious. But on the pretext of washing her hair or reading in bed she would often slip upstairs to their extension and make this call for romantic talk, while Raymond, her husband, watched television. A short whispered chat could occur. She always used the land line, regarding mobiles as insecure after that famous tapped conversation between Prince Charles and Camilla Parker-Bowles. The point was, Graham had to be at the other end, waiting every night in case Alison came through, and this had begun to bug him. He felt cornered, utilized. Wasn't he larger than that?

It was the same when Alison decided to visit. He had given her a key to his place and she would drop in without warning and expect him to be at home, vivid with welcome. Generally he managed this, but lately had come to feel he was too available. Surely it should be women who sat anxiously, hopefully waiting, not men. His sense of meek passivity seemed worse because Alison and Raymond had all that money: three-dimensional, metropolitan-scale money.

As for himself, Graham ran an adequate business selling novelties: love-spoons, cards, and London-scene water-colours, mostly to tourists from overseas. However, he was making no pile and, since his divorce, lived solo in the Brixton flat. It might also be termed adequate, yet lacked all the grandeur of Ray and Alison's property – and you could call that a property without sounding absurd. The area boasted many such places. Yes, boasted. He had driven past a couple of times to gaze at their home, as much as he could through those thrivingly thick hedge ramparts.

On the other hand, Graham's own street and district were . . . say, problematical. It was true that parts of Brixton had shaken off their harsh image and become almost fashion-able, especially among those who despised far-out suburbia but could not afford Kensington, or even St John's Wood. Upgrading had not quite reached the patch where Graham lived, though.

As a means of upgrading *himself* – since he could not on his own upgrade one whole segment of London – Graham planned to make two changes: he would acquire some new business allure, and he would arrange to become more scarce. Just before the time that Alison might ring, he took to dialling a number he knew would be unanswered – the office of his accountant, Jack Brabond, in the nearby district of Lewisham, sure to be empty so late. This gave Alison the busy tone. To take the receiver off the hook would not do because eventually that produced the 'unobtainable' wail to callers, and she would deduce what he had done, and be hurt and/or ratty-contemptuous – most likely ratty-contemptuous – and become sexually punitive for at least weeks. Not to answer would have produced interminable questioning from Alison on why he was out late. She could be darkly possessive.

He would leave the call ringing at Jack Brabond's for twenty minutes or so at about the right time, then replace the receiver. It did not always work, but often when Alison was eventually able to get through on these nights she asked why his phone had been engaged. He would reply that he'd had a fairly urgent business call from Seattle or Denver, where they were hours behind us and still in their offices. He felt this arrangement gave him commercial brilliance: internationalized him, as well as ensuring that he was not endlessly and gratefully on tap. Also, in some mysterious, even mystical, way the imperturbable steady ringing tone at Brabond's office brought a sense of contact with the world, and a fiscal, important world, at that. It told him he was not, after all, discarded and alone and flimsy in his drab corner of the city. Never mind that the call remained unanswered. It was specifically targeted and *would* have reached someone, had someone only been there. This potential communion buttressed him. Occasionally, if Graham awoke around dawn, miserable again in his deeply unshared bed, he would re-solace himself by dialling Jack Brabond's number again, sure it was now only a few hours before someone would reply. Clearly, he did not let the ringing go on for that long, but having been soothed by the prospect of an answer, he would put the receiver back and find sleep once more as morning arrived.

Now and then, Jack Brabond took women back to the office after an evening at a club or the casino. He was married and supposed to be seeing important clients in their houses on these nights, so patently could not ask the women home. He kept some drink at the office and had a five-seater leather sofa in his room for when he might be conferring with several client directors. Jack needed regularity, a stable, reliable pattern: from home to work at the office, home again at the end of the day, then out to the club or casino in the evening, perhaps to the office once more, but for a delightful sojourn now, not work, and finally home again. He had a dread of what he termed to himself the 'Outside', meaning more or less anywhere or anything in the city – in cities generally – which did not fall within the tidy, charted realm he'd fashioned. He recalled Sodom and Gomorrah, the Bible's 'cities of the plain', locations replete with danger and uncorralled evil. Jack feared cities, although he had to live in one: knew they were trouble, knew you must look after your defences.

Recently, on some occasions when Jack had returned to the office late in the evening with a woman friend, his direct-line phone would ring very close to the sofa at unfortunate, crux moments. God knew who would be calling now. It enraged and unnerved him: perhaps an intrusion from that threatening Outside. Without interrupting anything major, Jack would reach down behind the sofa and yank the plug from its socket. Whoever was ringing would get a 'no reply' sound, and never know they were cut off. Several women found his decisiveness with the plug ferociously sexy and grew even more loving, otherwise he might have pulled it before they began.

Tonight, though, he was having trouble with a murderously articulate, very beautiful woman called Helen, whom he had asked back for the first time. Jack gave her a couple of brandies and patiently listened as she elaborated a thesis she'd begun in the Grand Manner club about the way to achieve solid poise in badminton by playing well back from the net and wearing heavier training shoes. He blamed himself for this impasse, since he had mentioned to her that his only child, Ivor, played badminton for Leeds University: with Jack, it was an unwavering rule to be honest and let women know early that he had a wife and admirable family, and was devoted to them. His family were as much an antidote to the infected Outside as were these cheery episodes after hours in the office.

In fact, now and then, if a girl had come back more than once with him and seemed liable to grow what he termed 'clingy', Jack would take a few moments of relaxed, post-coital time to ring Ivor – reconnecting the phone briefly, if necessary – while she looked on and listened. The lad seemed to be living these days with his girlfriend, Sally, which was fine by Jack, and he might chat comfortably to one or both of them on such late-night calls. Ivor's student flat, full of love, sporting gear, and academic industry, was one part of the Outside Jack felt happy about, akin in some ways to his own setting. Ivor, like Jack, had to contend with the perils of a city – a smaller, northern city, but still a city, with all its accumulated peril. Jack was glad Ivor had established a refuge for himself and Sally there, just as Jack had built a couple of refuges for himself in *this* city: his home and the office.

When Jack put his hand on Helen's skirt now, as the survey of badminton footwear seemed about to close, she did not tangibly flinch or freeze but glanced down at it and smiled momentarily, as if indicating that this advance was laughable enough and anything additional would be grotesque. As summing-up, she listed again some brands of heavier trainers she favoured and then said: 'I must be off soon, Jack, dear. I only came for a last drink and to see your set-up here. AS YOU KNOW.' The telephone rang. Jack, alert for it, leaned over the back of the sofa and, using his free hand, would have disconnected with standard, aphro-disiac flair.

'Don't do that,' Helen snarled.

Shamefaced, he removed his other hand from her thigh area, while continuing his effort to kill the phone.

'No, keep doing that, you dolt, but don't do that to the telephone,' she went on, a throaty tremor touching her words. She picked up his non-plug hand and put it back on her skirt, rather higher up.

'It can't be anyone so late,' he said.

'Oh yes, so late, so late! A caller out there in the noble dark of the thrillingly complicit city trying to get through.' Her voice still thrummed with excitement. She put one of her hands over his on her body and pressed down confirm-ingly. 'Mysterious. It's as if there were a spectator, a witness.'

'You like that?'

'It's special.'

He felt terrorized by the continuing din but moved his hand from under hers, then down her skirt, then quickly up and beneath it.

In a moment she remarked: 'There. Now you see what I mean about it tuning me up. The brilliant clamour, Jack – that brutal insistence, the forlorn echo through an empty building. One loves it so.'

Christ, how long would this benign, lubricating racket last? On all previous calls he had disconnected almost at once. Urgently, he began to undress her, then himself. Seize the jangling moment.

'Oh, if only he knew the threesome he makes,' she cried. 'I'm sure it's a he. Perhaps somehow, somewhere in the city, he senses what's happening here.'

The ringing went on long enough, though Jack was not sure he did. After all, the circumstances produced some strain. Nevertheless, he felt there had been progress, and, in fact, a few nights later Helen agreed to return with him to the office. 'But no messing about,' she said.

'Certainly not.'

Things went pretty well exactly the same again, though: coolness, titanic discourse, and then those sudden hots from Alexander Graham Bell's bell. Above the sound of the ringing, she muttered into his ear on the sofa. 'You really reach me, Jacky, love.' Yet he feared that once more he had been too hurried, nervous all the time that a reversion to arid silence might abruptly end her zing.

When next he took Helen to the office, he found a smart way to avert this pressure. They were sitting sedately while she gave some detailed, very up-to-date, rather uncompulsive news on a great-aunt in Tasmania and her knitting prowess. He said suddenly that he must check he had locked the outer door. In fact, he hurried down the corridor to the room of his partner, Hugh Stitson. Hugh had a separate outside line and on it Jack dialled his own office number. Then he left Hugh's receiver off. When he returned to his room, the telephone was doing its fine, now wholly reliable bit, and Helen had shed her clothes and forgotten Tasmania.

'He's with us again, Jack – our blessed adjunct,' she sighed contentedly. 'Never, never stop, dear Wonderman,' she cried, gazing at the telephone.

'No, I won't,' Jack replied, but short of breath.

When Graham Campion, as usual, called Jack's office number that night, he found it busy. Crazy. This did not interfere with his tactic for stalling Alison, since as long as he kept the call in to the accountant she would still get the 'engaged' note from him if she rang. But he loathed the aggressively sharp tone of Jack's 'busy' sound. It made him feel rejected rather than potentially in touch. Who the hell phoned an accountant at this time of night, except him? Or who the hell would be working down there and ringing out so late? He looked in the directory to check he had not made a mistake and found Jack's business had two numbers, obviously one for each partner. Immediately, he rang the other. Jesus, this was engaged, too. Did they now and then have big, emergency audit work, or similar, that kept them at it into the small hours? They actually bothered clients by phone around midnight? Replacing the receiver, he thought urgently of some second-choice number where there would be no answer out of office hours and decided on his solicitor: those buggers hardly ever turned up even *within* office hours. He was looking for the name in the directory when his own telephone rang. Answering was inescapable. Alison said: 'I got straight through to you. No big-deal calls tonight?'

'Later,' he replied. But he feared his image had taken a body blow. She did not talk for long and said she was going to bed. He felt diminished.

At the office, Jack and Helen eventually let things reach their rich conclusion, although his phone continued to ring; and then they began to dress. While she was putting herself to rights in the women's cloakroom, Jack went to Hugh's office and replaced the receiver.

'Oh, it's stopped at last,' Helen said, reappearing in his room, ready to leave.

'Farewell then, Splendid Presence,' he said, addressing the handset in Helen's reverential style. And he meant it. He was coming to terms. 'You look so lovely, Helen.' He put out a hand to touch her face gently, affectionately.

'Now, don't start all that damn smoochy stuff,' she snarled.

At home, Graham felt a mixture of curiosity, hellish disorientation and anger over what had happened earlier. He thought that when the night had gone he might give one of his dawn calls, confident that by then at least there would be access to Jack's office. Graham craved this reassurance and notional companionship. But in a while he decided he could not wait until dawn and must try once more now, immediately, in the hope of settling himself for sleep. This time the number rang. Thank heavens! Had he been misdialling both numbers before?

In the office, Jack and Helen were about to leave. He had thought of giving Ivor a late call, just so that she would get no notions about eternal linkage with Jack on the basis of a few office evenings, but felt all-in and eager for bed, meaning sleep. When the bell reblurted she cried warmly: 'Oh, he's with us once more, Jack. Does he never falter, never lose concern for us?' She put her arm around his neck and drew him back towards the sofa. 'We must not fail him.'

Fail, he thought. Possibly.

Graham decided there was no point in letting the phone ring at Jack's for long, since Alison would not be calling again tonight. The damage to his aura had been done. This call was merely a final, rather desperate check: he saw now that his earlier failures to get through must have been some sort of freak breakdown on the lines. He replaced the receiver and went to bed.

When the bell ceased in the office, Helen looked at her illuminated-dial watch – she never took that off – and said: 'I must get home, Jack. You, too. It's an outrageous time.'

'Not quite yet,' he muttered, into irreversible countdown again.

'I must.' As brusquely as his former unplugging, she drew away from him and swung her magnificent legs off the sofa.

26

'What was that?' he cried.

'What?'

'I thought I heard someone in the foyer. An intruder? Wait here, darling.'

Jack ran swiftly, naked, still creditably aroused, down the corridor to Hugh's office and dialled his room again. He took true solace from these little in-house trips – part of a nicely managed, tidy life, over well-known ground, a portion of his wonderfully safe niche habitat. When he returned, Helen was lying back, haloed with appetite, and did not ask about the supposed intruder. 'Our eternal accompanist from some region of the grand Elsewhere,' she purred, pointing to the noisy phone. 'This time, lift the receiver off, Jack. Let him hear our joys. Let him be *truly* with us.'

'But, sweetness, it will stop the ringing,' he replied.

'It's not the bell that gets to my spirit, it's the sense of SOMEONE' – this was a big, pulsating, echoing word – 'some Night Person of our City, some Anon., some Enigma from the Streets, some Garnering Ear, yes, some Presence, as you so justly called him.'

Jack took the receiver off and laid it on the desk. Why not? The sounds would be going nowhere except to an empty office. Again, the sense of that small private circuit pleased him. It had nothing to do with Night Persons of their city. Night Persons of their city, or of any city, would scare him tremulous. In a while Helen gave some grand groans and shrieks, and so did he. Staring with affection at the receiver she said: 'Jack, wouldn't merely selfish ecstasy seem so skinflint? To share it is an act of blessedness.' She did not suggest actually speaking into the phone, thank heaven. He could imagine her asking the supposed listener in a Florence Nightingale voice if he'd taken therapy from his call.

Before they left, Jack carried out a quick but thorough examination to see that Hugh's phone was not switched on to Record. If it were, Stitson's secretary, Martha, would be expecting only workaday messages about self-assessment and allowable expenses. She had a weak heart and should be spared shocks.

A night or two later, when Jack and Helen were seated on

the sofa with drinks, he inadvertently mentioned he used to wear tooth braces as a child, and afterwards waited anxiously for a small break in her account of the many types of these now available so he could get down to Hugh's room and set up the contact. He had left her in mid chat the other night and felt it would be impossibly rude to do so again. His phone started to ring before she had completed her roundup. 'Ah!' she said. 'Take the receiver off, Jack.'

'But—'

'I must feel we are with him again, enveloping him, not just having him badger us through a damned meaningless bell. That's *so* one-way. Jack, don't deny me this. Don't shroud our love. I know you, too, yearn for this alliance with our plangent city.'

No, no, NO. But he lifted the receiver and placed it on the desk.

Shocked to have his call responded to, Graham almost dropped the phone. Covering the mouthpiece, he listened carefully. At first there was virtual silence, except for some rather feverish rustling noises and then, possibly, subdued voices, perhaps a woman and a man. He could not tell if the man was Jack: Graham usually heard Brabond pronounce words like 'docket', not the kind of word on his lips now. Shortly afterwards, though, came unmistakable sounds, and particularly from the woman. Graham realized, of course, that these exclamations were not directed primarily at him, yet also felt in some gratifying way implicated, welcomed, yes, embraced. This, too, was another life-extension for him. He decided it would be friendly to drive down to Jack's office and see whether he could approach a little closer, show extra fellowship. He did not replace his telephone, in case Alison rang and got no reply in his absence. To tell her where he had gone would be impossible, since that would give away his whole tactical system. She would hear a nice 'engaged' tone again.

Alison's husband Raymond telephoned her from Rotterdam to say there were delays in some deal and he would not, after all, be home that night. It seemed a lovely opportunity

to call on Graham. She took the Volvo and not long afterwards let herself quietly into the flat, gently cooing his name.
There was no reply but, standing in the little hallway, she
thought she heard sounds coming from behind the part-open
living room door. For a second she listened and then her
rage soared. Graham had a woman there – was having a
woman there. Bursting in, though, she was relieved to find
the room empty. Then she saw the telephone had been left
off the hook and went to pick it up. Meaningful noises still
issued. For a while she listened: it must be one of those
endless, dirty recorded calls for the lonely and maladjusted.
So this must be the number he rang every night – nothing
to do with love-spoon orders from the States! Graham
Campion was a pervert. Tonight, he had obviously grown so
excited by what he heard that he had been obliged to rush
out and gratify himself with a girl, too hurried even to put
the receiver back. She banged it down herself now.

Helen, in the office, was having a small spell of silence and
quiet enjoyment and heard a click from the receiver lying
out of its cradle on the desk as the call was abruptly cut.
Leaning across deftly from under Jack, she picked up the
instrument and listened. There was not the humming sound
of an open line but the *beep, beep, beep* that showed they
were no longer connected. 'Time we were away,' she snapped.
　'What?' Jack gasped.
　'Please. Don't be tiresome. This is an accountant's prestige premises, for Christ's sake, in close touch with the
Inland Revenue. Have some decorum.'

Graham arrived in the street just in time to spot the two cars
drive away. The office looked entirely dark. He knew he was
too late and sadly went home, feeling solitary. Entering, he
grew puzzled: he could have sworn he had not replaced the
telephone when he left for Jack's office, yet it was back now.
He rang Jack's number to seek a rerun of the previous effects,
but there was no reply. Inevitably there was no reply! Hadn't
he just seen the participants leave? He replaced the receiver.
　A little later, as he was preparing to turn in, his telephone
rang. When he picked it up he could hear vigorous sounds

very like those that had intrigued him earlier, though louder and even more appreciative. Between the happy yelps a woman eventually said: 'Sauce for the gander is sauce for the goose, Graham.'

'Alison?'

'So you like earholing this sort of thing, do you?' she replied. 'You deserted me, bastard. I was bereft.'

'Where are you, darling?'

'In a public phone box, with a friend I've just met. It's so easy to get a booth when you urgently want one these days and nights, because everyone's got mobiles. And this *was* urgent.'

'Which friend?'

'A friend in need and a friend in deed.'

Jack Brabond went home and climbed into bed with his wife, Olive. She stirred, half asleep, and low down put out her hand inquiringly towards him. He turned away, deeply spent. Not long afterwards, he was awoken by the telephone ringing with fierce persistence downstairs. After a while, to his amazement, he found himself aroused by it. Delighted, he realised he had at last learned the full, spirit-lifting lesson from Helen and come to see the city and, indeed, the world around, not as hostile but as an inspiration. A phone bell at night would turn him on. Lovingly he edged towards Olive.

'You'd better answer the call first,' she murmured.

'No, it will spoil things. I'll go in due course.'

'In due course it will have stopped.'

'I don't think so.'

'What?'

'Believe me. I've an instinct about such matters.' Like Helen, he'd come to feel that a magnificent source of desire and power out there was sending its restorative power to him: Elijah's mantle on Elisha.

The ringing stopped, then resumed, as if someone suspected they had misdialled. Olive said: 'Please, Jack. I can't relax while it's shrieking like that.'

'Doesn't it intrigue and thrill you? The Someone from the Brooding City. The Mystery from its Streets? The Presence?'

'You gone mad? Just get the blasted thing, will you?' she replied.

He would be considerate. One could not reasonably expect everybody – could not expect Olive – to be instantly in touch with these unspoken, vibrant messages from Outside any more than he had been instantly in touch with them himself previously. A slow revelation was needed.

He climbed out of bed and went down to the phone in the hall. Always he had resisted having an upstairs extension in case one of his more personal calls was overheard by Olive. Expecting no voice – this would be the magnificent Presence who was a Non-Presence, after all – he picked up the receiver. For Olive's sake he was committed merely to stopping the bell. He did not even lift the phone to his ear. Just the same, he heard his name spoken. It was a woman's voice, and for a moment he thought Helen's. What did she mean ringing him here at this hour, the wild cow? Now he did raise the instrument and said: 'Yes, it's Jack. What?'

'Mr Brabond? Sally. I'm phoning from Leeds.'

'Sally? Sally?'

'Ivor's girlfriend.'

'Oh yes, dear, of course. I was expecting a . . . But what is it?'

She seemed to be weeping. 'Oh, Mr Brabond, a terrible fight, outside in the street.'

'Outside?'

'In the street. They had broken into the flat to thieve. We came home and surprised them. Mr Brabond, there were three, with knives, and they held us prisoner for a while. They would have used me, but Ivor beat them off. So courageous. The fight spilled out on to the pavement. He wanted to draw them away from me, I know it. People saw, but by the time help came Ivor was—' She sobbed.

'Dead? Dead. Oh, why did you choose to live in a city?'

'What? Universities usually *are* in cities, Mr Brabond.'

'Just the same.'

'The police will tell you face-to-face. They don't telephone such news. But I thought you'd want to know even so late.'

'Yes. I'm used to late calls.' In those idiotically cheerful

31

telephone conversations from the office, why had he never stressed to Sally and Ivor the foul hazards of Outside, the de rigueur, galloping evil of cities?

'And the robbery was so pointless, so trivial,' she said. 'All they got away with were a couple of badminton racquets and his trainers.'

Trainers? Were they the heavy style? Although the crazy thought broke into Jack Brabond's head, he stopped himself from speaking it. The banal and the horrific could mingle, as everybody knew, but he did not have to cave in and help them do it.

When Jack went back upstairs, Olive was snoring. Why wake her? Keep the grief to himself till morning. He dressed and drove around the streets, pathetically hoping to escape his own grief that way. At dawn, he found himself near the office, went in and lay blankly awake on the big sofa. The phone rang. He picked it up and said: 'Look, Presence, this is no good to you now. I'm utterly alone.'

'What about me?'

# For Information Only

A s to grassing, it's not a career you would recommend to your children. No, not quite mainstream, yet surely of importance. You could even say crucial. In any case, few grasses, including this one, have children. The life's too what might be called up and down, meaning full of peril.

There's a murder now in these parts where some grassing – i.e., secretly slipping information to detectives – will be very much to the point, but even if this was generally known, which pray God it won't be, the skills would get no recognition. Obviously, grassing has what is sometimes referred to as a stigma, and even the ones you grass to, and whose front-page glories you create – that is, the police – despise you the same as everyone else. They have a truckload of grubby names for those taking mighty risks in their interests: terms such as 'touts', 'snouts', 'narks', 'earholes', 'whisperers', and of course 'grasses' – these last two being more or less the same, as a matter of fact, taken from 'whispering grass'.

This particular murder is like a lot of others, a villain exterminated by a villain, or villains. It is the kind of hellish crime where police run into what is always described in the tabloids as a wall of silence: nobody will talk to them, not even the friends and relatives of the corpse. You see, co-operation with police is something they have not been nurtured to, and no matter what happens, they cannot change their habits. Now, this is where the grass comes in. He will usually be on what is referred to as the inside – which clearly does not mean 'inside', as we sometimes refer to those doing a jail sentence, but on the inside of the communities concerned. As such, he might hear matters police never would. This boy can enter a club or pub without causing all conversation immediate cardiac arrest, which is what happens when plain-clothes police slink in, posing as humans. This murder is very messy and sick, as so many of them are when it's heavy against heavy, or heavies: singular or plural is one of the matters I'm not too sure about at this moment in time, but I'm working on it.

Now, the obvious question is, if most of the people in these communities will not open their mouths to the police, why does the grass, he being also a member of a community? Why does he defy the local culture? This is some poser, and, to be frank, it's where treachery comes in. Your true grass is a loner, but a loner pretending to be one of the band. A guise is what this is sometimes referred to as. It is not easy to keep up. After a few unexplainable arrests, some in the community may suspect or half suspect a certain grass is, well, a grass. But as long as they don't know it for sure and totally, the grass is usually safe. Safeish. It's an uncertain kind of career, though, there's no denying it – not at all like working in local government – which is why at this stage I would not think of marriage or a family.

To answer the question, then – why does a grass grass? – let's approach it from the side: a grass – this is to say, a decent-quality, experienced grass – is selective. He does not blab, blab, blab about every bit of criminality he knows of. He makes what could be termed a moral judgment. Example: he might not say a word anywhere about a burglary where nobody is hurt, and where insurance will take care of all losses anyway. This is even if the takings run into hundreds of grand. A grass is not like some priest or Bible puncher, pursuing an all-out holy campaign against every sin. His and theirs are quite different professions, though all worthwhile. As a matter of fact, I prefer the name 'informant' to 'grass', and to any of those other crude pieces of slang, informant having a weighty, rather civic sound.

But take this murder. The location is a children's playground in a public park, which gives a rather gross tinge from the start. Surely, there are some pieces of territory which should never be involved in crimes of violence and where everything to do with a murder is totally inappropriate. Think, for instance, of the gardens of a convent containing the pious, or the surrounds of a gallery which is filled with wonderful and timeless paintings – eminent names like Velázquez. Or think of this innocent children's playground. Yet, the fact is, here you have a number two or three in one of the local drug, pimping, and protection outfits pinned to the soil by a metal stake through the mouth and coming out at the back of his neck and into the earth to a depth of a full nine inches, unarguably sledgehammer work. That is my information – held back by the authorities from the press and broadcasters because of its acute unpleasantness, but discoverable to those like myself, for whom it is, if such a phrase is permissible in the circumstances, bread and butter.

Now, this is the sort of death nobody needs. This is the sort of death that would be out of order enough in the middle of a remote field or on the mud flats, but when it comes to Cedric Lyndon Chivers he is discovered naked alongside that harmless chunky green-and-red wood climbing-frame of the play area, and not so very far from the very smallest slide, meant for dear little toddlers.

My understanding is that, despite a gunshot wound in the chest, the forensic people say he was alive when that stake was forced into his mouth and thumped through. (The point about grasses – at least, about those of a certain stature – is that information moves two ways: mostly *towards* the police, of course, but this and that *from* the police, as well.) These findings could mean he was shot and disabled somewhere else, then brought here and throat-pinned in that barbaric fashion, copied, as I've heard, from the Vikings, who were famously short of what is known as compunction. Imagine the kind of mind or minds that would make a special effort to give Cedric this display in such a normally carefree setting.

This is my point about selectivity. Who's going to tell me that the perpetrator or perpetrators of the outrage should be allowed to hide behind a so-called wall of silence? I ask you, who? This is culture? Certainly not culture a chairman of the Arts Council would appreciate, or the late Dame Margot Fonteyn. Does anyone comprehend how those close to Cedric – business colleagues, as it were, or parents, who live locally – could keep quiet about what they know or suspect? With glossy first names like these – Cedric Lyndon – it is clear that the parents had bright hopes for their child. They certainly did not visualize this kind of unsightly end. Yet my information is that they will say nothing about his last known movements, nor about special enemies. To the press, they commented that they had no idea who could have done such a thing to their beloved boy, because he was so all-round popular and good-hearted, with a lifelong interest in the breeding of Sealyhams, those piss-everywhere white dogs with a big head and very short legs.

Grassing – you will be beginning to see – has its virtues; in fact, has its indispensable side, even if it will never bring a knighthood. Grassing in this kind of situation is a discreet public service. Surely it is reasonable to open one's mouth if another mouth has been prised open and a lump of steel rammed through it. Of course, I am not saying that Cedric's friends and relatives believe the murder should be accepted and forgotten about, and that this is why they make no disclosures. Here, again, we have a major point to do with grassing. Those who worked with and/or were even fond of Cedric – not easy, because he was a towering shit heap – those linked to him, I say, one way or the other, regardless, will look for means to put things right, as their evasive lingo goes. That's to say, vengeance. One reason they tell the police nothing is because these people want to deal with the problem themselves. This is referred to also as sorting it out.

Which suggests a kind of warfare – the gang kind. Society at large wants that? I take leave to think not. In war, all sorts can be hurt, not just the participants. You might get bullets on the busy streets, fast, murderous cars, even explosions. Is anyone going to tell me that there is no duty to prevent this happening, if at all possible? Who can do it but the grass? Obviously, police have a rough idea of who's in the gangs and how they operate and who might have been stalking Cedric. Rough ideas and might have been are no use to the courts, though. And they don't tell you where the next outbreak of bloodstained trouble might come. These, again, are matters that the grass can often assist with very materially.

A further important point is that revenge can be merely

approximate. People get hit, yes, but are they the right people? What revenge is often referred to in books of quotations and so on as is 'a kind of wild justice', which comes from some top-class thinker. Notice that 'wild'. This is not a controlled, proved matter. This is instinct stoked up with hate, obviously involving a big danger of mistakes. This is hardly the venerated jury system, with its 'If you please, my Lord,' plus wigs and innocent until proven guilty. But the grass can introduce that other element, the exactness, the rightness, the facts – well, the justice. Isn't his a vital role? (By the way, women don't seem to take to it much.)

Police will know, naturally, that this showpiece deterrent death is something to do with mishandling of drugs or profits by the late Cedric Lyndon, probably coke, maybe crack. It could be overmixing stuff with filler, or selling higher than is accounted for and holding back a juicy personal take, or even using some of the merchandise himself, then starting to mind-float and getting careless, and maybe doing some silly talking or, possibly, losing part of the consignment in a club or slag's room. This is the sort of important detail that can come a grass's way if the grass is on what is known as the *qui vive* and is fairly well trusted all round.

I will not hide the fact that one's own activities may, of course, benefit as a result of successful grassing. The rather coarse saying, 'You scratch my back and I'll scratch yours,' does have a bearing. Grassing is not entirely a selfless public service like the Samaritans. This mutual relationship need not always mean the passing of money from the police, but there can be a certain useful absence of pressure, instead. Example: there is an art dealer called Jack Lamb not far from here, generally thought to be a top-flight informant, and he goes from strength to strength, even though some of the works he buys and sells on the quiet could come from anywhere, meaning deeply illegal. Yes, what is known in the art game as provenance – signifying how the painting was got and where from – is assuredly not one of Jack's strongest sides. But, on account of grassing, he has other assets, such as the cop he talks to, who offers a certain powerful influence on Jack's behalf. Myself, I do a little commerce in various commodities, at a much lower level than Jack Lamb, obviously, but I admit there is sometimes a doubt or two over by what means certain items I have for sale originally came on to the open market. All right, maybe from theft. But, within reason, curiosity relating to these is not pressed by detectives. They are responding to my established ability to put helpful matter their way – often referred to in the eventual successful trials within the police-witness phrase 'acting on information received'. Hence my preference for the term 'informant'.

Harpur said: 'Francis Garland has a small-time but some-times reliable grass, sir, who's now reporting that Cedric was done by Gordon Hamm and Antichrist Jessop – sorry, Jeremy Lisle Vincent Jessop.'

'I want someone else for that. Don't we want someone else for that, Colin? Can we shut the bugger up?' Iles replied.

'Which bugger?'

'What?'

'Well, the grass or Francis, sir?'

The Assistant Chief Constable, who was bent forward over the desk examining some blemish on his wrist, nodded his fine grey head to acknowledge a fair point. 'I meant the grass. But you could be right. Garland's the very model of a thrusting Detective Chief Inspector and naturally wants his discoveries given due weight.'

'Especially when they could be true, sir.'

Iles held his hand under the direct beam of the table lamp and stared harder. 'Nothing genito-urinary first shows itself on the wrist, does it, Colin? Of course, you'll know that pox need not be just a simple trousers job.'

'I can probably explain our tactics convincingly to Francis.'

'Yes, do: explain them to him very convincingly, Col. We have someone else well and truly in the frame for Cedric, and don't want to be messing about with nobodies. Not at this stage. Can we take the grass in, to keep him quiet? Presumably we've been going easy on some of his own shady work as quid pro quo? We could stop blind-eyeing and get him celled? That would be one answer.'

'Well, it's much against the spirit, sir. The grassing code.'

Iles raised his head and smiled. It was that saintly smile

he sometimes graced the world with, a different species altogether from his more usual Herod smile. 'True, Colin. Commitments. Grasses are rubbish, but they're *our* rubbish.'

'This grass, talks exclusively to Garland, sir, so perhaps there is no real danger of word about Hamm and Antichrist getting out.'

'He talks exclusively to Garland as long as he sees some response. But if not? He's got information to sell. The press?'

'The press can't risk libelling Gordon Hamm and Antichrist just on the say-so of a grass, sir. Jessop's got social status. He wears handmade suits.'

'Jerk,' Iles replied. 'No wonder you're stuck at chief superintendent. Newspapers could still unleash their bloody specialist investigative people. They think they can find their way round libel, and often can. Look, I want Martin Gabalfa for Cedric Chivers's death, not a couple of hacks like Gordon Hamm and Jessop. And Martin did quite possibly give the orders for it. Press people, digging away, crowding, interviewing – they could very soon screw up the whole thing with red herrings.'

'Meaning with what might be true, sir?'

'Colin, what's true—'

'Is what a jury believes.'

'Is *still* what a jury believes – even after the Birmingham Six. We've built a sweet and almost full case against Gabalfa, yes?'

'Not bad.'

'All right, perhaps he didn't personally do it, but will we ever nail him for the foul things he does personally do?'

'Probably not, sir.'

'Including deaths?'

'Including deaths.'

'Perhaps not this specific death, but enough others. Many others?'

'Almost certainly.'

'I like your modest way with words, Harpur, you snivelling, quibbling also-ran. So, Col, if this is looked at intelligently, dispassionately, I'd say take the grass in for a while on something fairly minor, but definitely not bailable. Or even hint we'd leak a rumour to Gordon and Antichrist that he's shopping them. That should keep him quiet. We can do Gordon and Antichrist for something else when convenient. This is clean-sweep, strategic thinking – the long term. It's what's expected when you reach my rank, Col, which you never will, of course.'

'Well, I might be able to manage this business some other, less painful way, sir. I'll get Garland to let me see the grass and have a chat. It might take a few days to persuade Francis, though.'

'Manage it how you like. Manage it.'

What's known as sacrosanct, almost holy, is the relationship between a grass and his cop contact. This is totally private, one-to-one, what is sometimes also referred to as symbiotic, meaning they depend on each other. So I was more than surprised, you could say enraged, to see my police contact, namely Detective Chief Inspector Francis Garland, turning up to a secret rendezvous in certain disused railway carriages on a siding with another cop accompanying – viz., his boss, Detective Chief Superintendent Colin Harpur. This one was known to all, and, as police go, is straight in many ways, but also sharp and hard and, anyway, constantly leaned on to bend rules by that real piece of evil and merrymaking they've got down there, ACC Desmond Iles, i/c Operations – without anesthetic.

'Well, I've heard with admiration of your work,' Harpur said. 'You're totally anonymous to me, of course. Francis wouldn't ever reveal an identity. But the outline of your career is impressive and it's a golden comfort to us desk-based creatures that we have someone in the field like yourself.'

The word 'golden' I like a lot. It always sets up a promising aura, so I listen carefully. This carriage still had little patches of upholstery unvandalized, and the three of us sat spread around, avoiding the released, high, upthrusting springs, Garland at one corner, myself in another, and Harpur in the middle. He has that way of looking at you, even in this half dark, so you feel it hardly matters a damn he doesn't know your name, if he really doesn't, because he could find you straight off in a football crowd. As a matter of fact, he's the one who looks after Jack Lamb.

40

Garland said: 'Sorry I had to bring company. This has become an intricate matter. Higher authority was required.'

That sounded typical cop-shifty, so the thing was to let them know straight off I'm no pushover and had only that day picked up extremely recent and sensitive matter. 'The whisper I have currently is that you want Martin Gabalfa for this death, Mr Harpur. So, I'm a nuisance, am I, coming up with the certainty it was not Martin but Gordon Hamm and Antichrist?'

I listened to Harpur bring a wry chuckle out of his *Make Your Own Self-Confidence* kit. 'You say "certainly", and I'm sure you believe this, but we have some very strong evidence against Martin Gabalfa,' he replied.

'Planted? It's got to be phony. I can put you in touch with someone who'll say he saw two men carrying Cedric to the children's playground. The descriptions are Hamm and Jessop, to a T, Jessop in grand tweeds.'

You see, the grass must be able to stand his ground and speak his mind, regardless. Integrity and strength of character are so central. With police, you have all sorts of currents flowing, some murky, some liable to carry the facts away. Police like to what they call orchestrate information, which means arrange it to do the severest damage to the biggest people who have been messing them about, and Gabalfa is very big, Most Wanted.

'I've told Mr Harpur what you say,' Garland replied. He sounded fed up. It looked obvious he was getting squeezed to do it Harpur's way. Clearly, this was out of Garland's hands. He might be a whiz kid but even a whiz kid can only whiz as far as the system lets him, because it is the system that decides whether he is a whiz kid or a nuisance.

'To us, it doesn't look in the least like the style of Gordon and Antichrist,' Harpur remarked. 'Would they do a stake through the mouth, for Heaven's sake?'

'Have enough been found like that for it to be a recognized style then?'

'And you say you have descriptions,' Harpur sort of replied. 'Descriptions are fine, but any lawyer worth his breakfast can pull them to pieces. Okay, Antichrist likes calibre tailoring, but so do a lot of other people.'

41

'Not Martin Gabalfa. He's a ready-made and bomber-jacket man.' A worthwhile grass does not get pushed off his facts by Harpur-type, bully-boy argument. 'This witness has good eyesight. They were not moving very fast, humping a body.'

There was a pause and deep breathing, which with police always means, Look out, shit's going to fly.

'Mr Iles is very interested in your situation,' Harpur remarked nice and gently.

'The assistant chief? Himself?' That's what I mean about the pause. Christ, this was a development. You don't tangle with that one. 'Mr Iles? My situation?'

'To be blunt, your safety,' Harpur replied.

'I know how to keep my head down.'

'What I told the assistant chief, and so did Francis. All the same, he frets over you. To be specific, he worries that Hamm and Jessop might hear you're putting this story around about them, grow understandably resentful, and decide to instill eternal silence.'

'Might hear I'm talking? Might hear how?' Which, of course, was not answered and never would be, no matter how long and loud I shouted.

'This is Mr Iles's main anxiety,' Garland said. 'He would be very upset to lose you, or any part of you – thinking of your valuable work in the future. It's why Mr Harpur came with me. Personal security of a threatened individual requires at least a chief superintendent.'

'But I haven't been threatened.'

'"Threatened individual" is a category,' Garland replied. 'You qualify. Oh, very, very easily.'

'Mr Iles wants you to think extremely carefully about your safety,' Harpur remarked. 'Possibly even go away for a while. Certainly return eventually, say after Gabalfa's charged, or wait until conviction, but take a trip now.'

'You're telling me that Iles would get the information to Hamm and Antichrist that I'm naming them? My God. This is behaviour for a policeman, even Iles?'

Ignored, also, as you'd expect.

'Lie low somewhere distant and congenial,' Harpur continued. 'Not that I would dream of asking you to finance that yourself.'

'This is another reason for the attendance of a senior officer, you see,' Garland explained. 'Large money concerned.'

So 'golden' did bring a hearty message.

Harpur produced a fat official-looking sealed brown envelope and put it on top of one of the exposed curly metal seat springs, like an upside-down view of some big fish on a line. 'This would help take care of expenses for quite a time, as long as you don't choose the King George V Hotel in Paris. We keep a safety fund for our most distinguished helpers. It's the least we can do. And, look, you can be confident we won't start poking into those business activities – which I understand from Francis you have – looking for the dubious and prosecutable. That little enterprise of yours will be there intact when you return.'

Now, this is what's known as a major change in the picture. As will be obvious, I regard my grassing as a serious, worthwhile function, and the really responsible operator must take a very wide view of matters. There is no question that Martin Gabalfa has been a foul menace to the public good for an age, and deplorably able to make a monkey of law and order in all the run-of-the-mill modes – pushing drugs, killings, extortion, running whores. Probably, he gave the instructions for Cedric, including the methods. This, in fact, is beginning to look very much like a case where that matter of selectivity which I mentioned earlier will come in quite strongly. Clearly we have here a question of deciding how the interests of society will be best served and, considering everything, it will indeed probably be most useful if Gabalfa rather than Hamm and Antichrist is put out of the way. I like to think that Cedric himself – even such a bleak, fully paid-up arsehole – would feel consoled to know his terrible death was not entirely in vain, and that a large-scale, ungovernable rogue will probably be removed from circulation as a result. Further, some months in Portugal – not that glitzy Marbella dump where every bugger goes – would be very welcome, as it happens. Restorative.

Interestingly, Gordon Hamm and Jessop were in the club that very evening after my meeting with Garland and Harpur. Antichrist came over at once, wearing one of those brown-and-green check ensembles costing about fifteen hundred quid, including high-buttoned waistcoat, and grinning amiably the way he has, like a gashed refuse-bin. This sudden approach was gravely worrying. Grasses whisper but whispers get around about grasses, too. Things could happen very abruptly in that club, and they deliberately had tile floors now and no carpets, because of previous indelible staining. Antichrist remarked straight away: 'Do you know, we heard, Gordon and me, that we was temporarily top of the short list for that Cedric thing, but suddenly the heat's right off. A relief.'

Replying, I remarked: 'I should bloody think so. Something unseemly like that your style? Don't make me laugh.'

'Harpur wants Gabalfa for it. Correction, Iles wants him, which is even worse – worse for Gabalfa, I mean.'

'Oh, I hadn't heard any of this,' I responded.

'We'd feel better if the focus stays on Gabalfa. You hear anything at all that might affect this? Been picking up any drumbeats? Gordon and me, we had an idea you might be doing some personal investigating.'

'Me? Not a sniff. How would I? I'm home all day getting ready for a holiday. The Algarve. Packing my bucket and spade.'

'Nice. Expensive?'

'A bit, but I had this sudden feeling I deserve a break.'

'I think so.' Antichrist put his hand inside the lovely county-set jacket and came out with a rather Woolworthy cream envelope, but definitely not the smallest kind. 'I'd really like you to have a great time abroad. What with the wine and screwing and so on, it's bound to cost.' He passed the envelope over. 'Gordon thinks the same.'

'This is kindly, Jeremy.' Gordon glanced across from the bar and I gave him a grateful wave.

Antichrist said enthusiastically: 'What I gather, the Algarve is at its very best this time of year and for quite a few months ahead, also. Once they're over there, people want to stay, just can't break away to return home.'

'Exactly what I've heard myself, as a matter of fact.'

# War Crime

You'll be thinking, this is no place for an elderly woman, day in day out, haunting a building site, gaping at mechanical diggers. I'm certainly not interested in one of the 'six-bedroom prestige homes' they'll erect. I live alone now.

This was a Second World War Royal Air Force airfield at the edge of the town, abandoned years ago. Now, in 1994, they are breaking up the runways, ready for one of those 'executive' estates, and as a matter of fact, I'm here to see whether a boy called Peter Milton is found under the concrete. He will be wearing a wedding ring.

I call him a boy, and this is how I still think of dear, vile Peter. He was a boy when his life ended in 1943 and I put his beautiful body in the ground. They were just constructing this airfield. I was seventeen and Peter fourteen. At the time it seemed a mighty barrier, this difference in age – woman, child. Now, of course, the gap between him and me would be nothing. Perhaps I was wrong to worry about it even then. The thought harrows me. So do many others from those damned, imperishable days.

He was not local, but evacuated here from London to escape German bombing. Although by 1943 the blitz had slackened and many evacuees went back, Peter and a few others stayed. I was working in council Welfare, my first job after leaving school. While I began as just an office girl, senior staff were scarce in the war and soon I had to help with liaison – making sure the evacuees were happy. Peter and I were bound to have a lot of personal contact. Absolutely nothing untoward about this, believe me.

These Londoners seemed more grown up than children raised here – sharper and tougher, girls as well as boys. What

45

you would expect: big city against small town. I was still at school myself when they first arrived just after war was declared in September 1939, and some of the girls were put in my class. They knew so much: not about schoolwork, but other topics, grown-up topics, and Peter was the same, although only ten years old then. If he and his friends met you in the street they would sometimes shout crude, shocking, terribly intimate things.

When I came to know him better, I discovered he was not really like that. He could be sensitive, he had feelings. If not, he might still be alive and I would not need to wait near this disturbed ground every day, scrutinizing dirt. The workmen puzzle.

Peter disappeared near the middle of that year, 1943. At first, nobody bothered. People said he had run away, back to London. Occasionally, evacuees did that. He never arrived there, though, and eventually police here began a search. Peter and his friends used to play in sand dunes on the beach, making their dens, fighting battles, boiling crabs, and this was where police, troops, and volunteers concentrated their efforts, in case he had been buried by a fall. Finally, they dug out a place Peter had made with bits of driftwood and a sheet of corrugated iron. They did not find him, but some of his things were there: a Mickey Mouse alarm clock, army badges which he collected, and his autograph book. Very unfortunately, I had put my signature in that, and a line from a quite famous poem, 'Gather ye rosebuds while ye may'. The poem concerns girls, really, but it had seemed right for him when I wrote it. I told the police I had no idea where he might be, and it was absolutely true, then. They asked what the poetry meant, and I replied at once that it was only to fill up the page and came from another time, indeed, another century. Again, true.

It had been one of our good days when I wrote that. Peter could be so delightful, and he could be an utterly evil swine, with true London swinishness. When we had good days, I would take him on outings, such as watching military parades to celebrate 'Warships Week' or 'National Savings Week' or 'Tanks Week', displays meant to prop civilian morale. Sometimes we would go to the cinema, or to historical places like the cottages used by political agitators called Chartists for meetings last century, or we might gather wildflowers or blackberries in the country. This was simply part of my work and perfectly normal, believe me. You see, it was partly because we gathered wildflowers together that I wrote what I did.

His mother sent him the book from London for his fourteenth birthday and he said I must be the first to sign, because I mattered most. This was silly, but very sweet. That's what I meant – he could be really considerate. On these nice days he would talk to me as if I were his girlfriend, and he would try to use his hands and so on in the pictures or when we were blackberrying. Naturally, I had to stop that. He was too young. This is what I meant before: they were so grown up, these London kids. I don't know what went on between him and some evacuee girls, especially one called Joy. That used to make me horribly miserable and angry, though I never let him see I cared. It would not have been proper. In some ways, Peter was a right little shit. (That kind of language I would not have used then, of course. Women and girls didn't. But this is 1994 and things have changed, for better or worse I don't know. In any case, I and the rest of us in the town learned quite a bit from those evacuees, including some coarseness, I'm afraid.) There were bound to be times when I felt overwhelming hate for Peter, weren't there? At those moments it was as if I ceased to be myself and an appalling rage took over. It would always fade, but not always in time.

When I wrote that poetry in his book, we were behind the Chartist cottages on an afternoon out there, and he wanted to kiss me, I mean, really kiss me, on the mouth, bodies close, but I would not allow that either. I could not. I told him, I was like a sister or his schoolteacher. He replied that the poetry said something different – he could be so clever, that one – but I told him it was only poetry, from another, distant time. We had a laugh and he did not get at all vicious, not that day.

Then, just a week afterwards, he somehow found out about an entirely separate matter, and suddenly he changed. Peter could be fond, he could be a ripe peril. You see, I had kept quiet about certain new aspects of my life: I was sure

47

it would be exceptionally unwise to tell him I needed some-body more my own age. He would refuse to understand. So, in the street, he stood right in front of me and said at the top of his squeaky, wild voice, 'Some dirty ice-a-da-creamo Wop's sticking it up you, is he?'

I still feel ill when I recall those savage words. It was how they talked, the Londoners, even after years with us. And it was how they thought – vulgarity, aggression. You see, this was his sickening, glorious jealousy, which would lead to such a horrible end. I try never to think of it now, but the memories often force their way back. He had no damn rights over me. I was older, a woman, really. Good God, friends of my age were married and starting families.

The evacuees were not our only visitors at that time. Just outside the town stood a camp for Italian prisoners of war, who used to help the farmers. This was what Peter meant when he said 'Wop'. To be fair, everybody called Italians that then, and said all they could do was sell ice cream. These were the enemy, of course, like Jerries and Japs. But most of the Italians seemed gentle, not real soldiers. By this time, Italy was almost out of the war anyway. The camp had very little security, and prisoners worked unguarded on the farms. This was how I met Carlo.

It happened first when I went gathering wildflowers by myself one day on my bike. Peter should have come but failed to turn up, so it was absolutely his own filthy fault. I felt sure he was with one of the girl evacuees: Joy, I should think, the easy, scheming cow, giving joy to every boy she fancied, which meant most – I don't exaggerate. That really hurt me, but I decided not to look for him. Carlo was cutting a farm hedge near the patch of wildflowers. He could speak some English and was nice and funny and a bit dreamy, but not as beautiful as Peter. Carlo had quite a nose. The thing about Peter was his lovely long, soft, dark hair and brown eyes that could be so wonderfully warm. I was younger than Carlo, though only by a few years, and I felt quite happy with him. He could often sneak out, and I began to go to see him, especially on Sunday afternoons, and he would tell me about Italy. He came from a place called Bolzano and said he had been a boot repairer there, but was studying while a prisoner and might become a teacher or even a head-master.

One day he said we would marry after the war, and if they sent him away to another camp or back to Italy, he would come and find me the moment he could. I was not sure, but later he gave me a gold ring that used to belong to his mother, who was dead. Naturally, I was careful and wore it only when I saw him. Usually, I kept it hidden on a cord around my neck. I knew people would think it bad for a girl to be with an Italian prisoner, a kind of betrayal of our troops and Mr Churchill, and I never showed the ring or told anyone about Carlo. How Peter discovered his existence, I still don't know. He had this stinking London slyness, those lovely, stinking, miss-nothing brown eyes.

I think he began to watch me secretly. One Sunday after-noon, I was in some woods with Carlo, when he rolled away suddenly and sat up because he had heard a noise. Quickly, we began to dress. Then, out from the trees rushed Peter and four other boys, all of them London friends of his. They had hammers and iron bars and began to beat Carlo before he could get to his feet and defend himself.

They struck him on the head and face and lower, until he was unconscious. Peter hit him again and again, using some of that gross London language: 'See what we do to Wops who stick it up our girls? And on a Sunday, too. He's not kitted, I see. Are you? You'll be hatching a little Musso bastard – thought of that? And where d'you get that stinking ring?' I did not answer but was so upset and enraged that I told Peter I never wanted to speak to him again. He laughed and said I would soon come crawling, because I needed him so badly. But I meant it. That anger stayed with me quite a while, and I gave notice and left Welfare so I would not have to meet him.

That Sunday of the incident, I hurried to the camp and told Carlo's friends and they came to carry him back. He was unconscious. When I went on Monday to find out how he was, a prisoner said Carlo died from head wounds the previous evening, without coming round. I never discovered if they even brought a doctor. During the war, it was another time, and Carlo was only a prisoner. This was murder, of course, a horrible crime, but not one to interest the police much then. Troops killed Italians all the time in battle and nobody would worry much about another one dead. And, in any case, Carlo should not have been out of the camp. I knew the British commandant would want to keep it all quiet, or he might be in trouble. Probably he reported the death as due to a camp fight. And witnesses? I felt so sad but could never have publicly said the truth. People would think I was foully cheap to be like that with an Italian in the open air on what they termed the Sabbath. I never read anything of the killing in the local press, nor even heard of a funeral.

Two months later, Peter disappeared. I had seen him lurking near my parents' house, where I was living then, but avoided him by using back lanes. For a few days after the den was found, police and soldiers dug out more sand hills. They discovered nothing else. At the end, people said he must have gone swimming alone and drowned. I knew it was not true. Like all the London children, he hated the sea. I used to take him to the beach sometimes, but although he put his swimming trunks on, he never went near the water. He had a quite tall, slim body, yet not weak-looking. In any case, it was nearly winter when he disappeared and the sea would be too cold.

As a matter of fact, detectives came to see me four times about the autograph book, and kept on and on with their questions, but I still said the piece of poetry meant nothing special. And, perhaps, really, it didn't in the end. I wouldn't let it, couldn't let it. But, naturally, all their damn nosiness made me think back to that splendid day when we went to the Chartist cottages, and on a Sunday afternoon, one week after the search for Peter was finally abandoned, I cycled there. What I needed then was something to bring comfort through joyous memories of him. In winter the cottages would not be open to visitors, but that did not matter.

Arriving, I went around the back where I had written in the autograph book. That quotation had just come to me out of nowhere, and despite all the suspicion from police, I never regretted it. There was little I could regret in my contacts with Peter. What I regretted above all, and still grieve over, was the way I had broken those contacts, the way I had turned away from him in my fury after the serious banging he gave Carlo.

For a few moments, recollections of that happy day with the autograph book did rush back when I saw the cottages again. I felt pleased I had come. Sometimes a special location can create that sort of marvellous thrill, though it's all rubbish, of course: a place is only a place. Then, while I was still rejoicing at my decision, I found a window at the rear had been broken. That troubled me, but I did not know why. After a moment, I put my hand through and unfastened the catch. For a couple of minutes, I remained outside, no longer feeling joyful, yet knowing I must enter. Peter and I had gone inside last time, and this wish now was part of that deep urge to relive all the previous visit. I climbed in.

There was a strange smell, which I did not remember from before. The window led into a little larder, with dim-wit models of a nineteenth-century cabbage and loaf on the shelf, to show that in those days, too, people used to eat, and it was when I opened the door from this larder into the single downstairs room that I saw Peter.

I can think about this now and stay calm, but for years after that day, I was unable to speak of it. Thank God there was no call to speak of it. In fact, everything demanded silence. Some agonies are private.

To make visitors think they were having a real trip back in time, the council had kept these cottages as they were in history, and Peter Milton had hanged himself by the neck with rope fixed on a ceiling hook, once used for bacon sides too big for the larder. These hooks had to be strong because you did not want a great meat slab smashing down on one of the plentiful Victorian kiddies in its crib. There were some old chairs and other ancient furniture in the cottages and he had stood on a chair and kicked it away. It lay on its side now against the wall. He had brought the rope here, sure of what he intended. And he must have walked all that distance: I saw no bike outside. It all showed real determination, a real plan, and raw, unspeakable torment.

Of course, he had been there quite a long time. For a while I did not know what to do and thought of climbing back out of the window and cycling away. I could achieve nothing here, put nothing right. A section of my mind said this was nobody I knew, not now – this was nobody at all, not any longer: in the past, yes, someone sparkling and fine, with, admittedly, certain duff character aspects, but those were part of his liveliness, even if they meant someone else's harsh death. Now, no character at all.

And then I decided I could not treat Peter like that: leave him dangling on a pig hook, perhaps until the holiday season started again with all its sunshine and chattering folk on happy outings. I owed him more. This boy had killed for me. In many ways that was monstrous, of course, but it seemed also rather binding, in its way. Looking at him dead, I had to think even more than that: he had killed twice for me, for me alone. I brought back the chair he had used himself and, standing on it, tried to push the knot in the rope up and over the point of the hook so he would fall. When he was down I might be able to manage something. But I could not move that knot. This was the only way I could see to get him free. Free? How could he be free? But I had no other word. Because of the tautness, it was impossible to undo the knot. He had made an excellent job of that. I thought of him reaching up and taking care over it, jerking down a few times with his hand to test, so he knew there would be no mistake when it got his jolting though boyish weight.

I was working with my fingers above my head, which made things very difficult, and his body, spinning slowly now and then, pulled down on the rope so it resisted all my pushing up. I paused. Of course, I should have realized that a broken window meant bits of glass, and I could have found one and sawed the rope. My brain was not doing very well, though, that day. It was as if I felt I had to release him by my own strength and effort, and cutting the rope did not come into it, could not. This was something I needed to do for Peter, and it had to be difficult, a hard and worthwhile task for a dear, beloved crony. Standing on the chair, I had my face and head more or less level with his, and I knew that in a moment I would have to put my arms around his middle and try to lift him, easing the load off the rope while I attempted again to free him. In a grim way it was like the closeness of lovers, that merging into each other. How it always was with Peter and me: like lovers, only like.

If it were not for his clothes, he would have been difficult to recognize, what with the time he had been there and the quite noticeable disturbances throughout him that being hanged caused. I remember feeling war had taken me too fast into the adult world of ugliness and wise despair.

Bending my legs a little, I took hold of Peter around his waist, then tried to lift him and get the cruel tension off the rope. Peter's frame did not feel like a body, of course – so unyielding after the time he had been there. No, he could not be mistaken for a lover.

I managed to get a tiny bit of slack into the rope. Then, though, I had to free one hand, reach high again, and strive to push the knot up and over the hook point. This meant that I would have to keep Peter's weight off by clutching him with one arm only. I rested there for a few seconds, still pressing him to me with both arms – a kind of afflicted, unwholesome, very late farewell hug – then increased the pressure with my right arm and quickly raised my left hand to try to slide the knot up.

It did not work at once. I was gasping and my legs shook. Of course, I was not in the best condition for such a struggle and I feared I would have to release him before I had finished, or that I would topple from the chair. I needed help, and help was the last thing I wanted. Then, somehow, the knot did get over the hook's tip and the rope's end glanced against my shoulder as it tumbled. I think I laughed aloud at this little triumph. People must have giggled and had pleasure in this cottage when it was lived in, but probably nobody ever giggled in here before over getting a revered corpse unhung. I lowered Peter to the ground with as much control as I could – not very much. He hit the boards with two sharp, hard sounds. At first he landed on his feet and the noise came from his shoes. He actually stood upright briefly and for that second I could almost see him as he used to be, a cheerful, war-torn kid in a paisley pullover. His face was away from me then, so I did not have to look at the most telling aspects, and his shoulders and back of the neck and head could have been, just could have been, those of a living person.

Then, though, he tumbled to the side and struck the floor with a hard, heavy rap, the rope trailing from him like the lead of a break-away dog. I stepped down from the chair and went to him. Methodically, I searched his clothes. That seemed immensely necessary. There was not much, but in the pocket of his trousers I found a note in a folded envelope addressed to me with big capital letters, so there would be no mistake. It also said PRIVATE on the envelope in even bigger letters, which was thoughtful, but would have failed to keep other eyes out if I personally had not had the timeliness to find him. The note said: 'There will be no rosebuds for me to gather. You don't even talk to me any longer. Why should I wait?'

About this I had a cry, though nothing too long or too loud. Lately, I had learned ways to keep things in check. He was announcing, was he, that his life meant nothing if it did not include me, and I had shut him out through anger? He had been a child, but with the thoughts and hopes of a man.

Obviously, I burned that letter as soon as I reached home. It would be a memento of him now, but not at all the kind I want. This was a brutal accusation, and too bloody fair. I went to my room and then sneaked out of the house so my mother would not notice. I had found some old potato sacks in our shed, and I took them in my saddle-bag when I cycled back to the cottages. With these sacks I made what I think could be regarded as a duly respectful covering and, wrapping Peter in it, set out to drag him to where the airfield was under construction. This seemed an awful thing to do with someone who had been so comely, bumping and tugging him over rough ground. It took hours, mostly across fields. Now and then I had to pause with him under a hedge, through fatigue or because I heard people near. The sacks still smelled of potatoes. Fortunately, the blackout was in force then, and even when we came near houses light did not fall on us. No question, we were an unusual couple.

Men had left tools where they were constructing runways and I dug a small grave and carefully eased him in. I took the sacking off him first and burned that later at home, like the letter and the envelope. I knew it would be wrong to include such workaday stuff in his final spot. Before I covered his body with soil, I took the ring off the cord around my neck and put it on his marriage finger. That seemed absolutely right, and anyone would have done the same. I placed him face down. Always we think of people buried looking up, like seeking the light. I suppose it is a religious thing – the eyes sightless, yet directed towards salvation, heaven, God. I could not bear to think of the dirt falling in around his eyes and cheeks and nose, though. A week later they slapped on the concrete, thick enough for loaded bombers.

There are still these days when I cannot resist coming here, but I've no real hope now of seeing what's left of Peter or the ring again, though I will attend once or twice more while the machines are working near that notable area. You can see that the ring would have been a sweet reminder of both Peter and Carlo, not that I could care less about Carlo, with his dreary looks and endless, greasy talk about Italy, or Wopland as we used to call it in the war. He was going back to his drab work as a boot repairer, and all that business about making it to headmaster was sky pie. Thank God he never could come looking for me after the war. It is Peter I think of all the time, and his brilliant, ownership anger on finding us undoubtedly conjoint in the woods, his marvellous eyes so injured and agleam.

Fortunately, even without the ring I have something special and, yes, living, to remember him by. I am sure, unswervingly sure, that my son was conceived that day Peter killed the father. These are rare circumstances, I should think. I called my son Paolo, which I felt to be a happy combination of the two names, Peter and Carlo. I was quite lucky not to lose him through the contortions with Peter's corpse. By the time Paolo was born in 1944, Britain and Italy were at peace, so local folk would not be too bothered about an Italian name. I decided, sod what they thought, anyway. I don't consider it at all disrespectful to the dead to say Paolo grew up a lot better looking than his dad and luckily got my nose.

# Free Enterprise

These days Mansel Shale drove the Jaguar himself owing to the recent quick death of his chauffeur and bodyguard, Denzil Lake. Denz was found with the barrels of two Astra .38 pistols in his mouth. Both guns had been fired. Manse thought Denz deserved this. He did not replace him. Once you'd discovered a very trusted staff member secretly snuggling up to your enemies, you worried about putting somebody in that kind of close job again. Denz definitely had good aspects. Well, obviously, or would Manse have hired him and kept him on? All right, Denzil had sometimes refused to wear the professional driver's cap particularly bought for him, but Shale never went into a full rage over this. Betrayal was different. Anyone trying it had to go.

Afterwards, there'd been questions for Manse. Although the .38s belonged to Denz himself, not everybody thought suicide, because squeezing both triggers at exactly the same moment would be tricky. And some said if he'd done it himself, recoil should have jolted the Astras out of his mouth. However, by now inquiries were fading, luckily. Nobody beside his family would see Denz Lake as worth long-term fret, and possibly not them, either.

Shale drew up and took a good glance all ways before leaving the Jaguar. Since Lake passed on in that rather skull-wrecked style, Manse did his own look-arounds. The Agincourt hotel car park had a lot of shadows. It was a thing about car parks near buildings. You carried out some real squinting, especially at vehicles already standing here. Cars gave a lot of cover, above all cars in shadow. The point was, Denzil's dirty scheming and end came during one of those all-out territory battles that often happened in high commerce – the kind Manse operated. And battles might continue.

Always such heavy perils lay near. They could touch anyone in the trade, however major, not just slabs of shoddy like Denz.

Despite shadows, he did not mind the Agincourt too much. Every six months, or a bit less, Manse and Ralph Ember put on a great dinner in the hotel's restaurant for main people from their two firms. Business results and prospects could be talked over in quite a relaxed way. It was Ember who originally suggested these social meetings, but Shale would admit they could be useful. Tonight, there might be tricky moments. Manse knew this. Any bad difficulties – he would squash them, not by violence or gunfire but through personality. This was leadership. Manse believed in leadership – not frothing, Hitler-type leadership, but sturdy. He climbed out of the Jag and moved towards the rear entrance of the hotel. The Agincourt's name was considerably historical. Shale liked that. It gave weight.

Following the meal and after the accounts had been presented, guests were entitled and even encouraged to raise queries. Shale or Ember or both would answer. Hotel employees withdrew. Tonight, as Manse expected, some angry questions came about the way immigrant dealers from old Soviet Bloc countries had moved in offering all commodities – ganja to crack to big H – and stealing clients.

Although Manse recognized this was a tough problem, he would not discuss it now. Shale and Ralph always made sure they spoke only about convenient topics at these dinners. For instance, they would never disclose the firms' true profits, or plans by him and Ember to kill someone, or more than one, if a widespread approach grew necessary. They did always issue sets of figures for the previous months because very understandably it was expected, but these only gave what Manse thought of as a *wise* version of things, enough to take care of morale.

Shale and Ember had beautiful cooperation between their two companies, and the dinners were intended to help this happy arrangement. They took turns on a yearly basis to organize the meals, pick the wines and settle up. It was Manse's year as host. He loved it. In the two or three meetings he presided at, he could show he knew as much about grand vintages as that loud smoothie, Ralph, with all his glossy wordage and grammar.

The firms' dinners always took place on a Monday night. Normally the restaurant would be closed then, but it could be booked for private parties. Manse thought the room more or less all right. Ancient weapons and other items hung on the walls, such as swords, longbows, shields, suits of armour, boars' heads, and what Shale heard one lad call halberds, or something like that – some pieces real, most mock. The hotel put on imitation medieval banquets at weekends, and these articles were supposed to give atmosphere then. In Mansel's view this wall stuff was childish and naff and knocked dignity from the Agincourt name. He thought of that famous song: 'Bring me my bow of burning gold, bring me my arrows of desire.' This would be nowhere near the same if the bow and arrows were plastic. But Manse believed in tolerance, up to quite a reasonable point. You could not expect refined taste from everyone.

The firms asked for an ordinary menu and drinks, though, with ordinary crockery and ordinary service, not waitresses putting too much on show up top, as in the banquet ads. Manse heard this used to be the rule in wenching and roistering times way back – such as the famed Nell Gwynne wearing sketchy garments to get the king going. But, for God's sake, the firms' Monday sessions were serious gatherings, where Manse and Ralph, chairmen of a pair of work-together companies, reported fully to their best personnel everything they could be allowed to know. Friendliness and some jollity seemed right in Shale's opinion, yes, but not big skin.

Tonight, jollity was scarce because of the competition worries. As a sideline, some of the new, foreign dealers ran very young, smuggled-in, Eastern European girls who were fed drugs to hook them, and then put on the street. These girls sold the products, as well as themselves. This was a hellish tactic.

'Ralph and myself personally, we definitely got the whole situation in mind,' Shale said as the bleats piled up from members of both firms.

'Unquestionably,' Ember said.

'Yes, Manse, Ralphy, you say that, but these people are—'

'We definitely got it in mind,' Shale said. 'Ralph and self, we note all factors, you can believe it.'

'This goes without saying,' Ralph told them.

'But Manse, Ralph, if we don't—'

'This is an area known in boardrooms and such as "executive action", meaning leave it to Ralphy and me. You heard of executive action at all? A well know, corporation term you might of missed. The topics you mention are not for open talk at a meat and potatoes do.'

'Manse is right,' Ember said.

'But Ralph, Manse, these guys are hard, usually tooled up and—'

'So, we leave it now,' Shale replied. 'Right? Right?' He got really brickish brick wall into his voice. This was what he meant when he'd promised himself to squash nuisance people. This was what he meant by leadership. If you were host, you made them know you were. And you let nobodies know they were nobodies.

Naturally, the Agincourt was not the only time Manse and Ralph Ember met. These dinners could be happy sessions, Shale would never deny that, but they amounted only to extras, only to trimming. When he and Ralph saw each other alone, they would discuss large policy matters and decide their own rewards. It would be tactless to let folk at the hotel beanfeast know Manse and Ember each took pay of around £600,000 yearly from the firms. This might have led to unrest. Of course, anyone with deep experience of turnover would guess at the profits. Manse knew some believed it more – even a million. You could not control people's minds. But it was vital to take care nobody except himself and Ralph had the figures as actual, proved fact. Guesses, rumours and gossip would never be enough to cause really bad envy and scheming, except in someone like Denzil, and Denzil was gone. Shale had made sure the cap sat on his coffin in the service, another victory.

In fact, there had been a dip in income for Manse and Ember lately. And Shale knew the Monday night questions strangled by him told why. In their routine, confidential pre-Agincourt powwow a week earlier, Mansel had said: 'We got to do something, Ralph.'

'In respect of what, Manse?'

'In respect of overseas interests on the streets. We could be sliding.'

The two were in Shale's den-study at his home. This was once St James's rectory, and it pleased Manse to think clergymen might have prepared their sermons and tried on new dog collars here. Ember had brought a bottle of Kressmann Armagnac. He probably thought this made up for the refusal ever to allow Shale into Ralph's own place, what he called 'a manor house', named Low Pastures. Ember's residence and family must be kept clean, and always separate from the substance game, mustn't they? Oh, yes. The jerk was like that, hoping to seem gentry.

'I see these disappointing figures as very much a temporary matter, Manse,' Ember stated. 'There's been unhelpful publicity lately about bad addiction cases. That kind of thing always squeezes sales for a while. Only a while, though.'

'We got to hit one of these people,' Shale replied. 'Urgent.'

'One of which people, Manse?'

'They think they can sneak in here and set theirselves up, like entitled. We got to hit one of their high people. The one they call Tirana. It's the name of some town over there. Where he came from.'

'Albania,' Ember said. 'The capital.'

'Ah, the way they called George Washington after Washington.'

'Well, no, the—'

'If we hit him, this Tirana, the rest get to realise the situation – that they got no rights in this domain. But they also get to realize that what they *have* got – got from us – is big, smart opposition. Maybe then they'll all go back to their own country, or try it somewhere else – London, Manchester, Winnipeg.'

'This is extreme, Manse.'

Shale had tapped the genuine, For-Our-Eyes-Only accounts with a couple of fingers. '*This* could get extreme. I mean the slide.'

'I don't say there's no threat, Manse, but as I see it we need a more gradual approach. A measured strategy.'

'People at the Agincourt next Monday night will want to

know how we're going to handle it, Ralph. They wonder about what's known as their career paths. They thought they had a brill future and now here comes this Tirana and such.'

'I'm confident you'll dispose of any unhelpful questions at the Agincourt, Manse.'

'Oh, I can close down their bother, yes, but Tirana will still be around.'

'Perhaps we shouldn't exaggerate his impact, Manse.'

As Shale saw things, Ember was often like this – so dodgy about action. Many called him Panicking Ralph, or Panicking Ralphy, and he did get severe hesitation now and then, the way other people got rheumatism. He had to be helped along. 'If we slay this Tirana in a nice spot, the crew who work with him will know what we're saying to them, Ralph. They'll know it exactly.'

'What do you mean, "a nice spot"?'

'Like a sign.'

'In what way, a sign, Manse?'

'So that the way he been done and *where* he been done will show them they use business methods not at all suitable for here, not at all liked here.'

'I should think they already know that,' Ember said.

'But the slaughter of one of their generals – this would sort of clinch it for them, really light up the message. Or like with wolves.'

'With wolves, Manse? I don't—'

'Wolves. Shoot their pack leader and the rest are lost. We got something lovely here, Ralph. Two busy firms in agreement and the Assistant Chief Constable, Mr Iles, also happy as long as no violence from us where the public might get hurt. Oh, something like Denzil and the .38s don't affect that because it was out of sight and only Denzil, anyway. But now this Tirana and others arrive, and the whole thing, I mean the whole structure – the whole structure could be shook so bad it falls. *Our* whole structure.'

'These people, the Tiranas and so on, they fight among themselves, Manse, trying for dominance. It has to be possible they'll wipe out one another. This is probably why Iles hasn't smashed them. He thinks they'll do it for him.'

'Takes too long. By then our firms could be finished. This

Tirana, he got to be done, Ralph, and he got to be done by us and they got to know he been done by us.'

'Well, I—'

'Mr Iles – he would *expect* us to handle this. He would think it's part of the deal with him, like *understood*. Well, everything in the deal's understood. It's not going to be written down and signed like buying a TV, is it? Most probably Mr Iles is waiting to hear this Tirana been took out of the scene so the scene can get back to what it ought to be, meaning gorgeously peaceful and with our firms gorgeously climbing, not slipping.' Manse took a good sip of the Kressmann. It was great, no question. Ember owned a drinking club called the Monty, and got all his bottles cheap. He would not let Manse meet him there, either, though, because Ember hoped to turn the Monty into some high class joint one day like a grand, exclusive London club, for professors, judges, pin ball machine makers, bishops, boxing promoters. Mad. The Monty was a sink. Half the members had done jail and the rest would. Some called Ember 'Milord Monty', as well as Panicking Ralph.

'What you carrying?' Shale asked.

'In what respect, Manse?'

'Armament. I don't mean what you got aboard now, tonight. I know you would not carry a gun into my home and not just because it was a rectory previous. You would have more respect – in general. But what I mean, when you *do* have to carry something what is it? You used to like a Walther, didn't you, but then a Beretta? Still the Beretta? Myself, I'm into Heckler and Koch, same as the police. They know what's the best stopper, so why not copy? 9 mm Parabellum. But sweetly lightweight. Like you, Ralph, I hope I got some sensitivity about weapons and I would not bring them into this actual study where holy duties might have took place once. But I expect you noticed a painting in the other room by what's known in art lingo as a pre-Raphaelite called Arthur Hughes. I go for them pre-Raphaelites. Great on tresses. There's a combo safe behind that with Mr Heckler and Koch in and a fat box of rounds. I got another safe in this room, but only for cash and our private accounts.'

Next week, when the Agincourt function came and those niggles kept jabbing from some troops, Shale would have liked to tell them about the Beretta and the Heckler and Koch and the plentiful ammo, but impossible, obviously. All Manse could say over and over was he and Ralph had matters in mind – true, but not satisfactory. Just the same, some information had to stay buttoned. He would not even mention the name Tirana, and definitely not the spot where Manse considered it best to do him – best because, as he had explained to Ralphy, it would speak a message. During their meeting in Shale's house, working out the attack plans, he was afraid for a couple of minutes that Ember might go into one of his panics just at the *thought* of a shoot-out, and get so he couldn't talk and hardly breathe. Manse would hate anything like that on his property. But although Ralph had one big tremble, a lot of face twitch, plus a spurt of sweat on his top lip, things did not get worse, and after a minute he seemed more or less all right.

And he seemed more or less all right when they drove out towards the Morton Cross area at around midnight on Thursday to see off Tirana. Manse had picked this as the best location. To snuff him here would have a true meaning, and a meaning all invaders could read, even if their English was rough. Until now, most of the town's drug dealing took place in bars and caffs around the Valencia Esplanade area, or, for richer users, on a dockside floating restaurant called The Eton Boating Song, not far from there. This was where Shale and Ember's people did their pushing. Tradition.

But Tirana and other trespassers in their foreign, ignorant way had begun to work on the border of two different districts, Morton Cross and Inton. This was what caused those moans and snivels at the Agincourt. Some custom had already left the Valencia and moved to Morton and Inton. Manse tried to block and comfort them at the dinner, but he knew the trouble was grave. Clearly. And so that warning to Ralph in their rectory one-to-one. And so the need to fight.

Manse had researched Tirana. He took a jaunt most nights to Morton and Inton and did some dealing himself. But mainly he seemed there to scout around in the big BMW and make sure his people worked full out and got no peril from other crews aiming at take-over. Manse considered slaughter of

Tirana in this district at a prime trading hour would be the most vivid declaration that Morton and Inton were not the proper site for pushing, and that Tirana and his friends and enemies could never be right for this branch of established British business, anyway. They did not know the decent, accepted rules, and would not care about them if they did. Mighty gratitude was certain from Assistant Chief Desmond Iles when he saw the Morton-Inton development rubbished by first-class, point-blank salvoes into Tirana, and the selling once more nicely confined to its usual ground, and to Manse Shale and Ralphy Ember.

Manse had watched Ralph check his armament before they set out. 'So you *do* stick with the Beretta.'

'The same type. Not the same gun.'

Shale laughed gently for a while at this. 'Well, no, hardly. Traceable. A switch every so often, or even oftener than every so often, but always you renew with a model that's familiar. Sensible. You can trust it. Myself, I'm getting to feel something similar about the Heckler. Sort of companions, aren't they, Ralph? Reliable comrades?' Important to make him feel calm and strong, save him from one of his spasms now the operation had really started. 'There's Tirana. As almost ever.' The BMW was parked on a small grass island where three roads converged. From here Tirana could watch dealers and girls near the Morton Cross shopping mall and two side streets leading away to Inton. Shale cut the Jaguar's engine. 'I drive alongside, pull up and we both fire. All right, Ralph? Both.' Shale took the Heckler from a shoulder holster and put it ready on his lap under the steering wheel. 'All right, Ralph? I mustn't wait here. He'll see. It's a good moment. Not many folk about.'

Ember did not produce the Beretta. 'There's someone in the passenger seat,' he replied.

'A girl. That happens sometimes. One of the imported kids. He'll take her for the night. A perk. We can try not to blast her. We'll be close and OK for accuracy. All right, Ralph? The Beretta?'

'What's the matter with her?' Ember replied.

'What?' Shale said. Was Ralphy going to bits after all – making delays?

'Crying,' Ember said. 'Arms all around him, like life-saving in the sea. Really weeping. Listen. The driver's window's down.'

'They get excited, some of these kids. And they got to put on a passion act – especially she would for him, the master.'

'The way he's sitting,' Ember said.

'What about it?'

'Not right somehow.'

'What way's he supposed to sit then?'

'She's holding him up. I think he's hit already,' Ember replied.

'He's *what*?'

'Hit. He's dead. No movement.'

'Christ,' Shale said.

'Dead or on the way.'

Shale stared. After a minute he said: 'Yes. Sharp, Ralph. One of his own lot done him?'

'I told you. They fight. They snipe. They all want control.'

Shale thought. 'Yes, well we should vamoose, Ralph. Quit. They might be around still. Or we could get hauled in for doing him, which would be sick when we didn't, only wanted to.' He reached to restart the Jaguar. Ember gripped his wrist and stopped him. Shale said: 'We can't do anything now.'

'The girl,' Ember said. 'Wrong to leave her like that. A kid, a foreign kid.'

'She's only a—'

Ember had already opened the door of the Jaguar and begun to walk fast towards the BMW. Shale put the Heckler and Koch back into its holster and then followed him at a trot. God, was this Panicking Ralphy? Backbone transplant? How? Pity for this teenage tart did it? Yet he couldn't be *all* panic, or he'd never have landed his club and his manor house.

They reached the BMW. Ember pulled open the passenger door. The girl was sobbing. She turned to them, terror all through her. The movement made her release Tirana and he slumped to the side. As he did, Shale had time to see a tidy bullet wound in his forehead and a blood trickle. 'What happened, child?' Ralph said, his voice full of caring and grease, like a priest's.

'They came.'

'Who?'

'Yes, they came,' she replied. She made a pistol shape with one hand. The hand shook. It could be fright. It could be her coming down from a fix. She was plump-faced, pale-skinned, perhaps fifteen years old, her speech slow, her accent massive. 'But so quiet,' she said.

'A silenced gun,' Shale said.

She leaned across and put her cheek against the fat shoulder pad of Tirana's pin stripe jacket. 'He dead, oh, yes. But I loved,' she said. 'I love him. And he love me. Much. Very much. He said this. He said love.'

'Yes, I expect so. Leave here now,' Ember told her. 'At once.' He took out a wedge of money and gave her what looked to Shale like five twenties. 'Get clear.' Shale searched his own pockets and found six tens and a twenty. He handed these to her.

She folded the money, counting it. 'You pay. You want threesome?' she said. 'Coke after?'

'Just go,' Ember replied.

'That your Jag? I been in Jags before. Many. And Mercs. Once a Roller – Roller Royce. You see, I know threesome.'

'This is talk and more talk,' Ember snarled at her. 'It's dangerous for you here. Disappear.'

'Ah, talk? You want talk? You want me talk dirty? Yes, me, I have many, many dirty English words. Prick. Clit.'

# Body Language

O ne Tuesday afternoon, when Professor Cameron Phelps was nearing the end of his lecture to a Contemporary Fiction class on The Detective Story in Modern Novel and Film, a man he certainly recognized from drinks parties given by the English Society a while back suddenly appeared in the doorway near him, stood for a moment scanning the undergraduates, then stepped forward, pointing some sort of handgun at Geraldine Marques, sitting two students in on the third row, and shot her through the head, shot her twice.

When the first bullet hit her, Geraldine's face did not disintegrate or explode, as that hanging melon does on screen during the famous target practice scene in *The Day of the Jackal,* but it certainly seemed to Cameron to lose all the conventional qualities and lineaments of a face. For what might have been a quarter of a second, one of those looks of surprise, and yet at the same time of almost serene resignation, which in quite a few thrillers comes over the features of those about to be wasted, did register around Geraldine's eyes. That, though, must have been before the gun went off. Afterwards, nobody could have read anything in her expression because there was none, only this sudden dishevelment of the bone structure.

It was an old-fashioned lecture theatre, with long, curved, narrow mahogany benches going the full width of the room, except for the aisles, and steeply tiered to the back, where there was another door. Geraldine slipped down under the bench after the initial shot and, from his spot behind the lectern at the front, Cameron could not see much of her, only the whiteness of a cricket sweater she had regularly appeared in lately, and the grey-streaked, fairish mass of her hair. The man with the pistol went to the aisle, stepped up two tiers, jumped onto the third bench, and walked a few steps along it, scattering the books and papers of the couple of students between the aisle and Geraldine. He stood over the place where she lay and aimed the gun at her again.

'No,' Cameron yelled. 'Why? Oh, why?' He moved out from behind the lectern, the copy of *The Friends of Eddie Coyle,* from which he had been reading to illustrate irony, still in his hand. The man turned and stared at him for a moment. Her husband? Geraldine was a mature student with sons, from one of whom she might have borrowed the sweater. Didn't Cameron recall drinking Chianti with this man at some social evening for students and partners in her first year? A plumber? A roofer? 'Mr Marques,' he shouted, 'you'll never get away with this. Why don't we just talk it over like two sensible people?'

The man turned back, then bent down as if to get a better sighting of Geraldine on the floor. She must have rolled partway under the seat. In a moment he did something very extraordinary, which to Cameron carried a kind of sparkling symbolism. The attacker actually kneeled on the third bench, his back to Cameron, the gun pointed down in front of him at Geraldine. The contradiction seemed to Cameron heavy with meaning – this traditional attitude of subjection, even supplication, yet also this attitude of terrible dominance. In his teaching he always stressed the suitability of crime as a novelistic subject, because of its multitudinous complexities: hence today's look at Irony, for instance.

The man fired again, and soon Cameron glimpsed a large, spreading red rectangle appear on the shoulder and back of the cricket sweater. Again that seemed to him significant: this garment of a rigidly formulated, indeed venerable, game now touched by deep disorder. He could smell what he knew must be cordite, sharp, pleasant, lingering. The man straightened, then walked swiftly, assuredly, back along the bench towards the door. Yes, perhaps a roofer. He had on what looked to Cameron like remarkably expensive brown fashion boots, possibly even Timberland. Roofers made a bomb, and plumbers. But how absurd, he thought, to be noticing such things when a woman lay dead and the murderer was escaping. Yet the mind was ungovernable, following its own streams of consciousness, not exactly regardless of events, but only contingent to them. He would diary his reactions with exactitude.

To his classes he had continually pointed out that action, action, and more action was the essence of crime writing: explicit philosophizing, even character analysis, had to be brief, if not actually sketchy, in the interest of pace. Yearly he quoted to his pupils that saying of – or was it about? – Len Deighton, the spy author, stipulating that if a narrative grew slack, the way to recover was to have somebody barge through the door holding a gun. And now it had really happened – and yes, by God, it worked: the whole tempo of things had changed. This lecture theatre's atmosphere no longer seemed even vaguely comparable with what it was when he had been skillfully elaborating on the fierce irony in the title of George V. Higgins's *The Friends of Eddie Coyle* – where 'friends' meant the reverse. No question, it had been a well-prepared and genuinely felt lecture of very bright insights, but certainly the students had reacted much more vividly to the interruption by the armed man and the shooting of Geraldine. In fact, they were still tense, still white or flushed, many of them, some weeping.

So, then, action. The only relevant contribution he could think of now was pursuit of the gunman, who had left the room by the upper door, slamming it behind him. Cameron raced up the tiered floor after him. 'No!' an undergraduate cried. 'My God, Professor, he's armed. Let the police deal with it.'

Yet that was not how these things were shaped at all. If some innocent bystander is drawn in during a crime, he is drawn in and has no choice but to become involved, though fearful. This crisis was what in Hemingway – an occasional practitioner of crime fiction – would be called 'the moment of truth', and one could only put one's manliness on the line and hope it was of due quality. Cameron still carried the paperback George V. Higgins novel. Would he throw this at the gunman should he encounter him now? It was a paradigm situation: the pathetically ill-armed, run-of-the-mill, even insignificant man – one of life's ordinary Joes – willing to confront the violent brute, and able to offer against this threat only a farcically negligible missile, plus, though, his courage, determination, and the blessed instinct of good's resistance to evil. He remembered Fredric March coping with Bogart and other hoodlums in *The Desperate Hours*. Somehow and eventually this good and typical figure always won: art's pressure towards tidiness ensured it. He felt wonderfully heartened as he ran, and considered it not foolhardy but obligatory to ignore the well-intentioned, frantic, yelled warning.

Then, as Cameron neared the door, it was flung open again and the man stood there once more, his gun raised. Jesus, had all that rubbish stuff about Hemingway and blessed instincts knackered this narrative so badly that the technique of an armed intruder bursting through the door had to be given such an immediate second run? Cameron stopped, horrified, and they stared at each other. This was the instant, wasn't it, when a fictional character would think lovingly of all those precious things that constituted the texture of existence – bird song, children's laughter, a modicum of Turkish delight, Mozart and/or Randy Crawford, plus, of course, the clean smack of a ball hit perfectly into the pool pocket.

'Why? You ask why?' the man cried in a strangely hollow, yet at the same time immensely powerful, voice.

'Yes, why?' Cameron answered. There could be a remarkable strength from repetition in dialogue: the strength of incantation.

'I'll tell you why. Oh yes, I'll tell you why.' Perhaps this man attended evening creative writing classes and also knew about incantation.

One of the more promising students shouted: 'What we are seeing here is violence as an outcrop of fundamental psychological disturbance. Character blazoned in action.'

'Come,' Cameron replied, leading down towards the lectern. He turned his back on the gun, knowing somehow that this was a gesture which could not provoke a shot. It would have been hopelessly outside the mode. 'We are a university and everyone is entitled to his point of view. Tell me, are you Mr Marques? Did we not take wine together, sir, on some earlier occasion?' Often elaborate politeness darkened prevailing menace even further, by showing the formalities of society in peril and so indicating their extreme fragility.

'It doesn't matter who I am.'

'But may I call you Mr Marques?'

'Call me what you will. See me simply as someone with a mission. I have fulfilled half of it.'

'Half?'

Cameron felt a terrible fear grip him. If this were fiction it would have been an example of that storytelling trick of not giving the reader too much too soon: standard in crime writing, where narrative flair was the art of holding back. Lord, what was the other half of the mission? *Who* was the other half? As to halves, for half of half a term in Geraldine's second year Cameron had been banging her three or four times a week, after which she moved on to, he thought, Graham Liatt in the History of Political Ideas. The kind of ferocious sexual guilt that waylaid the hero in both *Presumed Innocent* and *Fatal Attraction* ravaged Cameron for a moment, though the actual circumstances in those tales were very different, naturally.

Marques followed him down to the lectern. Cameron replaced *The Friends of Eddie Coyle* on it and addressed the class: 'This is Geraldine's, well, husband. Was. We're often left without a full statement of the murderer's point of view. Perhaps we get excessively preoccupied with the restoration of legitimacy, the efficacy of the detective as agent of civic recuperation. Today this can be corrected. I don't know whether Mr Marques will agree to take questions later.'

Cameron could see Geraldine's body again, exactly as it had been, except that the red rectangle on the sweater had grown. The greyness in her hair had almost put him off that liaison in her second year, and had ensured that he did not grieve irreparably when, after a few weeks, she grew restless for Liatt, or some other teaching ram. Perhaps he should have forgone even that short affair. Regret, vain second thoughts, incomprehensibility at one's own actions – these were the essence of the grippingly dramatic. Watching her, inert, he realized she was what Martin Amis in his novel *London Fields* would rather jokingly call the murderee – the passive figure, to whom something is done, namely death:

71

it could be significant that the term was applied to a woman, the exploited sex – feminist critics might like to mull that. Geraldine's body bellowed body language.

'She was moving away from me, losing me,' Marques declared. 'That's why I am here.'

'Geraldine was?' Cameron asked.

'And so I decided to bring her to rest. She is mine again now, only mine, forever mine. Reclaimed at last.' Passionately, his voice rose to even greater force, easily reaching people in the back row, with which Cameron himself sometimes had difficulty, and Marques lifted both hands in a kind of agonized yet victorious declaration.

He had placed the pistol on the copy of *The Friends of Eddie Coyle* on the lectern, within a couple of metres of Cameron. While Marques was stretching like that, it might have been possible to snatch the gun. This did not seem at all the proper way things should go, though. Instead, there ought to come a moment – a moment when all the talking had been done, all the explanations covered, all the over-tones and wider issues hinted at – when Marques would voluntarily surrender the weapon in a telling gesture and Cameron would shake his hand, look once more squarely into his eyes, seeing only agony and loneliness there, and then take him regretfully but unswervingly to justice. It was important to round off matters, hit a note of tragedy rather than of banal *force majeure*. This kind of touch was what produced resonances, lifted even brutal crime to a signifi-cant plane.

In any case, Cameron was not sure he would be able to manage the automatic usefully even if he did grab it. It was of dark blue metal, horribly like the tint of a bruise, Cameron thought – upsettingly so, disablingly so. But how wimpish a reaction! Was this a sign of the essential impotence of the scholar and academic as against the Man of Action – the Man of Action whom scholars and academics battened on: historians with Attila or Wellington or Rommel; himself – Cameron – in this particular course, with murderers, bank robbers, roofers?

'How do you mean she's yours again now, only yours, forever yours?' Kate Bilton called from the end of the back row. 'How can she be yours, only yours? She's stone dead. This is surely sloppy thinking. She's not anyone's now. Blast someone's skull to establish possession? A bit roundabout, wouldn't you say?'

This kid Bilton had always suffered from a foul dose of literalism. Why she was doing an English course at all Cameron found it hard to tell. Realizing he had to say something to help Marques out of his probably limited articulation, Cameron replied: 'Death can supply a kind of resolution, surely, Kate. It has its own awful, majestic neatness. Take the end of *Bonnie and Clyde* – painful, yes, and yet in its oblique way triumphant.'

'Oh, that's Emily Dickinson-type crap,' Bilton said. 'What we've got here is a middle-aged, tireless shagger-around lying broken up on the floor of room B117, knocked over by a husband scared of scandal, AIDS, pox, and performance comparisons. End of story.'

Oh, how wrong she could be, with her rough, youthful common sense! The end of Geraldine, certainly, but not at all end of story.

'Moving away from you?' Cameron asked him. 'Do you mean socially and educationally through her degree course here? Believe me, I do understand. This is a theme in so much bitter and fierce crime: the class battle localized in some terrible, emblematic love dispute. Her new cultural acquisitions – literature, scansion, critical theory, familiarity with the *Faerie Queen* – made you feel excluded and uncontrollably envious, yes? Shut out? I see. Social class – the root of almost all major conflict in the British novel, including the crime novel. Its motivating power not always easy to grasp for those in foreign cultures – the USA or Japan – yet so vital, for all that.' Cameron turned sympathetically to him. 'Yet being a roofer is a fine and noble trade, Mr Marques, not to say indispensable.' Then, after a moment, Cameron switched back to the undergraduates and gave a small, apologetic smile. 'But, of course, you will have spotted that even as I enunciate this I sound patronizing, false, a slave of that very concept of social class. I don't even know this man's first name. Mr Marques. That form of address indicates I am addressing a mere artisan.'

'Roofer? Who's a fucking roofer?' Marques replied. 'I'm in the Foreign Office, passed out second in Great Britain.'

That use of the expletive really intrigued Cameron. He always gave two full lecture hours to the function of swearing in crime fiction. So often it could be used to compromise and amend the very class categorizations they were discussing here now, bringing magnificent ambiguity. It was exactly right for Marques to employ that demotic, briskly consonantal term when, at the same time, he was announcing himself virtually part of the establishment through his work and his, clearly, first-class intellect. Of course, the word had lost a good deal of its impact now through widespread use in prose of all genres. In the States, as Cameron told his classes, it had been necessary to augment its power a little by adding 'mother': 'a motherfucking roofer?' might have had an extra punch about it, and created yet more fascinating uncertainties of the social ranking of the speaker.

'Moving away from you in which sense then?' Cameron asked.

'I couldn't satisfy her any longer.'

Cameron immediately felt easier. He had failed to satisfy Geraldine Marques also, so if this was a jealousy job, her husband's rage should not fall on him. In fact, Geraldine had advised Cameron to try sex therapy, or some cock-specializing pseudo witch doctor she knew in one of the city's mean, multiracial, ghetto streets where a man might go who was not himself mean but who could not get it – or keep it – up. That standard weight of guilt was lifted and he no longer even vaguely thought of snatching the gun for self-protection. Was Marques after Liatt then? This was the second half of the mission? Cameron had heard Graham gave women as good as he got, in the current phrase, and then a bit more. Two girls in this class spoke rapturously of him, including the formidable Bilton. Had Geraldine told Marques of Liatt? His extermination was to come next? Among the political ideas Liatt taught, he favoured radical, old-fashioned Toryism and wooed women with a mixture of haughty surliness and extravagant charm. The best eternal triangle plots always had some thematic, possibly stylistic, aspects, as well as the mere clash of rival lusts, and perhaps Marques was Social

Democrat or even Labour. Then again, the sound of his surname – did it have yet further ambiguities: Marques, Marx? That also would distance him from Liatt. This could be altogether a marvellously layered situation.

Cameron wondered whether he should try to get a warning to Graham Liatt that he was about to have at least his face shot off and maybe worse. Yet there was a kind of unfolding inevitability about the way things seemed to move this afternoon. He felt it would be the behaviour of a philistine, even a vandal, to interfere. Matters had to take their sombre course, hadn't they?

And then the upper-lecture-theatre door was flung open again. A man stood there. 'Him!' Marques cried, in obvious, appalled recognition and anger.

It was not Liatt, but Albert Quant of French, bald, stooped, wet-nosed, filthy-jacketed, stained-trousered, greasy-breathed, loud-shirted, cheap-sandalled, who should have gone through early retirement years ago, but who somehow hung on and on and was now almost too late for late retirement. Alby (Froggy-Boy) Quant? It seemed unbelievable that he should have been giving it to Geraldine, or anyone else postwar. Alby, not Liatt, was the second half of the mission?

'I heard you were in the building,' Albert remarked, in that hesitant way he always affected, the sod, pretending that English was unnatural to him because of his deep immersion in the cross-Channel parlance. 'I am here.'

'Bursting through the door like that. So, where's your bloody pistol?' Cameron asked.

'You told Geraldine she deserved to live among gods because she was so lovely,' Marques cried. 'Where did that leave me, even though I spent hundreds on these boots she admired?'

'I taught her the works of de Musset,' Quant replied. 'That is true. She seemed impressed by certain poems.' He fell into that creepy, lopsided, reciting stance which could clear the senior common room. 'One work in particular impressed her. It begins, *Regrettez-vous le temps?* I'll translate, shall I, very loosely, and I'll telescope? We enjoyed together those lines, Geraldine and I. They go like this: *Do you regret having missed that past period when the classical gods descended and inhabited this very earth? Our trouble is that we have come too late, you and I, into a world that is too old.'*

Marques cried: 'That's it! She told me I was no use to her any longer, because I was of a hopelessly faded era. Damn it, she had come to regard you as a kind of deity – Zeus himself, for God's sake, as it were.'

Alby dealt fingerwise with a string of snot that swung suddenly from one nostril. 'I'm afraid this enhancement of my identity does happen now and then with women when we're into de Musset,' he replied. 'Especially mature women students. I don't encourage it.'

'She said she had come to imagine you as a great, beautiful, thudding-winged swan,' Marques complained. 'Took the kids' white sweaters to mock up appropriate plumage and improve her attractiveness.'

'As a swan Zeus did get it very effectively and significantly away on Leda,' Quant replied. 'I'm sure you know that. Yes, that was an example of when a god did indeed come on earth.'

Cameron was delighted. 'Oh, this is a murder with a definite classical flavour and, thus, right in the central British tradition. So many of our most distinguished crime-mystery stories are aimed at those with a thorough public school and Oxbridge humanities training. These books are intended, as the phrase goes, I think, for the fine mind momentarily at leisure, eg, in works by Dorothy L. Sayers. Classical, Biblical, archaeological references may abound, bringing a brilliant richness.'

Marques reached out for the pistol, then replaced it on the lectern, as if the thought of doing Quant, with his special status, was preposterous, especially from a distance of more than thirty metres and up the slope.

'You must flee now,' Quant remarked.

'No,' Cameron said, aghast. 'Things have surely come full circle. It is the juncture for retribution, for surrender, for completeness.'

'Those considerations are the banalities of a merely terrestrial, law-and-order-obsessed, sickeningly tit-for-tat-orientated society. Go, Marques. Go now,' Quant cried. 'Run free, follow your impulses, as did the glorious gods of old.'

'I do not deny the classics, Albert,' Cameron replied, 'and in fact I embrace one of their prime concepts: catharsis – the purging, the sacrifice. This now is due. This is the necessary culmination.'

'Balls,' Quant remarked.

Kate Bilton, looking from the lecture theatre window, said: 'Too late, anyway. Our friends the cops are here, with flak jackets and dogs – using the term "friends" ironically, of course. The porter must have been on the phone, hearing the shots. Marques is never going to get out.'

'This just had to be the final chapter,' Cameron said sadly, yet with satisfaction, gingerly confiscating the pistol. Then he leant forward to shake hands formally, meaningfully, almost mournfully with Marques. As he did so, some inadvertent pressure was applied to the trigger of the gun in his other hand and it went off. Marques fell. Dying, he gasped: 'I am truly with her forever now.' To Cameron, decorum seemed admirably present in this flourish of reconciliatory rhetoric. Blood welled.

'Christ, doesn't he spout, though?' Bilton said.

# Rendezvous One

Harpur detested running undercover jobs. In any case, Desmond Iles, the Assistant Chief, had put an absolute ban on these operations. Now and then, though, Harpur decided to ignore that. Of course, it could be dangerous to ignore Iles, and not just career dangerous: physically dangerous, limb and/or eye dangerous, life-expectancy dangerous. But Harpur had always realized policing was a risk game.

Most of his inner-city, hardened officers were too well known to trick their way into a gang. So, it usually meant finding someone from an outlying station, preferably someone young and new to the Service: no big, publicized cases in their CV. That is, they were novice cops, and normally might still need some lumps of guidance from a venerable Detective Chief Superintendent like Harpur. Not always possible, once they began to play crooked. They had to live a role, like an actor, and contact with them might imperil this pretence. A good undercover man or woman infiltrated the highest and most secret corners of a villain firm, and had to be faultless in their part. In those highest and most secret corners, a rumbled snoop could be most secretly tortured and done to death. It had happened a while ago to a detective called Raymond Street. For ever, this darkened Iles's soul. Thus the ban.

At present, Harpur had a youngster in one of the drug outfits on the west side of the city. Half in. Don't rush. Louise Machin came from one of those rural outposts. He had asked for her secondment, allegedly to help with youth club liaison. Yes, allegedly. If Iles got a whiff of that he'd know the real ploy instantly and come looking.

But a minimum connection with her had to be kept. Harpur

met Louise at pre-fixed times to talk method and information, if she had any, not at her place or his place or headquarters or any of the supposedly safe but predictable rendezvous sites such as supermarkets, art galleries, swimming baths, cinemas, the opera. Instead, he liked to use the rippling turmoil of Parent-Teacher Association get-togethers at a school somewhere. This would not be his own children's school, naturally. At the start of every term, the local paper printed a schedule for PTA gatherings, and he settled dates and places with Louise then. He reasoned they could blend with the parent crowd and nobody would realize they had no offspring there.

Tonight, talking at the back of a geography room, Harpur said: 'Listen, Louise, at every meeting I tell undercover officers that, if they get the smallest sense of something wrong, ditch it. Leave. Go fast to headquarters or any nick or my house or even Mr Iles's house. Abort. Don't return for belongings.' Meteorological maps heavy with wind arrows crowded the walls.

'You sound like a fire-drill, sir,' Louise replied.

'It *is* a fire-drill.'

'"The smallest sense of something wrong" meaning I feel they've spotted me?'

'There's been something like that?'

'Don't get het up, sir. No.'

He tried to read her eyes and face, in case she was acting off-hand and brave and fucking mad. But one reason he had picked her was she could thesp and knew how to deadpan. 'I say this to everyone, every time,' he told her.

'You said.'

'Routine. I don't want you to feel alarmed.'

'No, right,' she replied.

Her detachment, even jauntiness, scared him. She was gazing about the room, more interested in the maps and chatter than in Harpur's warnings. Another reason he had picked her was she did seemed calm and full of self-belief. 'Or if you can't get out, ring the urgent assistance number. Always a help team there. They'll come and get you. You've memorized the number?'

'Haven't I poll-parroted it often enough for you?'

'Standard check, that's all.'

'Routine,' she said.

He longed to ask her to repeat the number once again, but decided she might be right and he was into hyper-fret. Did she realize how fast your memory crumbled when you were screwed by fear? Did British Telecom realize, loading us with all those fucking digits? 'So, is there anything?' he asked.

'I think they may have clipped someone.'

Harpur didn't mind Americanisms. All languages searched for softer ways of saying killed: a kind of woebegone, daft delicacy. 'We've no unexplained deads reported.'

'Just the same, that's what I'm picking up. They could lose a body, couldn't they – sink it, concrete it, burn it?' she said.

Yes, they could. He did not say this. He wanted the silence so she would work aloud at justifying her guess to him. At the other end of the room, two teachers talked to parents, with a good-sized queue on chairs waiting. A whiteboard still had part of a rainfall lesson on it, the words DO NOT ERASE big in the bottom right-hand corner. Harpur liked schools, at least as an adult. They spoke of continuity, suggested things might be long-term OK. Stupid, and he knew it.

'I can't work out who,' she said. 'Yet.'

'One of their own people? Or the competition?'

'Nobody's missing in the firm, as far as I can see,' Louise replied.

'What's it based on?' Time for the head-on questions.

'What?'

'Your . . . your feeling someone's dead.'

'Based on a feeling,' she said.

'Something heard? Something seen?'

'Based on a feeling.'

'Yes, but—'

'A feeling,' she replied.

'Or maybe not heard, but do people go suddenly quiet when you're around? In that case, get out now. Now.'

'I'm only middle rank in the firm, so far. If they've killed they might want it kept boardroom, so when they clam it needn't mean they've sussed me.'

'Is it top people who go quiet when you're around? You get close to them?' Harpur asked.

'What the job's about, yes – getting to the chiefs? I've learned to tell the men from the boys. No good infiltrating flunkies.'

God, she was so magnificently assured, the dodgy, arrogant young cow. She could look like a teenager but talked like a veteran. Harpur must learn how to tell the women from the girls. Harpur knew he could not have selected better, unless she finished slaughtered.

When their talk paused he caught occasional fragments of conversation between parents and teachers: '. . . been all over the main rivers in Africa with Celia, Mr Green. When I say "been over" I don't mean like in a canoe, but at home, learning . . . Nile, Congo, Limpopo. Celia will never sell rivers short.' Harpur was afraid the queue would run out soon and then the teachers might call Louise or him for a consultation about non-existent pupils.

'If you're that near to getting something sizeable, we should have an earlier meeting than our schedule says,' Harpur suggested. 'As soon as you've found a name and possible location for the body we'll close you down. A three weeks' wait after this is too long.'

'I'd prefer things as planned. I'm used to the pattern. I don't want to feel hurried.'

'No, but—'

'Best as it is, sir.'

She was offering a cold lesson in how not to panic. All the same, he felt panicky for her. She was a biggish, wide-faced girl of twenty-three, not pretty, not especially bright in appearance, though *damn* bright. At least, he hoped damn bright – above all, bright enough to spot the difference between getting treated as a run-of-the-mill exec in Dubal's organisation, and being lulled as a spy. She was dressed to suit her supposed career: jeans, brown leather bomber jacket, trainers. Her fair/mousy hair had been chop cut, tufted all directions.

The route into Dubal's firm had been to buy from one of his dealers for a time, then offer to sell to pals. Dubal's people gave her small amounts at first and, when she came back with the money, increased her stock. She disposed of this, too, and brought the takings, without going junkied herself. Main folk in the firm might want to meet her soon, even Dubal personally.

She didn't actually sell to pals, but to anyone. What she couldn't sell she stashed and made up the money with some Harpur provided from his informant fund. Supervision of that was woolly. The ACC knew Harpur would never tell him about his grasses, regardless of the rule saying keep superiors briefed.

'This will upset Mr Iles, won't it, sir?'

'What?'

'Dubal murdering, or Dubal's minions, on his say-so? Isn't there a kind of deal?'

'Deal?' Harpur replied. He made it come out as true puzzlement.

'Dubal, Mansel Shale, Ralphy Ember can do their drugs business as long as they guarantee peace on the streets, and especially no deaths. Isn't that Mr Iles's arrangement?'

A brilliant summary. Harpur chuckled a bit. 'Policing could never function like that, Louise.'

'I don't think I understand Mr Iles – his mind – what I've heard of him.'

'No great problem,' Harpur replied, sticking with a fragment of chuckle. Oh, no? Christ, Harpur would love to understand the ACC's mind himself. Much of it stayed a mystery, although they had worked with and against each other for so long. Iles's competing spells of highest calibre brutality and highest calibre tenderness; his adoration of his wife and infant daughter, his lust for teenage girls, on the game or not; his uncrackable loyalty, his gross subversiveness; his radiant brain, his interludes of screaming mania. These made the ACC quite tricky to profile, possibly a little more than other Assistant Chiefs. Using a special, large voice from somewhere central in him, Iles had once recited a line of his favourite poet, Tennyson, to Harpur: 'Trust me all in all or not at all.' Harpur did not read much Tennyson and decided it was better to give Iles a *bit* of trust, but only a bit. In fact, when it came to the sexual safety of Harpur's fifteen year old daughter, Hazel, he trusted Iles that 'not at all' option.

'The Chief would never permit deals with people like Dubal,' Harpur told Louise.

'The Chief doesn't control things, does he? Mr Iles does. That's what I gather.'

A brilliant summary. 'Policing couldn't function like that,' he replied.

'Is that why you put me into Dubal's team?'

'Is what?'

'You had an idea he'd started to stray from the agreement – getting rough? You think there've been earlier killings?'

A brilliant summary. Harpur had never fully accepted Iles's doctrine of controlled trading in exchange for urban tranquillity. Now, Harpur wanted evidence of violence to push in front of the ACC and force a change. Louise might find it. Very occasionally, Iles could be reached by reason, even from an underling. Despite the ACC's baffling elusiveness and spasmodic blood surges, Harpur believed two consistent obsessions were present which made Iles's character partly comprehensible. The first of these was relatively minor and Harpur didn't give it much notice. In any case, it was bound to embarrass him and he would rather soft-pedal this area. Iles never forgot, and would never let others forget, that there had been a time when, to use the ACC's own brisk phrase, Harpur was 'giving it in the backs and fronts of cars, by-the-hour hotels and similar' to Iles's wife, Sarah. Occasionally, the ACC would still yell unhinged, near-frothing condemnation at Harpur, and to anyone else around. In headquarters, people loitered about the corridors if they saw Iles speaking to Harpur at any length, in case the Assistant Chief suddenly soared to one of his gorgeous, noisy fits of rejuvenated jealousy.

Harpur pushed these uncomfortable notions under. It was time to get out of the PTA. Louise had no more for him now. 'Look, I know we've been over and over this, but just recite the assistance number again, will you?' he asked. 'Another routine.'

She groaned but did it.

'And watch your substance intake,' he said. 'Only enough for credibility. Too much and you'll get daring and slack.'

'Is that what happened to Ray Street?'

'I don't want Street darkening everything all the time, like a threat,' Harpur replied.

'He does, though, doesn't he?'

Yes, he did, mostly because of Iles. The second of the Assistant Chief's ruling impulses concerned Street's death. This Harpur preferred to regard as Iles's truly crucial fixation. It dated from when the ACC allowed Harpur to put Street undercover in a drugs syndicate, where he was one day somehow exposed as a cop, beaten and murdered. Harpur and everyone else at headquarters knew this terrible memory never left the Assistant Chief: the regret and sick guilt. Iles was into guilt, most particularly the guilt of others, but also his own. Although the two heavies reasonably regarded by the ACC as responsible for Street's death escaped conviction when sent to trial, they were soon afterwards found dead, one shot, the other very picturesquely garrotted. Harpur and others felt it might well have been Iles who personally saw them off. Iles possessed many deep, interesting skills. There had never been charges against him: Iles knew about evidence: how not to leave any.

But even those neat vengeance killings failed to quell the ACC's self-blame. And so this present eternal ban on under-cover work, which Harpur would blind-eye. He believed Iles saw himself as the caring guardian of all subordinates. When he failed one of them, the humiliation and pain were so appalling and permanent he could not load the risk on others or himself again. Harpur felt some of the guilt, too, certainly, but could not accept the absolute embargo. To conceal such matters from Iles was hard: he had his own hidden network of tipsters and whisperers, his own Satanic intuitions.

And his own way with reprisals. Harpur considered it chillingly feasible that, if an undercover officer were murdered again, Iles would in his agony and rage hatch something for Harpur because he flouted the ban. The ACC's enduring anger about Sarah and Harpur sharpened the possi-bility, plus his rabid frustration at being successfully fenced off from Hazel by Harpur. Or as far as Harpur knew. When he thought about the chance – likelihood? – of being targeted by Iles, he thought garrotting. Although one of the men acquitted of Street's death had been shot, Harpur felt Iles probably preferred strangulation by wire above all other means of finishing an enemy. The ACC would adore the physicality and necessary extreme nearness to the victim.

Harpur took to walking late in the evenings around the Valencia Esplanade district, where the bulk of the city's drugs dealing was done. He needed to see Louise. That was all: see. It would be lunatic to approach her or talk to her here. They were certain to be noticed by someone in touch with Dubal. Possibly it was lunatic for Harpur even to walk here alone. Everyone recognized him. Trading stopped as soon as he left his car – club trading, shop-doorway trading, alley trading. Mobiles clamoured. Dubal would hear he was about and might wonder why. Pushers in these designated streets were supposed to be left alone, as long as they stayed in these streets. This was part of Iles's peace-in-our-time bargain with Dubal and the rest. In any case, Harpur was too big a rank to start chasing pushers. Dubal would suspect these walks were policy walks, might even mention them as a breach of protocol to the ACC. Just the same, Harpur felt driven to come. Had Louise stayed alive? It was ten days since the PTA. Although he had been down to the Valencia three times since, he never saw her.

He did not see her tonight, either, and went home. The phone rang as he was taking a couple of night cap gin and cider mixes.

'Col?' Harpur knew the voice immediately. He did not answer, waited. 'Col, I pick up a buzz about one of your troupe.'

'What buzz?'

'Grave, Col.'

'Who?'

'We need to act.'

'We?'

'Now. Last few days they've been leading her on, setting her up. No longer. You'll need my help. I don't suppose you're carrying anything.'

'What sort of thing?' Harpur asked.

'The ordinary sort – muzzle, trigger, full chamber.'

'I've heard of them.'

'Louise. That's the name I get in the buzz.'

Jack Lamb heard a lot of buzzes, had a lot of impeccable knowledge. He was possibly the greatest informant in the world, and belonged to Harpur, only to Harpur. Because of security, Jack would hardly ever talk as fully as this by phone. Things must be . . . must be grave, as he called it. 'What buzz?' Harpur asked. If Lamb had heard it, Dubal and those around him could have heard it. This buzz might have started there. God.

'She's installed, right?' Lamb asked.

Harpur said: 'I don't completely understand what you're—'

'Louise Machin. You put her there, defying the Iles prohibition? Oh, dear. I gather she sensed a killing but didn't know where or who. She was right – a routine punishment death inside Dubal's conglomerate, as I hear. There've been others, haven't there? The victim this time someone minor – lowest rung street trader – but Louise pushed too hard for detail and now they know what she is, Col. Know she's yours.'

Yes, God.

'And I'm told you've turned night street walker.'

'Just looking around our ground.'

'You won't see her,' Lamb replied.

'Just looking around our ground.' Harpur hated to have his intentions read.

'When I say now, I mean tonight. Within the next half hour. They've been keeping her in, but tonight they—'

'Right,' Harpur replied. Always he said 'Right' to any instruction from Lamb. If Jack told you something you'd better believe it.

'It'll be dicey. But you can't bring help.' Lamb sounded joyful. 'After all, Louise Machin is not supposed to be there, is she?'

'Yes, I can bring help, if it's bad.'

'Of course it's bad. Would I ring if not? But, no, don't bring help. We can manage it, Col.' Lamb liked that: Harpur's dependence on him alone, Harpur's gratitude to him alone, if things worked all right, whatever they were. Harpur thought he knew what they were. Jack adored the word 'we' when applied to him and Harpur. The link, the bond. 'Are you carrying something?' Lamb said.

'You asked me that.'

'Meaning, no.'

'Right,' Harpur replied.

Harpur walked to the gates of a park not far from his house and Jack Lamb picked him up in a van. Once before, Harpur had been in this vehicle at Lamb's invitation. He used it to carry pictures to or from customers. Lamb ran a toweringly successful art dealership, and when Harpur last entered the van it was to look at some canvases: good stuff, apparently, by people with names Harpur certainly half knew, and still half remembered – Tissot, Hunt, Mellais or Millais or Molière. He never asked Lamb where or how he came by his rare items. This was the essence of their relationship: Lamb brought Harpur brilliant information – but not art information – while Harpur did nothing to shatter the picture business, and discouraged investigation proposals. To entangle Harpur more thoroughly, Lamb liked to show him valuable paintings now and then.

Jack drove hard out of the city. 'The shits,' he said.

'Who?'

'Do you know where they've taken her?'

'Who?'

'Dubal's people.'

'Taken who?'

Lamb didn't think this worth a reply.

'Where?' Harpur asked.

'To Rendevous One. To *our* fucking Rendezvous One, Col. It's a message.'

Normally, when Lamb had something to tell Harpur, they met at one of four, listed, pre-arranged rendezvous spots, the same sort of system as with Louise. Rendezvous One was what had been a World War II anti-aircraft gun site on a wooded hill above the city. Concrete emplacements remained, and metal rails for ammunition trucks. It was remote and atmospheric: Jack adored old military installations and sometimes dressed in army surplus gear for these meetings. The site had always seemed safe. But was it known about by

87

villains like Dubal all the time? This would be what Jack meant when he spoke of a message. Was Dubal saying: 'We've rumbled your undercover girl, as you see from her corpse, and we know where you meet your grass. So how now, Harpur?'

But did they also know that Jack, in his bonny way, knew they knew and knew they were out there with Louise now? If not, there was a chance of saving her.

'I'm not an all-round mouth, Colin,' Lamb said. 'I grass only when I'm nauseated, and to hear they'd terrorise and waste a kid like Louise Machin from the sticks nauseates me.'

Always Jack stressed he did not inform for the sake of it or for favours. Find the moral factor. Even with this choosiness, Lamb was still the best in the world. 'You've got a leaker at the top of Dubal's outfit?' Harpur asked.

They left Jack's van well down the hill and began to walk quickly up through trees towards the former gun positions. It was very dark. Harpur found himself hoping the people with Louise would knock her about before the finish, to make her talk. He and Jack needed time. Harpur had the feeling she would hold out for at least a while, and this could keep her alive. The arrogance might help. What was she able to tell them, anyway? They knew it all. He climbed faster. Thank God the ground was familiar. Jack led. Although he weighed about 260 pounds and stood six foot five, he moved nimbly, swiftly, silently. Now and then when Harpur came up with him for a few yards, he could see that Lamb held some sort of semi-automatic in his right hand, perhaps a Glock 9mm. Good taste: police used these, especially armed response vehicle crews.

Harpur thought he heard voices, or a voice, male. It was distant and no words carried, but he sensed a question. Interrogation. Lamb seemed to have heard it, too, and slowed a little, grew even more careful about where he trod, and crouched like a jungle soldier. Harpur did the same. He loathed firearms, yet wished he were holding a Glock as well. The trees began to thin and there was slightly more light. Nice for locating targets, nice for being located. He heard the male voice again. This time he made out one word:

'Harpur'. Or 'Harpur?' – another question. For a second it dazed him. Then came a female voice, too faint for clarity, and very brief, the tone suggesting denial. She was still holding them off, then, still saying she wasn't run by Harpur. Holding them off mentally, that is. He heard something else: what could be a blow, a heavy fist blow, even a pistol whip blow, not a slap. There was no cry of pain. Perhaps he had it wrong and she had not been struck. But perhaps, also, that's how Louise was: someone who'd never yell. Or perhaps she had been dropped unconscious.

Jack Lamb turned for a second and pointed forward and to his left. Harpur took it to mean he could see the anti-aircraft emplacement and possibly a vehicle and people. Harpur nodded and moved faster. Suddenly, though, Lamb began to run, putting more space between him and Harpur, despite the gradient, his pistol out in front. It was as if he had noticed some change in behaviour and judged it too late for stalking and subtlety. Possibly someone was about to end it for Louise.

Lamb bellowed: 'Stop! Armed fink!', still galloping hard. Harpur rushed to get with him. He heard a shot from the emplacement and a bullet banged into a tree near him. Lamb abruptly stopped and went to one knee, a two-handed grip on the Glock. He fired four rapid rounds. As far as Harpur could recall, the Glock would give him seventeen if full.

Mark Lane, the Chief, liked to look at the scene of any crime he considered significant not just as itself but as a symbol of the general state of law and order. Harpur drove him and Iles out to the hillside. The two bodies had been cleared from there by now, naturally, but Lane wished to see the setting. A concrete road laid for troop supplies in the war survived, and Harpur took the car the whole distance and parked.

Iles went forward on foot and said: 'Here and here, wasn't it, Col?' He stepped from where he'd been standing between the truck rails to a place four or five yards on the right. 'Well, the blood's still visible.'

'Yes,' Harpur replied.

Lane said: 'And their status you say, Desmond, is . . . ?'

89

'Oh, Dubal thugs, sir. Enforcers. Percy Kellow, Jerry Henschall, almost always known as Mildly-Sedated.'

Lane climbed up on to an earth wall surrounding the emplacements. From here he could gaze down at the city. 'A place constructed to protect people,' he said. 'And now? Now, it is foully tainted in this way. Oh, a decline, Desmond, Colin.'

'I rather like it, sir,' Iles replied.

'Like? Like?'

'Two bits of rubbish removed,' Iles said.

'But what does it mean, what does it signify?' Lane cried.

'Oh it signifies Percy and Mildly-Sedated had offended somehow and were brought up here and executed,' Iles replied, 'either by colleagues or trade competitors. It's tidy. Hygienic.'

'We're talking of two murders, for God's sake, Desmond,' Lane said. 'What I mean by taint.'

'They'll do less tainting dead, sir,' Iles replied.

Lane waved an arm towards where the bodies had been found. 'But why, exactly? Who?' he said.

'I don't think we're getting very far with that, sir, as yet,' Iles replied.

Harpur said: 'As Mr Iles suggests, we assume some sort of gang battle or a disciplinary episode within the Dubal firm. We're working on both possibilities.'

'I will not accept this contempt for legality,' Lane said. 'It could spread, become uncontainable.' Always the Chief feared chaos, or Chaos, might start on his ground and from there gallop out and corrupt at least the cosmos. The dread had brought him to breakdown not long ago. 'I cannot, will not, rest, until—'

'Quite nice shooting, I gather,' the ACC said. 'Two bullets in each heart, and not half an inch between either pair of them.'

'And found, how?' Lane asked.

'A New York Bronx-accented anon call from a public box, sir, telling us where to look,' Iles replied. 'Standard sort of thing.'

Lane groaned. 'My God, Desmond, do you realize what you say? That this kind of incident has become a customary part of life now? Is this the beginning of—?'

'Of Armageddon, sir? Oh, Col here has it all in hand. He often knows a fucking sight more than he lets on to you and me.'

'Colin?' Lane said.

'We're really working on it, sir,' Harpur replied.

The Chief walked away along the top of the earth wall, perhaps for a better view of the city, in case there were actual signs of break-up. He went slowly out of sight.

Iles said quietly: 'When she was struggling one day to think what the hell ever made her see anything in you, Col, do I remember Sarah telling me you could do a very witty Bronx imitation?'

'My own feeling, sir, is there'll be terrible problems resolving this case,' Harpur replied. 'Perhaps insurmountable.'

'A kid girl I heard you brought in from one of the border stations – was she involved in it somehow here?' Iles said. 'And then the tale's around that you were looking out for her down the Valencia? That it?'

'Kid girl, sir?' Harpur replied.

'Have you been playing some undercover game?' Iles said.

'I understand the Chief's feelings about this place,' Harpur replied. 'It's—'

'I don't want his remaining sliver of sanity disturbed by the truth of what happened, Col – as I see it, one of our girls dragged out here and brought close to finale. Did she tell you Dubal or his people might have blitzed someone? What I hear.'

'You hear a lot, sir.'

'At Staff College I was known as Listening Desmond.'

Harpur said: 'So, perhaps these two *were* eliminated in a discipline thing.'

'Fuck off, Col. You know how they died. I also heard of this kid girl – Munching? Machin? Moocher? – this kid girl, chatting with you in a PTA meeting at a school your children don't go to. Wouldn't I be familiar with Hazel's school – that charming uniform? And now I'm told this girl officer is off sick with head and facial wounds. Not irreparable. Am

91

I right, they were going to kill her, Col? A Ray Street reprise? You bypassed me? The Chief would see insurrection in that.'

'Sir, it—'

Iles said: 'These two, Perce and Mildly, done by our favourite Glock. Were you out here, gallant and ballistic on her behalf? You? But you could never shoot like that. Some capable, secret chum?'

Yes, Harpur would like to understand the ACC's mind, but knew he would never get near. Also, he was curious about Iles's gifted sources: perhaps not in the Jack Lamb league, but with twenty-twenty vision, just the same, the sods. Harpur said: 'I—'

'Two down, Perce and Mildly-Sedated. Great. Possibly I can forgive, Col, if the kid girl is really all right. At staff college I was known also as Desmond the Merciful.'

'Ah, here's the Chief now,' Harpur replied. Lane approached. He looked appallingly haggard.

Iles called out to him: 'That's totally right for you, sir, if I may say – the stark prominence on a wall. Eloquent. Something elemental, grand, marvellously reassuring. Don't you glimpse a happy emblem of leadership in the Chief's position there, Col?'

# Fancy

'Yes, I'm around places like this at night a lot – and waste ground, several London stations, heaths, student accommodation.'

'Same myself. Funny we've never met.'

They were sitting at opposite ends of a wooden bench in this Hampstead bus shelter. It was after one a.m., and no bus would come.

'Better than idling at home.'

'Every few nights I need this sort of outing.'

'Call me Charles. Obviously, not my real name.'

'I'm Vernon. As it were.'

Charles said, 'Frankly, I'm the Wolfman rapist you've read of in the press, doubtless.'

'That's a laugh.'

'I'm telling you. Seven women hereabouts. I itch somewhat for Number Eight tonight.'

Vernon's voice rose in rage: 'You've got what I'd call a steaming cheek. You're talking to him, old son: me, I'm Wolfman.'

'You're what?'

'You heard.'

Charles said, 'He's nearly six feet tall and thin. Pointed, cruel face – well, like a wolf's. Obviously. All the girls say that. You're a chubby, gross little object, for God's sake.'

'I don't like your tone.'

'Lump it, then.'

'Anyway, Wolfman's got a refined, super-cool accent,' Vernon replied. 'It's been frequently mentioned in the press. Listened to yourself lately? You're slum rubbish.'

'I can turn on class. It's a cover.'

'I'm much, much taller than you'd think,' Vernon said. 'And slimmer. It's the way I'm sitting.'

'You know what? You're sick, that's all,' Charles said. 'Who the hell claims to be a rapist when he's not?'

'You.'

Charles stood angrily. 'You push your luck. I'll see you off.' He took a step towards Vernon, who also rose. 'You're standing now?' Charles enquired.

'The Wolfman rapist's got a word tattooed on his – on his person,' Vernon replied. 'This has been observed by victims and publicized by police, in case it's fortuitously noted in, let's say, a Turkish bath.'

'"Excelsior". I'll show you. There's light enough.'

'Yes, and *I'll* show *you*.'

In a moment Charles snarled, 'You had that done after hearing of it.'

'You can talk. You're pathetic. Just a mimic.'

'Sod, I'll—'

They began to fight then, punching each other's face and head ferociously. Charles was cut over the eye. Vernon's nose and lip bled heavily.

A young blonde woman, in miniskirt and bulging blouse, suddenly appeared from the road. Her heels towered. Rushing forward, she pulled the two apart and flung them casually to separate ends of the shelter, where each folded down exhausted on the bench.

'Zip your trousers, boys,' she said. 'You'll get chilled. Then out of here, smartish.'

'Who the hell are you?' Vernon asked, standing again, his voice pugnacious, lip wound or not.

'Police,' the woman said.

'You what?' Charles replied.

'Decoy for the Wolfman rapist. I have to lure an attack. Goons like you will mess it up.'

'You've struck lucky, girl,' Charles said, 'for I'm Wolfman.'

'Take no notice, officer,' Vernon told her. 'I am he.'

'With "Excelsior" on your respective members?' The woman sighed. 'Blokes like that here every night, acting out their would-be sex lives, haunting his ground. Everyone to his own kicks. It's harmless. One tattooist's bought a Porsche from the extra work. Off you go now, gents.'

As they walked away, Charles said, 'Some fool, that one.'

'Too true.'

'It's because you were there.'

'How?' Vernon asked.

'She saw straight off you couldn't be Wolfman and decided we must both be nutters. Thus, despite a brazen confession, I outwit the Fuzz once more.' Charles chuckled rather heartily.

'And I'm a nutter?'

'What else?'

'I'll show you what else, you lying prat.'

They began to fight again in a side street but, when the policewoman neared on her stilts, they stopped and made their way towards an all-hours coffee bar. At one table a couple of pretty girls sat talking, and, in a while, the redhead drifted over to sit with Vernon and Charles.

'My friend and I think you two must be boxers on your way home from a late-night tourney,' she said. 'The marks on your faces. Though not unbecoming by any means. I believe they're called tourneys.'

'Tourney's fine. You should have seen the other guys,' Vernon replied.

'I knew it,' the girl cried, thrilled. 'My name's Louise.' She turned and called her friend: 'Oh, we were right, so right, Elaine! A tourney. Elaine's absolutely mad about boxers.'

Elaine, dark-haired and taller, joined them.

'I'm Rocky Blaze,' Charles remarked.

'Jabs Bison,' Vernon said.

'We're nurses,' Louise explained.

'Jabs really flips for nurses,' Charles said. 'He's famous for it in the Fancy – as we pros call boxing.'

'What about you, Rocky?' Elaine asked, leaning over and gently touching one of his cuts.

'Whoever comes,' Charles answered.

'Oh, invariably,' Elaine said.

Towards three a.m. they made their way to the nurses' home and sneaked in through a ground-floor window. Charles went with Elaine to her room and Louise took Vernon to hers. The men arranged to meet near the same window again later.

When they rendezvoused at five a.m. it was still dark. For a moment, the two stood tidying themselves. Charles, gazing from the window, suddenly said, 'My God, I saw someone dash through the grounds and disappear near the front of the building. It's the hunt. The Fuzz has traced me after all. I'm a golden prize.'

'Louise is eager to meet me again,' Vernon replied.

'Same with Elaine and me.'

'But I'm not sure,' Vernon said. 'I'm so busy.'

'I told Elaine similar,' Charles replied.

'I didn't say why, naturally, but being Wolfman – there's so much preparation and lying in heated wait,' Vernon explained, 'with buckets of excitement burned up.'

'Oh, for Christ's sake, you're not still on about that? Honestly, can't you understand, you're not Wolfman? It's a delusion, all in your tortured dreams, like being Jabs Bison. For I'm the Wolfman rapist. If anyone's been traced, it's me.'

'Like hell,' Vernon said.

'Excuse me, but did she comment on "Excelsior"?' Charles asked.

'It was dark. I didn't mention same as I was not on Wolfman duty.'

'Me, too,' Charles said.

'But you never are on Wolfman duty, you foul fraud.'

Charles punched him in the ear and once more they were about to fight when a series of brilliant searchlight beams slashed the blackness, playing fiercely on the nurses' home. A loudspeaker voice blared: 'Come out, Wolfman. This is the police. We saw you enter. You're surrounded. Your raping nights are over.'

Vernon and Charles climbed out jointly, bravely, competitively, through the window and four harsh beams swooped on them. They walked with dignity towards the cordon. When they reached it, a uniformed sergeant genially took each by the arm. 'Get out of the way, laddies, will you,' he said. 'The Wolfman rapist's trapped in there. Heard of him? Big stuff. Yes. You've had a bit of nurse nooky? You'll be needing your prunes and Cornflakes, I expect.'

Vernon and Charles stood behind the cordon and watched. After not very long, a thin man about six feet tall, and with a narrow face, came out from the front of the building and strolled smiling defiantly in the lights towards the police. 'It's a fair cop. I've had a decent run,' he drawled. 'Pity Wolfman couldn't enjoy one last fling, though, damn it, you fellows.'

'I don't like this at all, Vernon,' Charles said, 'Life's lost its purpose.'

'It's going to kill my evenings out stone dead, Charles, if he drops from the news.'

'There's Elaine, of course.'

'And Louise,' Vernon remarked.

'They're very nice, but I need something with, well, a bit more substance,' Charles said. 'Something for the mind.'

'I know what you mean, Rocky. Look: don't forget the Fancy.'

'Right! Maybe a bit of road work together and sparring, Jabs?'

'Sounds good to me, Rocky. We could be contenders.'

# Big City

There was an agreement. Rhys and Jill had spelled it out together. They told each other it was for the sake of the children. Rhys told himself that, too. But he knew it was for his own sake. He must not lose Jill. To keep her he had accepted terms. They would be pals, living together with their family. For passion she would go elsewhere. It was painful, she said, but they must accept change. It could happen in a marriage. Look at most of their Cardiff friends! She suggested people were becoming more sexually independent, confident, and generally 'big city', now the London government had given Wales *almost* a Parliament, *almost* independence. The Welsh Assembly, as this cut-price Parliament was called, had housed itself in a waterside building on Cardiff's dockland. Jill said this transformed Wales, made it a *real* country again and brought the city the status of a true, world-scale capital at last. Small-town negativeness, small-town prudishness, narrow moralizing, were no longer on. She considered the new attitudes were especially evident in folk from their circle – journalists, politicos, lobbyists: those most in tune with the reborn Wales. She said she still loved Rhys, but was not *in* love with him. She had met someone else.

Although Rhys was hurt, he rejected the difference between love and *in* love. Or, at least, he did not believe that side of it would last. He must wait it out. Nor did he see why political devolution from London should mean rampant adultery, but he let the point go. And so, the agreement. He considered it a workable pact and not necessarily humiliating. Later, looking back, he was sure nobody could have foreseen so much tragedy.

When the arrangement began, Jill used to offer fairly plausible tales beforehand to cover an absence, in case Rhys tried to ring her. She'd say shopping or a drink with Beth Postern. That stopped. It obviously sickened her to lie. She had a wonderful honesty: one of the things he loved her for. Now, she would announce only that she'd be out from midday. He did not ask where. Silence was part of the agreement. He noticed she never put on her smartest outfits for these meetings, nor wore jewellery he'd bought her. This meant she refused to rub his nose in it by festooning herself for someone else. He felt grateful. He could not tell her that, though.

In fact, it was when Rhys and Jill called the babysitter and went out as a couple to a restaurant or party that she dressed up and appeared at her most elegant. A room full of people shone if she was among them, shone *because* she was among them. As her husband, Rhys felt pride. Just as much as emotions and sex, her sparkle offered the essence of Jill, and could never be withdrawn from him. This helped Rhys accept the agreement. She remained his: he owned that wondrous social side of Jill. He exulted to read the covetousness in men's faces.

Part of the agreement was that if he found somebody else, he should be free to go to her. Rhys felt sure he would never want that. This certainty enraged Jill, possibly increasing her sense of guilt. Too bad. He could not alter. Jill was the only woman for him. Once – only once – she tried to explain what had drawn her to the other man. Apparently, he relayed non-stop ferocious desire for Jill. This was the word she picked, *ferocious*. Rhys was embarrassed by it, not injured. He felt she sounded quaint. Yet she said this man's passion had left her no choice.

When the arrangement was new, he did not allow himself to think much about where the two of them went, and at that stage he would never have secretly tailed her. Although this was certainly not banned by the agreement, it would have seemed shady. He assumed they generally had an early lunch in a restaurant, and afterwards . . . Gross to speculate on that, and probably unhealthy. She liked to be home soon after the girls returned from school.

Rhys and Jill still visited restaurants themselves. Looking brilliant, she would talk and radiate at full power, and anyone watching would surely have supposed them alight with joy in each other, perhaps even lovers, not man and wife. It thrilled him. This was Jill as Rhys's, her jewellery very much in place. Occasionally, they bumped into acquaintances at these places and would perhaps make up a four or even push tables together for a party of six or eight. The more the better for Jill.

On one of these evenings, they came across friends and colleagues at The Celtic Bistro, and, while helping rearrange the furniture, he felt the back of a hand, a woman's hand judging by size, pressed for a few seconds very firmly against the inside of his left, upper thigh. Very upper. At first, he thought it an accident amid the little confusions of aperitifed people reshaping the restaurant. Soon, though, he corrected: the contact was too prolonged. He yearned to believe it had been Jill. Was she telling him in a sudden, uncontrollable, almost shy fashion she was his after all; totally his, not just her public self? Perhaps her affair and therefore the idiotic agreement were dead. Time had righted things?

But, he must not dream. Really, he knew Jill was never near enough to touch him as they shifted the tables and chairs. He decided only Beth could have done it; Beth, strapping young wife of busy, inaugural Welsh Assembly member Jeremy Postern. No apology or joke came from her about the contact, though. That seemed to confirm the incident was intentional. Yet she did not attempt to sit next to him for the meal, and when he talked to her and studied her as the evening went on, he found no personal message, no readable explanation in her blue-black eyes for knuckles wilfully nudging his nuts. The incident shook Rhys. It made him realise that the notion of 'another woman' could be more than a notion. Perhaps someone else *was* available. To his amazement, this interested him. Was Jill correct, after all, to resent his self-righteous dismissal of the agreement's clause entitling him, also, to sexual liberty? Curiosity about the significance of the act dogged him. Perhaps it was part of the new sophistication: a woman would hint and wait.

Early one evening, when he was having a semi-work drink with Jeremy Postern, other Assembly members, and press friends in The Referendum cocktail bar, Rhys went outside briefly and mobiled Beth. She seemed warm, pleased to hear him, unsurprised. He wondered if they might meet one evening, and she thought they might. They fixed a time. Rhys went back to the bar feeling not excited or victorious but, yes, more *wholesome* than for ages, more manly.

Beth and he seemed to need no preliminaries. It was as if they had been waiting for each other. She went halves with him on a bottle of Dubonnet and the charge for a room overnight in the plush new Capital Hotel in Cardiff Bay, though they would be using it only for a few early evening hours. They made fierce, prolonged love. Yes, it was even *ferocious* prolonged love. Afterwards, while they lay relaxed, he reassured Beth about the care he would take with her reputation, explaining how he had phoned only when certain Jeremy was not at home.

'The smug sod wouldn't care,' Beth replied. She sounded defeated. 'He's too deep in all the superlative Assembly crap for love life. We go our own ways.'

'You don't like that?'

Hurriedly, she turned towards him: 'Darling, of course I do. I wouldn't be here with you now, otherwise, would I? Aren't you and Jill permissive with each other, too?'

'Good God, no. I couldn't tolerate the idea of her seeing somebody else, screwing somebody else.'

'I adore jealousy in a man,' she said vehemently. 'It means he cares. It's what makes you so damn irresistible, Rhys. *You* wouldn't doze through a marriage. God, but Jill's lucky.'

This encounter revolutionized Rhys, gave him vision. Jesus, might Jill think he did not care because he showed no rage and put up with the agreement? Was this why she had discarded him sexually? But he *did* care. He must show it. He was not like Jeremy – and like many men Rhys knew: by piffling career obsession and bed coolness they forced a wife to seek fulfilment elsewhere. He decided he must watch Jill discreetly when she went to one of her meetings. Although he still loathed the idea of gumshoeing, he had come to loathe apparent indifference even more. He would annihilate this disgusting, arid agreement. But agreements were only words and sentiments. He wanted something solid to smash. He needed a look at the opposition.

Luckily, he could take time off work as he wished. He was part of the newly hatched lobbying industry around Mount Stuart Square in Cardiff Bay at the docks, and ran his own hot public-relations firm. Surveillance was sure to be difficult, though. Jill would soon notice his Citroën. And so, next time she said she would be out for the afternoon, he took a company Vauxhall and went to wait near their Cowbridge, Vale of Glamorgan, house until she left at around noon.

She drove to a side street in Splott, an undazzling region of Cardiff. She parked. Rhys drove on a bit and also parked, then watched through the mirror. Soon, a Toyota arrived and drew in not far from Jill's VW. At once, Rhys sensed this was Lover Boy and turned in the driving seat now to get a proper look through the back window. He kept his face partially obscured by the headrest. A middle-height man left the Toyota and walked twenty yards to Jill, opened the VW passenger door, and climbed in. For a few minutes they kissed and talked, all excited smiles, arms locked around each other, as if they'd fought their way across ice floes after years of forced separation. Probably they were here every week.

Lover Boy's hair was grey, but cut in a bristly, young-thruster style. Boy? Palely aglow with the tired beams of Indian summer, he must be at least ten years older than Rhys. It hurt. She could prefer someone this age? He had a round, pushy face with heavy eyebrows. Although he could have had these trimmed, he must regard them as part of his image, proving verve. Image was vital in this jumped-up metropolis. His face was full now of . . . full of what Rhys longed to dismiss as raw, lucky-old-me triumph. This was someone in his fifties at least, all set for a nice afternoon with a beautiful woman of thirty-four. Horrified, though, Rhys found he could not honestly describe what he saw like that. His view was imperfect, but he glimpsed . . . well, damn it, yes, he glimpsed *love* there – maybe ferocious, maybe just intense, but in any case enough to terrify him. He sensed the power of their relationship, almost admired it, certainly envied him, the spry jerk. God, Beth had it so right, and Rhys could switch on the jealousy. He was delighted at how well he hated. He might tell Beth about this whole unpleasant sequence.

The man's clothes recalled some 1970s sports commentator's – three-quarter-length sheepskin coat and a crimson scarf. Still, he was presentable. Naturally. To think otherwise would be a rotten insult to Jill. And it would be mad to feel jealous if the rival were pathetic.

The lovers left the VW and began to walk. They turned into the main road. Rhys went after them on foot, staying well back. He saw Jill take the man's arm for a while, as though feeling anonymous in this unfashionable spot. But then she suddenly let go and put a little gap between them. She probably realized that, down-market or not, people who knew her could be driving through. To be observed at all would be bad, but walking arm-in-arm was an utter giveaway. They kept the distance between them until vanishing into a rough-looking eatery. Never would Rhys have taken a woman to such a place, and certainly not a woman like Jill, even in run-of-the-mill clothes. At first, he thought Lover Boy must be short of money. But no, it was clearly part of the cleverness. This pair were unlikely to meet anyone they knew in such a dump, and especially not Jill. Secrecy above hygiene. After about ten minutes, Rhys walked past on the other side of the street and looked in. They were at a table near the window, too bloody tied up in themselves to notice anyone else.

He was sick with distance and rage and helplessness. The agreement came to seem contemptible. Bloodless. He returned to his car intending to wait until they appeared, then drive behind them to their next destination, presumably a room somewhere. But he found he could not face this. The old tenderness towards Jill, the old reluctance to snoop on her, ravaged him, made any further dogging impossible. Briefly, he contemplated vandalizing the Toyota. In the Citroën boot he had a tyre lever which could have made an impression. But he was not driving the Citroën and, in any case, that was a crazy, infantile thought – vehicle-breaking by day-light in a well-peopled street. Instead, he walked to the Toyota and glanced inside. On top of the dashboard lay an opened envelope showing a name and address. It seemed

Lover Boy must be G. Lowther and lived in the Pontcanna district of the city. This comparatively chic spot was home to many loud people from independent television companies, presently coining it with innumerable worthy films about Welsh identity. Rhys thought this lad looked like a Geraint rather than a Glyn or a Gwyn. He couldn't have said why. Perhaps G. was on the technical side, or Rhys might have recognised him through work.

Rhys went back to the office and, as he sometimes did, stayed late. There were papers to deal with after his spell away. Some routines had to continue. But, obviously, his mind was badly troubled and he did not operate well. Would he ever operate well again if he stuck with the emptiness and degradation of the agreement? He finished, went out to the Citroën in the yard, and decided to drive home via Pontcanna. When he eventually reached Cowbridge, he was surprised to find Jill still up. She seemed desolated.

'Jeremy Postern rang,' she said.

'Some sparkling speech he wants puffed? Am I to call him back? At this hour?'

'He rang *me,*' she said.

'Oh, yes?'

'Beth told him you and she have an affair going.'

'Why the hell would she do that?'

'To make him jealous, I expect. Compel him to want her.'

'But he couldn't care less, Jill.'

'You fool. He's frantic at the thought of losing Beth. He asked me what we can do about it, he and I.'

'Just like Jeremy.'

'Maybe. Anyway, I won't tolerate this. Rhys, I'm leaving you. Tonight. Now. For keeps. I've sent the girls by taxi to my mother's.'

'But, Jill, darling, why?' he cried. 'It was only the agreement.'

'The agreement is finished.'

'It is?'

She wept. 'It's not needed. Gaston and I ended things today. It all came to seem ludicrous, barren, mean. The relationship just dropped dead while we walked to a restaurant. We both sensed it, though neither of us understood why.'

'Oh, a restaurant where?' Rhys asked.

'I intended a new start.'

'But this is wonderful!'

'Not now. Impossible. It's unfair of me, maybe, but I can't stay since hearing of you and Beth. Unbearable. I'm going.' Jill went out to her car. He walked urgently after her, and saw that the VW had suitcases on the rear seat. She climbed in, keyed the ignition, and music sounded from the radio. He stood by the side of the car, the driver's door open. She seemed to remember something and went hurriedly back into the house. She left the engine running, as if to tell him she had not changed her mind. He waited. The music ended and a local news bulletin began on the radio. It reported the discovery of a so-far-unidentified middle-aged man dead on the ground in a Pontcanna street. He had been killed by head wounds. Jill returned with another small case, which she placed in the back. She climbed into the VW again and reached out for the door, which still stood open. She said: 'Rhys, how in God's name could you betray me with someone like Beth Postern?'

'But it was Beth who taught me the way to hold on to you, love.'

Jill pulled the door to and drove off. She did not wave.

# Like an Arrangement

Not everyone realized that the thing about Assistant Chief Constable Desmond Iles was he longed to be loved. Among those who did realize it, of course, a good number refused to respond and instead muttered privately, 'Go fuck yourself, Iles.' A very good number. On the other hand, there was certainly a young ethnic whore in the docks who worshipped the ACC unstintingly, and he would have been truly hurt if anyone said it was because he paid well.

What Iles totally abominated was people who came to esteem him only because he had contributed or helped in some way: say a piece of grand, devastating violence carried out by the ACC for them against one of their enemies. He despised such calculating, *quid pro quo*ism, as he called it. Once, he had told Harpur he utterly disregarded love that could be accounted for and reckoned up. Harpur felt happy the ACC received from his docks friend, Honorée, and from Fanny, his infant daughter, the differing but infinite affection he craved. Also, Iles's wife, Sarah, definitely possessed some quaint fondness for him, quite often at least. She had mentioned this to Harpur unprompted in one of their quiet moments.

To Harpur, it seemed that much of Iles's behaviour could be explained by this need for completely spontaneous, instinctive, wholehearted devotion. Think of that unpleasant incident at the Taldamon School prize-giving, for instance. Although Iles would regard the kind of physical savagery he was forced into there as merely routine for him, it had made one eighteen-year-old girl pupil switch abruptly from fending off the ACC sexually to offering an urgent come-on. This enraged Iles. He had been doing all he could to attract the girl, probably as potential stand-by in case Honorée were working away some time at a World Cup or Church of England Synod. Totally no go. And then, within minutes, the Taldamon girl suddenly changed and clearly grew interested in Iles, simply because he had felled and disarmed some bastard in the stately school assembly hall, and kicked him a few times absolutely unfatally about the head and neck where he lay on the floor between chair rows. Colin Harpur instantly knew the ACC would regard this turnaround by the girl as contemptible: as grossly undiscerning about Iles, as Iles. That is, the essence of Ilesness, not simply his rabbit punching and kicking flairs, which could be viewed as superficial: as attractive, perhaps, but mere accessories to his core self. Harpur saw at the end of this episode that the ACC wished to get away immediately from the girl and return to Honorée for pure, unconditional adoration, even, if necessary, on waste ground.

It was some school: private, of course, and residential, and right up there with Eton and Harrow for fees. In fact, it cost somewhere near the national average wage to keep a child at Taldamon for a year, and this without the geology trip to Iceland, the horse riding and extra coaching in lacrosse and timpani. Harpur and Iles – Iles particularly – were interested in Taldamon because the police funded one of its pupils during her entire school career. This was an idea picked up from France. Over there, it had long been police practice to meet the education expenses for the child or children of a valuable and regular informant, as one way of paying for tipoffs. The scheme convinced Iles and others. It was considered less obvious – less dangerous – than to give an informant big cash rewards, which he/she might spend in a stupid, ostentatious way, drawing attention to his/her special income. That could mean the informant was no longer able to get close to villains' secrets because the villains would have him/her identified as a leak. It could also mean that his/her life was endangered. A child out of sight at a pricey school in North Wales would be less noticeable. Or this was the thinking.

They had put Wayne Ridout's daughter, Fay-Alice, into Taldamon, from the age of thirteen, and now here she was at eighteen, head prefect, multi-prizewinner, captain of lacrosse, captain of swimming and water polo, central to the school orchestra, destined for Oxford, slim, straight-nosed, sweet-skinned, and able to hold Iles off with cold, foul-mouthed ease until . . . until she decided she did not want to hold him off, following a gross rush of disgusting gratitude: disgusting, that is, as Harpur guessed the ACC would regard it.

Harpur and Iles would not normally attend this kind of function. The presence of police might be a give-away. But Wayne had pleaded with Iles to come, and pleaded a little less fervently with Harpur, also. It was not just that Wayne wanted them to see the glorious results of their grass-related investment in Fay-Alice. Harpur knew from a few recent conversations with Wayne that he had felt down lately. Because of her education and the social status of Taldamon, Ridout sensed his daughter might be growing away from him and her mother, Nora. This grieved both, but especially Wayne. His wife seemed to regard the change in Fay-Alice as normal. Harpur imagined she probably saw it on behalf of the girl like this: when your father's main career had been fink and general crook rather than archbishop or TV game show host, there was only one way for the next generation to go socially – up and away. Regrettable but inevitable.

Wayne could not accept such sad distancing. He must reason that if he were seen at this important school function accompanied by an Assistant Chief Constable, who had on the kind of magnificent suit and shoes Iles favoured, and who behaved in his well-known Shah of Persia style, it was bound to restore Fay-Alice's respect for her parents. And it would impress the girl's friends and teachers. For these possible gains, Wayne had evidently decided to put up with the security risk in this one-off event. Harpur doubted Fay-Alice would see things as her father did and thought he and the ACC should not attend. But Iles agreed to the visit and addressed Harpur for a while about 'overriding obligations to those who sporadically assist law and order, even a fat, villainous, ugly, dim sod like Wayne'. The ACC was always shudderingly eager to get among teenage schoolgirls if they looked clean and wore light summery clothes.

It was only out of politeness that Wayne had asked Harpur. As Detective Chief Superintendent, Harpur lacked the glow of staff rank and could not tog himself out with the same

108

distinction as Iles. In fact, the ACC had seemed not wholly sure Harpur should accompany him. 'This will be a school with gold-lettered award boards on the wall, naming pupils who've gone on not just to Oxbridge or management courses with the Little Chef restaurant chain, but Harvard, Vatican seminaries, even Time Share selling in Alicante. There'll be ambience. Does ambience get into your vocab at all, Harpur? I know this kind of academy right through, from my own school background, of course. I'd hate you to feel in any way disadvantaged by *your* education, but I ask you, Col – do you think you can fit into such a place as Taldamon with that fucking haircut and your garments?'

'This kind of occasion does make me think back to end of term at my own school, sir,' Harpur reminisced gently.

'And what did they give leaving prizes to eighteen-year-olds for there – knowing the two-times table, speed at dewristing tourists' Rolexes?'

'Should we go armed?' Harpur replied.

'This is a wholesome occasion at a prime girls' school, for God's sake, Col.'

'Should we go armed?' Harpur said.

Iles said, 'I'd hate it if some delightful pupil, inadvertently brushing against me, should feel only the brutal outline of a holstered pistol, Harpur.'

'This sort of school, they're probably taught never to brush inadvertently against people like you, sir. It would be stressed in deportment classes, plus during the domestic science module for classifying moisture marks on trousers.'

Iles's voice grew throaty and his breathing loud and needful: 'I gather she's become a star now as scholar, swimmer, musician and so on, but I can remember Fay-Alice when she was only a kid, though developing, certainly . . . developing, yes, certainly, *developing*, but really only just a kid . . . although . . . well, yes, *developing*, and we went to the Ridout house to advise them that she should—'

'There are people who'd like to do Wayne. He's helped put all sorts inside. They have brothers, colleagues, sons, fathers, mothers. Perhaps the word's around he'll be on a plate at Taldamon, ambience-hooked, relaxed, unvigilant.'

'A striking-looking child, even then,' Iles replied, 'despite

Wayne and his complexion. A wonderful long, slender back, as I recall. Do *you* recall that, Harpur – the long slender back? Do you think of backs ever? Or was it the era when you were so damn busy giving it to my wife you didn't have time to notice much else at all?' Iles began to screech in the frenzied seagull tone that would take him over sometimes when speaking of Harpur and Sarah.

Harpur said, 'If we're there we ought at least to—'

'I mean her back in addition to the way she was, well—?'

'Developing.'

This long back Fay-Alice unquestionably still had, and the development elsewhere seemed to have continued as it generally would for a girl between thirteen and eighteen. A little tea party had been arranged on the pleasant lawns at Taldamon before the prize-giving, out of consideration for parents who travelled a long way and needed refreshment. It was June, a good, hot, blue-skied day. 'Here's a dear, dear acquaintance of mine, Fay-Alice,' Wayne said. 'Assistant Chief Constable Desmond Iles. And Chief Superintendent Harpur.'

Iles gave her a true conquistador smile, yet a smile which also sought to hint at his sensitivity, honour, beguiling polish and famed restraint. Fay-Alice returned this smile with one that was hostile, nauseated and extremely brief, but which still managed to signal over her teacup, *Police? So how come you're friends of my father, and who let you in here, anyway?* Was it just normal schoolgirl prejudice against cops or did she have some idea that daddy's career might be lifelong dubious – even some idea that her schooling and Wayne's career could be unwholesomely related? This must be a bright kid, able to win prizes and an Oxford place. She'd have antennae as well as the long back.

'Fay-Alice's prizes are in French literature, history of art and classics,' Wayne said.

'Won't mean a thing to Col,' Iles replied.

'I wondered if there'd been strangers around the school lately,' Harpur said, 'possibly asking questions about the programme today, looking at the layout.'

'Which strangers?' Fay-Alice replied.

'Strangers,' Harpur said. 'A man, or men, probably.'

110

'Why would they?' the girl asked.

'You know, French lit. is something I can't get enough of,' the ACC said.

'Mr Iles, personally, did a lot with education, right up to the very heaviest levels, Fay-Alice,' Wayne said. 'Don't be fooled just because he's police.'

'Yes, why are you concerned about strangers, Mr Harpur?' Nora Ridout asked.

'Are you two trying to put the frighteners on us, the way pigs always do?' Fay-Alice said.

'I recall Alphonse de Lamartine and his poem "The Lake",' Iles replied.

'Alphonse is a French name for sure,' Wayne said. 'There you are, Fay-Alice – didn't I tell you, Mr Iles can go straight to it, no messing? Books are meat and drink to him.'

Iles leaned towards her and recited: '"Oh, Time, will you not stop a while so we may savour the swiftly passing pleasures of our loveliest days?"'

'Meat and drink,' Wayne said.

'Don't you find Lamartine's plea an inspiration, Fay-Alice?' Iles asked. 'Savour. A word I thrill to. The sensuousness of it, together with the tragic hint of enjoying something wonderful, yet elusive.' He began to tremble slightly and reached out a hand, as if to touch Fay-Alice's long back or some conjoint region. But moving quickly towards the plate of sandwiches on a garden table, Harpur put himself between the ACC and her. He took Iles's pleaful, savour-seeking fingers on the lapel of his jacket. In any case, Fay-Alice had stepped back immediately she saw the ACC's hand approach and for a moment looked as if she was about to grab his arm and possibly break it in some kind of anti-rape drill.

'Or the history of art,' Wayne said. 'That's another terrific realm. This could overlap with French literature because while the poets were writing their verses in France there would be neighbours, in the same street most probably, painting and making sculptures in their attics. The French are known for it – easels, smocks, everything. It's the light in those parts – great for art but also useful when people wanted to write a poem outside. In a way it all ties up. That's the thing about culture, especially French. A lot of strands.'

'And you'll be coming home to live with Mother and Father until Oxford now, and in the nice long vacations, will you, Fay-Alice?' Iles asked.

'Why?' she replied.

Iles said, 'It's just that—'

'I don't understand how you know my father,' she replied.

'Oh, Mr Iles and I – this is a real far-back association,' Wayne said.

'But how exactly?' she asked. 'He's never been to our house, has he? I've never heard you speak of him, Dad.'

'This is like an arrangement, Fay-Alice,' Nora Ridout replied.

'What kind of arrangement?' Fay-Alice asked.

'Yes, like an arrangement,' Nora Ridout replied.

'A business arrangement?' Fay-Alice asked.

'You can see how such a go-ahead school makes them put all the damn sharp queries, Mr Iles,' Wayne said. 'I love it. This is what I believe they call intellectual curiosity, used by many of the country's topmost on their way to discoveries such as medical and DVDs. What they will not do, girls at this school – and especially girls who do really well, such as Fay-Alice – what they will not do is take something as right just because they're told it. Oh, no. Rigour's another word for this attitude, I believe. Not like rigor mortis but rigour in their thoughts and decisions. It's a school that teaches them how to sort out the men from the boys re brain power.'

'So, does the school come into it somehow?' Fay-Alice asked. 'Does it? Does it? How are these two linked with the school, Dad, Mum?' She hammered at the question, yet Harpur thought she feared an answer.

'Linked?' Iles said. 'Linked? Oh, just a pleasant excursion for Mr Harpur and myself, thanks to the thoughtfulness of your father, Fay-Alice.'

'A business or social arrangement?' Fay-Alice asked.

'No, no, not a business arrangement. How could it be a business arrangement?' Wayne replied, laughing.

'Social?' Fay-Alice asked.

'It's *sort* of social,' Wayne said.

112

'So, if it's friendship why do you call him Mr Iles, not Desmond, his first name?' Fay-Alice asked.

'See what I mean about the queries, Mr Iles? I heard the motto of this school is "Seek ever the truth", but in a classical tongue which provides many a motto around the country on account of tradition. You can't beat the classics if you want to hit the right note.'

The ACC said, 'And I understand swimming has become a pursuit of yours, Fay-Alice. Excellent for the body. You must get along to the municipal pool at home. I should go there more often myself. Certainly I shall. This will be an experience – to see you active in the water, your arms and legs really working, wake a-glisten.' Beautifully symmetric circles of sweat appeared on each of his temples, each the size of a two-penny piece, although the group were still outside on the lawn and under the shade of a eucalyptus. 'The butterfly stroke – strenuous upper torso exercise, but useful for toning everything, don't you agree, Fay-Alice? Toning *everything*. Oh, I look forward to that. Wayne, it will be a treat to have Fay-Alice around in the breaks from Oxford.'

'Aren't you a bit old for the butterfly?' she said. 'I hate watching a heart attack in the fast lane, all those desperate bubbles and the sudden incontinence.'

Iles chuckled, obviously in tribute to her aggression and jauntiness. 'Oh, look, Fay-Alice—'

'We don't really need *flics* here, thank you,' she replied. 'So why don't you just piss off back to your interrogation suite alone and play with yourself, Iles?' Harpur decided that, even without pre-knowledge from its brochure, anyone could have recognised this as an outstandingly select school where articulateness was prized and deftly inculcated.

In the fine wide assembly hall, he appreciatively watched Fay-Alice on the platform stride out with her long back et cetera to receive prizes from the Lord Lieutenant. He seemed to do quite an amount of congratulatory talking to and hand shaking with Fay-Alice before conferring her trophies. All at once, then, Harpur realised that Iles had gone from the seat alongside him. For a moment, Harpur wondered whether the ACC intended attacking the Lord Lieutenant for infringing on Fay-Alice and half stood in case he had to move forward and try to throw Iles to the ground and suppress him.

They had been placed at the end of a row, Iles to Harpur's right next to the gangway, Wayne and Nora on his left. To help keep the hall cool, all doors were open. Glancing away from the platform now, Harpur saw Iles run out through the nearest door, as if chasing someone, fine black lace-ups flashing richly in the sunshine. He disappeared. On stage, the presentations continued. Harpur sat down properly again. The ACC's objective was not the Lord Lieutenant.

After about a minute, Harpur heard noises from the back of the hall and, turning, saw a man wearing a yellow and magenta crash helmet and face-guard enter via another open door and dash between some empty rows of seats. At an elegant sprint Iles appeared through the same door shortly afterwards. The man in the helmet stopped, spun and, pulling an automatic pistol from his waistband, pointed it at Iles, perhaps a Browning 140 DA. The ACC swung himself hard to one side and crouched as the gun fired. Then he leaned far forward and used a fierce sweep of his left fist to knock the automatic from the man's hand. With his clenched right, Iles struck him two short, rapid blows in the neck, just below the helmet. At once, he fell. Iles had been in the row behind, but now clambered over the chair backs to reach him. Harpur could not make out the man on the floor but saw Iles provide a brilliant kicking, though without thuggish shouts, so as not to disturb the prize-giving. Often Iles was damn fussy about decorum. He had mentioned his own quality schooling, and this intermittent respect for protocol might date from then.

But because of the gunfire and activity at the rear of the hall, the ceremony had already faltered. Iles bent down and came up with the automatic. 'Please, do continue,' he called out to the Lord Lieutenant and other folk on the stage, waving the weapon in a slow, soothing arc, to demonstrate its harmlessness now. 'Things are all right here, oh, yes.' Iles was not big, yet looked unusually tall among the chairs and might be standing on the gunman's face. A beam of sunlight reached in through a window and gave his neat features a good yet unmanic gleam.

Afterwards, when the local police and ambulance people

had taken the intruder away, Harpur and Iles waited at the end of the hall while the guests, school staff and platform dignitaries dispersed. Wayne, Nora and Fay-Alice approached, Wayne carrying Fay-Alice's award volumes. 'Had that man come for me?' he asked. 'For me? Why?' He looked terrified.

'My God,' Nora said.

'Someone hired for a hit?' Wayne asked.

'I'd think so,' Iles said.

'All sorts would want to commission him, Wayne,' Harpur said. 'You're a target.'

'My God,' Nora said.

'Someone had you marked, Wayne,' Harpur said.

'He'd have gone for you in the mêlée as the crowd departed at the end of the do, I should think,' Iles said.

'But how did you spot him, Mr Iles?' Nora asked.

'I'm trained always to wonder about people at girls' school prize-givings with their face obscured by a crash helmet and obviously tooled up,' Iles said. 'There was a whole lecture course on it at Staff College.'

'Why on earth did he come back into the hall?' Nora asked.

'He would still have had a shot at Wayne, as long as he could knock me out of the way,' Iles said. 'He had orders. He's taken a fee, I expect. He'd be scared to fail.'

'Oh, you saved Daddy, Mr Iles,' Fay-Alice replied, riotously clapping her slim hands. 'An Assistant Chief Constable accepting such nitty-gritty, perilous work on our behalf, and when so brilliantly dressed, too! It was wonderful – so brave, so skilful, so selfless. I watched mesmerized, but *mesmerized,* absolutely. A privilege, I mean it. Thank you, Mr Iles. You so deserve our trust.' She inclined herself towards him, the long back stretching longer, and would have touched the ACC's arm. He skipped out of reach. 'We shall have so much to talk about at the swimming pool back home,' she said. 'I do look forward to it.'

'Let's get away now, Harpur,' Iles snarled.

'Yes, I must show you my butterfly, Mr Iles,' Fay-Alice said. 'Desmond.'

'Let's get away now, Harpur,' Iles replied.

# At Home

Carthage,
Tabbet Drive,
Exall DL2 4NG
May 20

My dearest mother,
I would have replied sooner but – well, Dennis is in and out of the house at odd times and I don't feel safe with pen and paper. It's all right this afternoon. He's definitely gone to town and I'd hear the car early enough. I'd still argue there's a lot to be said for Dennis, as long as you make allowances.

It was lovely to hear your voice on the phone recently. Nobody speaks my name in quite the loving way you do. But please don't ever say anything . . . I mean anything DIFFICULT. There are three extensions here which make it unsafe, and we are all the time plugged into a recording machine that clock-logs any disconnections, and he would want to know why, wouldn't he? Damn crazy, really, isn't it – all this brilliant electronic stuff for communication by phone makes it necessary to use olde-worlde letters!!! Mobiles? Don't trust them for security. Remember Prince Charles and Camilla! E-mail? Don't trust *it* for security. Just think that previously people used to write stories – whole novels – entirely in letters, like that play from the book, *Clarissa*, on TV. Those days, they really took their time getting raped!!! Well, I hope nobody ever makes a book out of *our* letters, Mum!!! In his little way, he often reads.

Glancing back over, I don't know why I said I don't feel safe. I'd hate to give you worry. Safe is such a *major* word. I don't think he would go beyond, not in a *major* way. My

116

feeling is, deep down he's yellow. In any case, I'm careful not to antagonize. I do things absolutely as he wants now, more or less, and he can really be quite sunny. Well, obviously!!! This was the side he used to show. I know I could still love him, KNOW IT, if only he would stay like that for a little while. There are these sudden falls into – well, call it turbulence.

Yes, of course, OF COURSE, it would be fine if you came to visit. Don't worry. He'd be fine. Yes, September or October, fine. I don't keep your letters – so they'll never make a book!!! It's wise not to have them in the house, given his filthy rummaging. I read each in the neighbour's house where I asked you to send them – as less dodgy than to here. Alice is a real gem, or 'Care of Mrs A. V. Ward' to you when you write!!! I bought her an azalea. Alice leaves me alone in her sitting room with your letters for as long as I like – tea and croissants. Lovely.

Sometimes she likes to be called Alice, sometimes Veronica. How she sees herself that particular day. It's harmless, and, as I remarked, she's a treasure, though heavyish in the hips. I'd say she's got her eye on Dennis, the quaint old leching cow, and I know she'd love an invite to some of these weekend things we organize. Women do take to him, Mother, even a woman like Mrs A. V. Ward, who's in line for an OBE medal, as I hear, for services to memos and agendas in some *worthy* job, maybe to do with hospitals or the police committee or 'meals on wheels' for the old.

I go over and over your lovely writing – and then it's down her toilet in teeny bits. Sounds horrible, but advisable. By then I've read it so often I can remember all the lovely, lovely words and this is enough until the next one, and Alice lets me know via a nod in the Drive or at, say, the supermarket, but not by phone, naturally, because he might be about and earholing – that chummy little way he has. Their flush doesn't always take everything away first go, but Alice doesn't mind, no matter how often I work the lever. She understands that I would not want some of your lovely words to be lying there under the water or stuck to the pan and thus treated inappropriately.

But when you write about coming, Mother

I'll break off now because I hear the car. I'll post this as it is, half a letter being better than none!!! Please don't fret.

Your loving daughter,
Jill


Dear Ma,

Well, I didn't post the earlier bit after all, but hid it in my bra and pants drawer. Not sure how impregnable that is, but where else???!!!

Continuing. If you are in touch about your visit, you must write to me here at Carthage, not at Mrs Ward's – well, clearly. This would be an *un*confidential letter, a family letter about arrangements, and one for Dennis also to see, without danger of comeback. So, re weather and family only, and nothing DIFFICULT. Address it to both of us and refer to his broking work and things that interest him, such as making hedge animals and birds through topiary, or the films of Alain Delon.

Naturally enough for any human being – which Dennis definitely is – I've seen his birth certificate!!! – he loves to believe there are certain positive aspects to his personality, the damp cut-out. I don't understand how he's turned against me like this. Do you realize, we've been married twelve years – yes, TWELVE!!! – and if you've got a poisonous nature, this is quite a while for stuff to build up. The side hedge is a peacock now, a marvellous wide tail and sort of aristocratic beak. He's really safe and sunny when he talks about these things, and that marvellous old smile gets through. He can look wholesome then, I don't deny, and this is what possibly gets to women, plus the jauntiness he can put on.

But, oh, mother, the terrible savage thing that happened last week was


Mother, I'm sorry the paper is scrunched up a bit and has a blot or two, but he came back sooner than I thought and moving so quietly. Well, he does. I had to push it all away, under my clothes once more, and then into the special drawer. I had quite a job getting the ink off my let's say thighs!!! I've been worried about the letter these last three days, and

118

this is the first safe chance I've had to bring it out – there's that purple word again – 'safe' – so I'll say sorry. I'm going to close now, not being sure where he is today and wearing those damn rubber-soled running shoes.

We are very well and hope you and Father are. I know Dennis would wish to send his very best. We've been having fair weather, though not *really* summery.

Your loving daughter,
Jill

Carthage,
Thurs

My dearest mother,

I find myself with a few moments, so can continue where I had to break off hurriedly. I was discussing the weather. Yes, it has already been a really warmish May for once.

This will be a short letter because soon I must get on with one or two 'chores', such as the stairs. We have people here at the weekend and everything has to look sparkling. On parade!!! Not neighbours. In these weekend things, I feel anything can be regarded as normal as long as both participants – or more than two, in some instances – yes, as long as *all* participants agree without threats or bullying. Some pleasure can certainly be got by 'extending boundaries', as it is referred to. After all, normal is just a word and *so* relative. We have good lined curtains and are careful in all respects not to offend neighbours.

I think I shall do an extensive buffet meal for this occasion, with many types of meat and fish. My social life will certainly brighten up over the next few weeks for, in addition to this weekend Carthage symposium, I intend going for the first time to a reunion of my school class at the Sage Park hotel.

Trust you are both well. Dennis would certainly like to be remembered and we are jointly looking forward to your visit.

Your loving daughter,
Jill

Carthage,
Tabbet Drive,
Exall DL2 4NG
May 31

Dear Cindy,

Are you sure it's OK for me to write to you at your home address? Things must be very different there from what I'm used to. It was wonderful to see you and the other 'girls' at the reunion after all these years. It made me wish I'd come to other sessions, but, as I mentioned, it is often difficult to get away. Such an 'eye-opener' to hear from someone of my own age that the kind of weekend things which happen here from time to time are not unique. Although I had often suspected this, I could not be sure until I spoke to Cindy Porter (née Rayner) of Florence Nightingale House, Moss-Bribant School, now Dr (!) Lucinda (!) Porter, with inside knowledge of all sort of lives via Casualty, as well as her own adventures!!! (Excuse the handwriting. I must write this quickly and have a little damage to my arm and knuckles – in part my own fault, I admit, the thug.)

Please don't feel anxious about me. I thought afterwards I might have made things here sound too dark. That's sherry!!! It's worrying – the electric-powered topiary shears and so on, but I have to believe in my ability to talk a hellish crisis back to a spell of peace. All that joking and gossip which used to irritate our teachers were not completely a waste!!! I remain certain that, regardless of what he may *suspect*, he does not one hundred per cent *know* about the happy matter I mentioned to you, and he would never push to the ultimate unless absolutely forced. Gutlessness is Dennis's long suit. You'd think jealousy would have died after the behaviour at these weekends, but no doubt his measly mind would distinguish between unmeaningful knockabout and a serious liaison. Seems much of a muchness to me.

Many cheerful and amusing memories of school came back upon seeing you, Cindy. I'd like to ring you some time from a public booth, and possibly arrange to meet. I do a big shopping trip every week, and an hour or so stuck on the beginning or the end is not noticed. I know because I already use

120

that bit of time elasticity for other 'get-togethers' with you-know-who, as spoken of. Mainly it's backs of cars or, during this kind of weather, in the open air. Of course, PLEASE DO NOT, REPEAT NOT write here or telephone, because of Dennis's little ways. The trouble with our place and its damn wall-to-wall carpeting is it's hard to hear him moving about. Beigeish mostly.

Must close. Grand to hear of your fine holiday in Biarritz, a spot I've always admired, beloved of Edward VII, I believe. Following the recent weekend, I'm going to give the carpets a good sprucing up with a new, most effective liquid cleaner. Obviously overnight anywhere with you-know-who is out of the question. Isn't the weather gorgeous for spring? Some complain about lack of rain, but I think this tiresomely ungrateful.

Yours, with so many happy school memories,
Jill

Carthage

My dearest mother,
In haste. Well, as ever!!! I think it would be cleverer if you put off your visit. There are difficulties. But please, DON'T WORRY, just difficulties. It was lovely to hear about the new octagonal conservatory, which is so 'period' and chic. I've always thought of chicness as your forte. He'd better remember, electric powered shears don't just cut one way and they can go wrong. What I think would be cleverest is if you could write and say certain matters have come up at *your* end making a visit in September or October as planned awkward. This would be one of the formal, joint letters, sent here to Carthage for both of us, not 'Care of Mrs A. V. Ward', of course.

Illness as explanation would be all right, or redecoration. It will be cleverer for you to say you can't come than for me to tell him we ought to postpone the invitation due to difficulties here, because he'll reply, in his special slimy way, 'What difficulties?' Leave it till the New Year? He's always one to claim there are no difficulties, yet being the whole disgusting cause of them.

How touchingly appreciative of the remarks about the Alain Delon films and his hedge clipping he was!!! So, further material along those lines would be beneficial. It makes him feel *noticed*. There's an Alain Delon film called *Red Sun*, which you did not refer to last time but which you could mention in your next letter. It's a Western, but to do with a samurai sword somehow as well, if you could highlight these facts. But perhaps it would seem unusual if you knew the name of this obscure 1971 film, so possibly just say about Delon and the samurai sword and he will be able to comment in his little way, 'She means *Red Sun*, and this will build him up temporarily. A kindness.

Another weekend party a few days ago, including some new people. This can make things more interesting, as long as they behave within bounds, though showing stamina. I hate brashness or vulgarity in physical matters, as you will recall, but, on the other hand, a certain disregard for restraint is a plus. All were deeply appreciative of a large peach flan. The noise is kept reasonable. I don't consider it inhospitable to ask guests not to groan or cry out like a porn video. This regard for control is in my upbringing, I suppose. Dad always hated indoor noise. I know Dennis would wholeheartedly wish to be very warmly remembered to you if he knew I were writing.

Your loving daughter,
Jill

Carthage

Dear Greg,
Can't make it this weekend. Please don't be angry and please keep him zipped up. Will definitely be in touch soonest.

All my love,
Jill

Dear Tim,

I trust you'll not mind my troubling you with a personal matter. I've nowhere else to turn. I put off bothering you, but now feel unable to continue in this alone.

You will deduce it's about Jill. There are some things going on which I do not understand and others which, perhaps, I do, and wish I didn't. Tim, think of this letter as like the old days – your younger brother, Dennis, approaches for advice, which you always generously gave. I suppose I could talk to you about it all on the phone or by e-mail, but I feel more at ease (and more secure) setting things out on paper.

Jill seems to have developed a terrible and, need I say, utterly inexplicable fear of me? I know this will seem absurd to you – as, indeed, it does to myself. If anything, I've always thought I need more aggression in life – and you used to tell me so. Just the same, I sense a constant dread in her of what I might do. Once or twice when I must have come silently to the door of a room – we have fitted carpet throughout – I've opened it and found her obviously tense and straining to hear where I might be in the house. It is as if she's – as if – well, the only word I can regard as right, Tim, is *terrified* – yes, terrified of being confronted suddenly by me. But why? Once, when leaving the house, I glanced back and spotted her part concealed by upstairs curtains, a look of immense relief on her face as she watched me. Imagine the hurt, even dread, I suffered.

Perhaps your first reaction will be that your brother is imagining all this – has flipped. I could sympathize with that reaction, though I think I can claim to be one who does not generally fantasize. But there's something else. Recently, I found buried deep in Jill's underwear drawer an uncompleted letter to her mother. It was much crumpled and must have been hurriedly concealed in her handbag or under the clothes she had on, and ultimately transferred to the drawer. It was a letter she had started, then put aside, then resumed, though still not finished.

Obviously, Tim, this is not a drawer I usually open, but I felt such a strangeness in the house that examination of all potential hiding places was justified, even vital. When I looked again later, the letter had gone, of course, possibly completed and sent. What the fragment said shocked me so much that I transcribed some of the more worrying parts and I'll include them now, so you may judge for yourself. It was the end of one passage that upset me – a sentence broken off, as if she had been disturbed, or simply could not bring herself to go on. It said, 'But, oh, mother, the terrible, savage thing that happened last week was—'

When I read this I searched my mind for what she could mean, and still do. No 'terrible, savage thing' happened here. Or not that I know of. And that is the point, for her letter was almost entirely about me, the suggestion being that I had perpetrated this terrible, savage thing on her. The letter said, 'Dennis is in and out of the house at odd times and I don't feel safe with pen and paper.'

Now, Tim, perhaps you'll begin to understand fully my disquiet. She went on to lay out ways of communicating secretly and then seemed to descend to a note of outright hatred and contempt. Having referred slightingly to my interest in certain films and hedge care, the letter continued, 'he loves to believe there are certain positive aspects to his personality, the damp cut-out.' Why would she describe me in this tone?

Of course, I've already considered the obvious – that my Jill, as I used to call her – yes, that *my* Jill has found someone else, and therefore feels not only cruel loss of affection towards me, but guilt causing her to fear I'll seek revenge. Obviously, I don't refer here to casual, harmless, playful encounters with weekend guests, but a relationship of depth. It would devastate me if I found she were unfaithful in that fashion, yet it's a possibility I must face. But even if such a dreadful supposition were proved as fact, I trust I would not turn in my sorrow and rage to savage reprisals. It is one of the most wounding elements in the whole situation that Jill does not seem to know me – fails to understand my nature.

Do you think you could write a word and tell me how these matters strike you, Tim?

Your affectionate brother,
Dennis

Carthage

Dear Tim,
Thanks so much for your prompt reply. I'm all the more grateful since I realize your natural instinct is to telephone, not write, but you'll understand it would be awkward to receive that kind of call here, or through the switchboard at work.

No, there have been no further developments, simply the continuance of this stifling tension. I still feel all my movements around the house and garden are anxiously monitored by Jill, as though I were a murderous intruder. This is all the more baffling because in the letter she referred to me as yellow deep down and incapable of anything she called 'major'. I will not allow this to provoke me, rest assured. Again no, I have not come across further correspondence in her underwear drawer, though I've been thorough in my searches, unpleasantly furtive as this has to be, as you say.

Your suggestion about secretly intercepting letters from her parents won't work because all correspondence containing what she calls 'difficult' matters go care of a neighbour. We do get some letters from her parents, but on formal, trivial matters, and I think Jill tells them what to write. They were to have visited in the autumn, for instance, but cried off, giving some absurd excuse about her mother's duties at the Oxfam shop. I believe Jill asked them to cancel because of the situation here. These letters throw a deliberate veil – discuss politics and the weather and inquire politely about my interests in film and hedge art, blatantly humouring me. Jill feeds them topics. See what lengths she'll adopt to hoodwink her husband. Oddly, she declares in her letter that she could still love me if only I'd remain what she terms 'sunny'. I fail to fathom this. I'm as I've always been and how most of us are – a mixture of moods, but never, I trust, offensive.

If you can bear to analyse these rather rambling remarks and let me have your views again, I'd be for ever grateful.

Your affectionate brother,
Dennis

Carthage

Dear Tim,
I dislike the tone of your last letter, just arrived. There are wise points but, reading between the lines, I feel you're really saying that what's happening is in some way my fault. You take the very same negative attitude as hers and you turn away from the dangers to me that may exist from her state. You imply I've been cold and devoid of understanding. Not true. One has tried so hard. There are even passages of your letter which hint I'm imagining everything, or lying, and that I found no letter in her drawer.

I should not have troubled you. Forgive me. I'll not write on these matters any more.

Yours,
Dennis.

Carthage

My dear mother,
I've written the envelope to you in advance today as I'm not sure of Denn's whereabouts, so if this letter is incomplete it's from necessity again. I'll just post it as before to show I'm all right. One does grieve re the continuing trouble in Iraq. I don't say at all that Denn does not feel the stress of the difficulties here, too. I would still argue I could love him if only

Carthage

Greg,
So sorry, this Saturday not poss. Perhaps Saturday fortnight. Will confirm, though.

J

27 Perdita Close
Amberchase,
Lancashire
July 16

Dear Mrs Ward,

As Jill Seagrave's mother, I feel I should write a note to you – I mean, to you personally, not merely 'Care Of Mrs A. V. Ward'. That has always seemed strange, as if I'm writing to you, yet not. I am very grateful for all you're doing for Jill, and for me.

I wish to raise a sensitive matter. Jill has always been a rather imaginative person inclined to dramatize and, really, I wonder sometimes whether the precautions with letters are actually necessary. Some of the things Jill writes to us about her husband don't chime with my own and Jill's father's impressions of Dennis. Always, he struck as a decent person, devoted to Jill and determined to make a good life for the two of them, and for children, should those eventually come along. Have things at Carthage changed so much that the reflections on him made by Jill week after week now are reality based? There is a reference to an electrically powered hedge trimmer.

We would dearly like to visit, to investigate for ourselves, but Jill is adamant that we come only when she considers it right. This, I'm afraid, will be never.

It would be such a help if, when you have a moment, you could drop me the briefest of lines to say whether, as a trusted neighbour, you observe anything *actual* that would account for Jill's anxieties and fears or does she invent and fantasize?

Sincerely,
Gwen Day (Mrs)

Carthage

Dear Cindy,

Just a line to say how much Dennis and I enjoyed seeing you and your hubby in our home recently. We both felt you

127

'lasted the pace' well for a first visit, and several 'regulars' have telephoned to speak appreciatively of the 'new acquisitions', meaning your good selves!!! Julian's wry humour in no way jarred, especially as he has so many other facets. Needless to say, you have facets also, and these were likewise generally admired.

Till soon,
Jill

Carthage

Dear patient Greg,
No, not Saturday, but almost certainly the following Friday, darling.

J

Carthage

Dear Tim,
It would have been out of place to speak of the following matter at the funeral (and thank you so much for coming, despite my ill-tempered letter in June) but I hope now you will allow me to say one more word or two about relations at the end between Jill and myself. Although I'm sorry I was harsh with you in my letter, I still feel you suspected I was the real cause of the poor state of things here, not Jill. What I tell you now will finally correct that misunderstanding.

Obviously, it could be seen as especially distasteful to go through Jill's private hiding places immediately after her appalling death, but I did think it even more obligatory than before, for fear the police might make blundering deductions from the kind of correspondence with her mother I have described. It was, indeed, fortunate that I did inspect her underwear drawer once again, for I discovered another uncompleted letter, probably hidden away as before because she was interrupted. Timothy, there were sentences here that I really do not like to speculate on too much, but I think you

128

will see their meaning. She referred several times to an electrically powered hedge cutter which I use for my topiary, and said that such dangerous tools had been known to turn lethal when connections in the cutter itself or the plug became faulty or 'had even been vandalized', causing electrocution of the user.

She added that such an accident to me would be 'truly and deeply rotten', but in case it ever happened would her mother be careful to destroy all Jill's previous letters in which the hedge cutter had been mentioned and, of course, this one – in fact, never completed and sent. I felt sickened and dizzy at these paragraphs, and perhaps you feel the same on hearing of them. Also, I noted down the broken-off end of the letter. It said: 'Cross your fingers but I think I might at last have found someone who'

That incompleteness – so tantalizing. Naturally, I shredded this letter at once. I want nothing to besmirch Jill's name further, following the unseemly nature of her death. But I don't think I need to spell out the implications of the hedge cutter references. They can only signify that, had she been allowed to live, she meant to dispose of me, or try to, by tampering with the cutter. No doubt Jill would have argued that whatever action she undertook would be only to pre-empt an attack from myself. Tim, I think we can both see the ludicrousness of this. And I feel we are both aware that the 'someone' she had found was intended as possible replacement for myself.

Do please believe me, Tim, that her letter, though now destroyed, did exist. I hope you will admit, in the light of its fortunate discovery, that blame for the ghastly fate of Jill can never rest with me. I write because I prize and, as always, crave your esteem.

Ever your affectionate brother,
Dennis

Dear Mrs Day,

I very much regret that there was no time at dear Jill's funeral for you and me to speak – me as the *actual* Mrs A. V. Ward, not 'Care Of'! I now regret, too, of course, that I had not replied to your letter asking for my views on Jill's letters.

I would like to make some sort of amends by passing on information that might not normally be available to you. I work in an administrative role with the local Police Authority and therefore sometimes hear unpublished background material to crimes. Detectives on the case say privately that Gregory Lave-Page, who confessed to the murder of your daughter, and will stand trial, loved her sincerely, fiercely, and was only driven to this ghastly offence because, finally, he felt unable to attract her away from her husband, and from the life they had made at Carthage.

Nothing I say will remove the pain you experience at her death, but perhaps you'll draw comfort from the fact that, in Lave-Page's view, at least, Jill was still indissolubly committed to Dennis and their marriage. She had apparently talked frankly and at length to Lave-Page about the nature of her relationship with Dennis.

Forgive me if I bring up dark detail, but, as you will know, Jill was stabbed to death with eight blows the instant she stepped from her car at the last rendezvous with Lave-Page, because – as he informed detectives – he sensed after several cancelled meetings that she had tired of him and would say the affair must end. He literally could not bear to hear this. Hence his ferocious attack. He told police that, although Jill and Dennis obsessively feared and distrusted each other, he – Lave-Page – had come to see it was this very obsessiveness which, in a strange, almost mystical way, kept them together, and would eternally – his word – yes, eternally keep them together, despite her affair with him, and despite, also, certain exceptionally liberated social occasions at their home, about which he had heard rumours. They gave him additional, intolerable pain. A mixture of these factors evidently pushed him into heartbroken, frenzied, violent despair.

He believed that at times Jill and her husband would actually fabricate or hint at frightening, brutal incidents and plots, hoping to increase the excitement they gained from this unique, binding tension between them. And he alleged her husband might even continue manufacturing and reporting to others such imaginings after her death, so powerful had that eerie link become. Perhaps this was what Lave-Page meant by 'eternal'. He obviously knew himself excluded.

In conclusion, may I say how much I feel for you at this time and also, of course, for Dennis, whom I will naturally seek to assist in any ways possible?

With all my sympathy,
Alice Ward

# A Bit of Eternity

Up at the other end of the air raid shelter an argument had started between two men Mark Milward did not recognize. They stood facing each other, close, too close. Most people in the shelter sat on the narrow, slatted wooden benches around the walls. There were about ten in the shelter altogether, including the two men. Mark was with his mother, his younger brother, Ian, and Clifford Hill from the house next door to the Milwards. Clifford was fifteen, older than Ian and Mark.

Occasionally, Mark could pick up some words of the men's argument above the noise of bombs and anti-aircraft guns outside. The quarrel seemed to be about money and nothing to do with the air raid. Mr Cartwright was sitting near them. Mark thought Mr Cartwright must have shut his chip shop on the corner of Chave Street when the bombs started.

Mark stared towards the arguing men. He could only see them dimly, but felt sure they were not local, because of the way they spoke. They were too old to be in the army. The shelter had one central, dim, yellowy electric light. Smoke from burning houses drifted in through the shelter's open doors at each end. Now and then the smoke almost hid the men. Mark thought sometimes they did not look real. They were like shadows or dark pictures of mysterious characters in one of his adventure books.

Ian sat on the other side of their mother, his face turned in against the top of her arm, as if he wanted to sleep or hide. He was seven. Clifford Hill sat next to Ian. When the bombing started, Clifford went down into the Hills' own private air raid shelter in their back garden. His mother and father had gone out to the cinema this evening. Clifford became scared by himself in their shelter and had begun yelling, to see if anyone was in the Milwards' house. Ian, Mark and their mother were sheltering under the big wooden kitchen table, just sitting on the mat, and Mrs Milward unbolted the kitchen door to the back garden and shouted to Clifford to come in if he wanted to. Clifford climbed over the wall between the two gardens and the three made room for him under the table. Mark's father was at work in the docks this evening.

After a while, when the bombing seemed to get worse, Mark's mother said it might be better to be with other people. And there was not really enough room under the table for four if the raid lasted a long time. The public shelter stood not far from their house, on what used to be a grass island in the middle of Chave Street. They got out from under the table and, when there was some peace for a few minutes, his mother opened the front door and the four of them hurried to the big shelter. It was brick with a cover of very thick cement. Searchlights swung about in the sky, hunting the bomber planes for the guns to shoot at. Anti-aircraft guns were known as ack-ack. Houses on fire in the next street, Milton Street, lit up the Milwards' own street – a strange yellow, red and blue light, with black smoke at its edges. Everybody knew that if the bombs made a fire it would be seen through the blackout by the next gang of German pilots tonight, who'd use it for a target. As they reached the shelter, Mark had heard a cracking sound, then a funny rushing, roaring sound, and he thought this must be a Milton Street house as it collapsed.

Near him on the bench, his mother watched the two men for a few minutes, then turned her head away. He could tell they frightened her – the phlegmy hate in their voices, but also poshness. She wanted to pretend they were not there, not even as shadows or pictures. She seemed more afraid of these two men than of the raid and German bombs. Mark, his mother, Ian, and Clifford had run to this street shelter because they did not like it on their own as the raid went on and got worse. Although his mother had wanted the company of the Chave Street public shelter, now she must think these two men were a new danger, extra. She put her face close to Mark's and whispered, 'Just ignore them.'

He heard it all right. A pause had come in the bomb noise and gun noise. Maybe she thought that if the men noticed Mark staring at them they would forget their argument and turn on him, although just a kid. His mother could be like that sometimes. She believed that if you did not take any notice of a bad thing it might go away. Of course, the bombs sounded bad and you had to take notice of them, and the sight and bitter smell of burning in the next street, and the glass bits under their feet from blasted out windows as they ran to the public shelter. But these two men – they might get tired of arguing if people ignored them. Or, if the quietness outside went on, perhaps they would leave the shelter and try to get somewhere else, such as to the pub or a lane where they could fight.

Now, the two men still argued. They would move even closer, as if about to fight, and then back away, but still grunting and muttering about money. One said half the money should be his, but the other said he was the one who found it and that was that. Mark did not know which money. He thought it must be a lot if it made them quarrel so badly, not caring who heard. Their voices did not seem like the voices of people from the streets around here, but more like the headmaster in the grammar school where Mark had just started, or even like people on the wireless with the News.

One of the men turned his back on the other, as if he'd become suddenly fed up with the argument, or as if he was sick of looking at the other man and did not believe him worth talking to any more. That's how it seemed when he turned his back – not just to walk away but to tell the other man he was not worth talking to any more. Perhaps the man who turned his back would go. The raid might be over. For the last few minutes Mark had not heard any bombs and the ack-ack was quiet, so there would be no lumps of shrapnel coming down from exploded shells. Mark's mother might be right, and as long as nobody took any notice of the men this trouble would end. Clifford said: 'He's got a knife.' He did not whisper. He just said it in an ordinary way, but trembling, and Mark could hear it, although his mother and Ian were between him and Clifford. Mark looked at the two men. The one who had not turned his back seemed really angry because the other one had. The one who had turned his back probably knew it would make the other one more angry. That might be why he did it.

The other one stepped forward two paces very fast and got his left arm around the neck of the one who had turned his back and pulled him against himself. They both had black or dark overcoats on and now they were together like that and in the smoke, they looked like a big, thick shadow. The one who had turned his back shouted something, or nearly a scream, but Mark could not tell what it was. It might have been just a shout of surprise or he might have been trying to say something but could not because of the arm inside the overcoat sleeve pressing so hard against his throat.

Through the smoke around the two men Mark thought he saw something shine. It was in the right hand of the man who had not turned his back. His other hand and arm stayed around the neck of the man who turned his back. The man who had not turned his back said in a loud voice, but still posh, 'You can't keep it all. Can't.' He said the 'Can't' really strong both times, but stronger on the second go. It seemed to echo right along the shelter, past Mr Chip Shop, and then past Mark and his mother and Ian and Clifford. And then the right arm of the man who had said 'Can't' went forwards and backwards four times, or maybe five, and Mark thought he saw that shining thing again and the man who had turned his back just slipped down and lay on his side by the other man's feet on the floor of the shelter. He did not have holes in the bottom of his shoes.

Before this big raid tonight, Mark and his friends used to use the public shelter as just somewhere to play in. There had not been any bombs near their street until now. Girls and boys kissed in here and similar, away from grown-ups, and played chase through the shelter. It had a door at both ends in case of being trapped if it was hit, and the locks had been broken and then mended and then broken again and left broken. When they built the shelter just after the war started, Mark had drawn a big heart in the wet cement on one of the outside walls and put in it 'J. P. loves C. L. This is true.' It was much better doing this in cement than in chalk on a door, because the chalk would be washed away by rain.

The cement soon went hard and the letters and heart would stay for years and years – until the end of the war when the shelter might get knocked down because of no more raids. Mark thought this was how love should be – for nearly ever, if possible.

J. P. meant John Payne and C. L. meant Carole Landis. These were real film stars, but in some of their games Mark used to pretend to be John Payne and Jill Mace, who was his girlfriend, also aged eleven, pretended to be Carole Landis, another star. A girl called Doreen was the actress, Betty Grable, and her boyfriend, Eric, was Don Ameche. These stars usually came in pictures about really cheerful, sunny places with music, such as South America, or about exciting ancient times, and Mark thought it seemed really nice to pretend to be in those places or a different time and not just themselves, around their own streets, now, in the war and the blackout and carrying gas masks to school in a cardboard box. Carmen Miranda, another star, also had the name 'The Brazilian Bombshell'. She could be very comical and sang in some of these pictures, but was not so very pretty, and none of the girls wanted to be her. John Payne smiled often with good teeth and had smooth, dark hair. Now, because of the raid and this man lying on the floor, and Clifford Hill saying 'He's got a knife' in an ordinary way but trembling, the shelter seemed different. It was not a place to play and kiss in, but to hide from the bombs and shrapnel in and watch two men get really in a rage about something, most probably money, and one of them turn savage.

The other man, the one not not moving on the floor, went and sat on one of the benches. 'He's got the knife in his hand,' Clifford said. 'Blood.' Cliff was still *trembling*.

'Ignore him, Clifford,' Mark's mother said. Mark could see the knife now. The man held it down against his trouser leg in his left hand. The knife would drip on his clothes and shoes. The man bent forward like somebody praying in church. Mark thought the man would run after doing what he did, but he stayed there, although outside everything still seemed better. The chip shop man, Mr Cartwright, said: 'Someone should go and fetch a police officer.'

'Well, you go,' Mark's mother said.

'I must watch this man,' Mr Cartwright replied. He meant the one with the knife. But Mr Cartwright was very wheezy and thin. He should eat more of his own fish and chips. He would not be able to stop the man if he wanted to go or if he became angry with someone else. 'The boy should go,' Mr Cartwright said. 'There'll be police in Milton Street because of the bombs there. He can wear this in case of shrapnel.' Mr Cartwright had a grey metal helmet by his side on the bench. Mark went and put it on. It was too big, but Mr Cartwright tightened the strap under Mark's chin. He began to feel grown up and necessary, as though he had become someone else. He liked this.

'No, Mark,' his mother said.

'I'll be all right. I'll come straight back,' Mark said.

'He'll be all right,' Mr Cartwright said. 'The other boy, the older one, has some shock.' He meant Clifford. Mark felt proud to be doing something with a helmet on that Clifford could not do, although fifteen.

'Well, *you* go,' Mark's mother said again to Mr Cartwright.

'Mr Cartwright has to be a guard,' Mark said.

It was very cold. He went through the lane to Milton Street. All one end of the street was flat or burning and half the big mansion at the end of the street had also been torn away. Mark could see a bed and a wardrobe upstairs, where the wall of the room had gone. Flames from one of the houses lit up the smashed mansion. The builder of these streets had put up this big home for himself, with a high wall at the back and a view of the river in front. Mark thought the builder must know now it had been stupid to put that mansion there, especially if he was in it when the bombs began. A big ammunition factory stood opposite on the other side of the river and the bombers had most likely been after that. Even at night and in the blackout they could see the river. They used it to find the factory and only just missed.

He saw a policeman without his helmet on who was helping look for people in one of the bombed houses. Doreen, aged twelve, who was Betty Grable, lived in Milton Street, but Mark did not know which house. It was not the mansion. He said: 'I think a murder. In the big shelter – Chave Street.'

'How many?' the policeman asked. His face had ash on.

'How many what?'

'How many dead?'

'Well, one,' Mark said. 'A murder.'

'There's three here. And four next door and three next door but one.'

'Murder,' Mark said. 'Money.'

'Maybe I'll come in a minute,' the policeman replied. Mark watched while two air raid wardens and an ambulance man brought out a woman's body under a blanket. He could see her stockings. They had slipped down her legs and were wrinkled and creased near her shoes. It was definitely a grown up woman, not Betty Grable. Doreen did not wear stockings like that and the legs were too thick, much thicker than Doreen's or Betty Grable's. Betty Grable had insurance on her legs because they were so important for a star in bathing costumes. 'Where did you get that helmet?' the policeman said.

'It's Mr Chip Shop's.'

'A kid of your age shouldn't have a helmet. They're not for kids. Helmets are not toys.'

'It was important. I had to come. He might run. Or go for someone else. My mother and brother are still there, and Clifford Hill. Clifford couldn't come because there was only one helmet and he's already a bit scared from being by himself in their own shelter at first.'

'All right,' the policeman said. 'I think that's all we'll find here.' They went back through the lane. The man was still sitting on the bench with the knife in his hand near the other man on the floor. It was a pocket knife that would fold up, but with a big blade, and it was not folded now. The policeman crouched and looked at the body. 'You did it?' he said to the man on the bench.

The man held out the knife in one hand. Yes, blood, as Clifford said. The policeman took out a handkerchief, wrapped the knife and put it on the bench. 'Evidence,' he said. 'Did you see what happened?' he asked Mark.

'Yes. That one on the floor turned his back and—'

'All right,' the policeman said. He brought out handcuffs from his tunic pocket and fixed them on the wrists of the man seated on the bench. The man let him. 'I'm going back to Milton Street to tell the sergeant I have to take this man and you to the police station. You're a witness.'

'Yes,' Mark said.

'You can both wait outside now. It's calm,' the policeman said. 'We don't want this fellow frightening the other folk. I don't think he'll run. He's not the sort. Anyway, in cuffs he'd look like a looter who's escaped and people would get after him. They've heard of looters.'

Mark and the man stood near the heart that Mark had drawn in the cement. The fires in Milton Street were still high enough to light up the heart and initials. 'What money?' Mark asked.

'Yes, money. It's always about money, isn't it?'

'What?' Mark said.

'Trouble. He found the money in our mother's house when she died. All the money. Behind volumes on the book shelves. She wouldn't go to banks. He knew that. That money's an inheritance, for sharing, isn't it?'

Mark would have guessed this man's mother was the kind to have volumes and book shelves.

'But I shouldn't be asking you, telling you – a kid in a helmet,' the man said.

'I was the one Mr Cartwright picked to go.'

'Even so,' the man said.

'Is he your brother?' Mark asked.

'He took it all.'

'Why didn't you run?' Mark said.

'Oh, I don't know. Where to? What did the constable say – I'm not the sort?'

'You'd be like Cain, after he killed Abel. Nowhere to hide.'

'You go to Sunday School, do you?'

'I don't think you live here,' Mark said.

'I came on the tram to see a lady. But tonight the raid starts before I reach where she lives and I have to get into the shelter. And who do I find here? My brother. Fluke. Good? Bad? When he scooped the money he disappeared. He must have taken a place around here to hide. It's not the kind of district I'd expect him to be in – especially now he's

139

got the money. I always bring the knife when I come this way to see the lady. Protection. Oh, look, sorry, you live here, don't you? I just meant that if I—'

'It was an accident we were in the shelter, too,' Mark replied. 'There wasn't room under the table when Clifford came. And it's only wood. It wouldn't hold up all the bricks if the house fell down. I'm glad we came to this shelter because I saw in Milton Street how a house could just tumble, even a mansion – so much really heavy stuff. Why do you see a lady here if you don't like this part of town?'

'I wonder who J. P. and C. L. are?' the man replied. He pointed at the shelter wall. He had to use both hands because his wrists were fastened together. 'They've got a bit of eternity here, J. P. and C. L. Very rare. They'll last as long as the shelter.'

'As a matter of fact, J. P. is me,' Mark said.

'You? I thought your mother called you Mark,' the man said.

'It's a game. J. P. is John Payne,' Mark said.

'John Payne?' the man said.

'Yes, I'm John Payne,' Mark said.

The policeman, pushing a bike and with his helmet on now, came back just then. 'You're John Payne?' he said. 'Like the film star?' He put his bicycle against the wall under the heart and went into the shelter for the wrapped knife. He came out and put it into his saddle bag. The three of them began to walk to the police station. The raid had finished. People were around the streets now, looking at the damage, watching the firemen. Water from their hoses froze in the gutters. When some people saw the policeman and Mark with a man in handcuffs they began to shout and shake their fists and spit. One of the women screamed he must be a dirty looter of bombed houses like she'd read about in the London blitz, and a good job the police had him. 'No, you're wrong, he only murdered his brother,' Mark shouted.

In the police station, the officer told an Inspector what had happened in the shelter. The Inspector produced a pad and said: 'Well, a knifing's still a knifing, even tonight. This boy can give a witness statement, can he? Then we'll make charges. What's your name, son?'

'His name's John Payne,' the constable said.

The Inspector said, 'Spelled like the film star?' and began to write it down.

'No, I'm Mark Milward, really,' Mark said.

'What's that mean?' the Inspector said.

'What?' Mark asked.

'"Really."'

# Night Light

A fter such a sickening find on the premises, Panicking
Ralph Ember began to fear he would never get his
drinking club in Shield Terrace up to the same level of exclu-
siveness and distinction as, say, the Athenaeum in London,
or even the Garrick or Boodle's. Through good, vigilant
patrols of the lavatories and odd corners, Ralph believed he
prevented pretty well all drugs use or dealing in his club.
And he made sure celebration parties for acquittals or releases
or christenings or bail virtually always remained unviolent.
But then came this appalling discovery, this appalling situation, that he could not possibly have guarded against.
Nobody could have.

On visits to London, Ralph had several times been over
to get the atmosphere of the Garrick in Garrick Street, the
Athenaeum in Pall Mall and Boodle's in St James's Street.
This would be from outside, of course, just the buildings.
He did not belong to any London club, and there were
doormen. He liked the idea of both the Garrick and the street
being called after the famed British actor centuries ago, David
Garrick. As a result of this long connection with the theatre,
Ralph understood that many present Garrick members came
from the arts, meaning not just the stage, but literary and
media figures. The Athenaeum possibly had some people
from the arts, but mainly it was major Civil Servants,
academics and business leaders. Boodle's, from right back
in the eighteenth century, would feature many very upper-
class names, some titled, on their list, and Ralph, standing
opposite the entrance, had twice watched members wearing
what were obviously first-class shoes, most likely off personal
lasts, going in and leaving. Ralph's club was called the Monty.
For a long while it had been one of his dearest aims to make

the social rating and general quality of membership and facilities equal to those of any top, renowned London establishment. The Monty didn't have a special type of membership, like, for instance, the Garrick. The Monty could be said to be more general.

At just after two a.m., on one of his usual closing time inspection rounds, it angered Ralph to find this slaughtered male – no question, male – this slaughtered male near the emergency exit door in the club's car park. It not only angered him. It made him almost despair. Although the Garrick, Athenaeum and Boodle's might provide private car parks, Ralph would bet nobody from any of those clubs – management or membership – had come across a naked dead pimp there lately – naked or even properly clothed, most probably.

Of course, Ralph recognized him, despite the absence of Claud's customary, vivid, un-British clothes, and the deep damage to his head and face. A club security light shone over the emergency door and gave the body some gleam. Ralph was very strong on security and safety – the security and safety of anyone at the club, plus his own. Clearly, Claud Montagne's security and safety were beyond Ralph's care now, yet he did not feel he had failed in his responsibilities because, almost definitely, Claud had been killed elsewhere, stripped, then brought here and left, out of malice, tactics or playfulness. Despite his concerns for security, Ralph could not risk closed-circuit television. It would disturb some members if they knew their movements into, and particularly out of, the club had been filmed and timed and dated. Ralph himself did not want that kind of exact data, in case police approached him to crack an alibi. Ralph had to stay uninvolved.

Claud Montagne had unquestionably been a member of the club and for a while sat on the Entertainment Committee, might actually have chaired it. Ralph acknowledged obligations to his members, even members like Claud, who would have been one of the first kicked out once Ralph began moving the Monty towards a nicer status modelled on the Athenaeum's. This was the club he really admired – full of true industrialists, scholars and administrators. The Garrick might be all right, but Bohemian, and you never knew where that could end up. And he considered the name Boodle's sort of deliberately unserious, oafish.

Ralph did not see how he could control what happened to members away from the club. In Claud's line, he might upset all sorts of people who would target him. Some of his girls could have parents who objected to the work he expected from their daughters. Or there were pimps from abroad now – Eastern Europe, for instance. They ran imported young tarts and might well want to displace traditional figures like Claud. His foul, expensive garments and lurid jewellery could cause very rough envy in immigrant pimps.

Almost always when the club shut, Ralph did a good, final, all-clear tour himself. This job he would not delegate and the staff went home. Ralph had enemies. Naturally he had enemies. Anybody who made £600,000 a year through drugs wholesaling, plus profits from the Monty, was sure to stir malice, just as in his minor, sleazy way, Claud Montagne was. Although Ralph wore fine but very conventional made-to-measure suits bought in London, and no jewellery beyond a fairly ordinary watch, he could not avoid being noticed. The £600,000 was easy for others to estimate, unfortunately. Some said it must be more. And then the Monty in addition. Ralph accepted the risks that came with wealth. On his early morning rounds he looked mainly for incendiary stuff, or people lurking before a break-in, or a booby bomb under his car. He had never discovered a body before, nor thought he might. But, clearly, this could be another way of getting at him. Perhaps some trading rival hoped Ralph would be nailed for the murder, dungeoned, and so put out of the commercial scene for a decade or so. In Ralph's view, life and trade had become increasingly competitive.

It puzzled him that Claud should have been placed so near the security light, as if meant to be found. Others leaving the club might have seen Claud, might in fact have seen him delivered, but few Monty members of the current flavour would report this sort of thing to Ralph or the law, for fear of getting implicated. They would notice, as Ralph did, the nearness to the light, and deduce they were intended to have a stare and then pass the word. So, a trap. Although Claud

144

had been elected to the Entertainment Committee, and possibly to its chair, he was not markedly popular. Not many Monty pimps were. Some said pimps did nothing for the Monty's image. People would not get anxious about leaving Claud's corpse unprotected.

This death made Ralph ponder that unless he could start transforming the club soon, he might have Albanian pimps applying for membership. Ralph did not regard himself as at all racist, but he foresaw difficulty when that happened. It had to be said, pimps were looked down on, and foreign pimps would probably be very unwelcome. The Membership Committee might reject them, and this could produce resentment, leading to more bodies in the car park.

Any deado on Monty ground would have been unsatisfactory to Ralph, but in an important way Claud rated as special, special even among pimps. One of the girls who worked for him was black and about nineteen, called Honorée. This might not be her actual name. Girls in their business looked for a glamour label and many re-christened themselves. The girl could actually be a Mavis or Flora. A name change also concealed their real identity and background. Ralph regarded that precaution as entirely reasonable. Some girls managed to run two separate lives, the so-called respectable one subsidized by the other. They would not want the two to overlap.

The main point about Honorée – the sickeningly main point – was that for quite a time she'd had a business liaison with Assistant Chief Constable (Operations), Desmond Iles. This had become pretty well known. Some said the relationship amounted by now to an affair, although, of course, Honorée saw many other clients. An unkind but humorous tale went around not long ago that she had given the Assistant Chief crabs. He stayed with her just the same. What perturbed Ralph was the possibility that Claud had turned brutal with Honorée lately, and so invited retaliation, revenge, by one of her admirer regulars: Iles, for example. Pimps often grew brutal. A girl might offend somehow. It would be either skimming from customer payments, or refusing certain customers, or not getting enough customers. It had to be likely that these days Honorée would turn down approaches she didn't fancy. When you were dealing regularly with an Assistant Chief (Operations), sometimes, apparently, in a hire car on waste ground in the Valencia Esplanade district – well, when a girl had that kind of polished devotee, she might grow choosy.

This could be serious, if, for instance, she declined a friend or friends of Claud, or big villains he lined up for her, ready to pay gorgeously from plump loot wads. For that kind of hoity-toityness, a girl could get ferociously knocked about. Girls were generally beaten with a broom stick on the soles of their feet by the pimp, so as not to disfigure them and reduce drawing power. The girl would be held down on a table by an apprentice pimp, or tied down, with her feet over the edge. Whoever beat Claud to death had not worried about making a mess of his face, possibly *post mortem*, but, then, Claud had no need of his face. Similarly, the soles of the feet were body areas rarely coming into play during tart activity. Girls did not have to walk much, just stood and waited and talked bill-of-fare, then generally went in cars.

Ember was known as Panicking Ralph, sometimes as Panicking Ralphy, because of the way he could suddenly fall into a kind of paralysis and uselessness when confronted by bad stress. Claud dead on Monty soil, plus his possible link to Iles via Honorée, brought exceptionally bad stress. As soon as he recognized Claud, Ember had felt that well-known rectangle of fright-sweat take up station across his shoulders. His legs did not want to do anything for the moment, and Ralph leaned against the emergency door. He had an old scar along his jaw line, and whenever a real panic hit him it felt as if this had opened up and was weeping something obnoxious and yellowy down his neck and on to his shirt. It never did open up, of course, but instinctively tonight his left hand went to check. His right propped him against the door.

One devilish possibility had to be that the body did not come to Ralph from a business rival looking for one-upness, but from one of Honorée's very best chums. Claud tipped here was the kind of mischievous little trick Iles might pull if the pimp had savaged Honorée and needed to be briskly killed in retribution. As Iles might see it, a girl called Honorée deserved to be honoured, although that might not be her true name. Iles could have dropped Claud here knowing that Ralph would feel compelled to make him disappear efficiently and secretly because of his mission to get the Monty up to a brilliantly élite rating alongside the Athenaeum. Media publicity featuring a bare, pulped pimp on club terrain could in no way help that plan. Ralph's panic came because he wondered what would happen if he failed to shift Claud to somewhere that gave no possible traces, and, instead, notified police headquarters about him. In that case, Iles might do everything he could to fix the death on Ralph. And Iles's everythings were a lot. You did not become ACC (Operations) without a flair for self-protection. Iles would know others might see a motive link from Claud via Honorée to him. Divert it to Ralph, then. Ember could become one of Iles's operations.

At present there was a very sensible, constructive arrangement between Iles and Ralph, and Ralph's colleague, Mansel Shale, in the drugs enterprise. As long as Ralph and Manse kept violence off the streets, Iles did not get difficult about the trade. He believed there would always be drugs and thought it absurd to fight the supply. National policy was gradually catching up on his view. But if Ralph failed to cart Claud off somewhere and fast, this sweet, discreet, commercial alliance with the Assistant Chief might end. Ralph would be persecuted, even prosecuted. Shale would slip into monopoly, a monopoly of £1,200,000 a year, untaxable.

Ralph bent closer to the body. He wanted to see whether Claud clutched a letter in one of his fists, such as, *Get rid of him, Ralph, there's a dear mate.* That would be the kind of fruity insolence Iles was capable of, wouldn't it? Wouldn't it? *Destroy this note after reading. Do not retain for your archive at Yale University.*

Ember found no message and went back into the deserted club. He took off his suit and put on a pair of dungarees kept in his office cupboard for maintenance tasks. He would burn these tomorrow. His panic remained ripe, but he could manage the change of clothes. He knew he would get back to normality in a while. This was why he detested the nickname Panicking Ralph, or much worse, Panicking Ralphy.

These spasms did come, but they never lasted, not long enough to justify the slur. As the sweat and the leg weakness and the jaw scar delusions faded, he brought his car around to Claud and opened the boot. Luckily, it was lined with a big plastic tray. That could go into the incinerator, too.

When, in the future, the undistant future, he began to raise the Monty to a more select category, one of the first club events Ralph would discontinue was the kind of après-funeral shindig that took place there for Claud. All right, he knew the proverb saying nobody should speak ill of the dead, but this did not necessarily mean you had to open your club to Claud Montagne's relatives, associates, girls and minder-muscle. Ralph felt a kind of surprise that Claud actually *had* relatives, or, at least, relatives who would want to proclaim they *were* relatives, through attending his funeral and follow-up. Possibly people went back to the Athenaeum after the funeral of a member in London, but the member would most likely be some sort of genuine dignitary, known at All Souls College, Oxford, or the Inns of Court, not a pimp. And if he *was* an Athenaeum pimp, it would be for girls who could ask really bumper payments on the best West End street corners, such as in Shepherd Market. Plus, his relatives would not look how Claud's relatives looked.

Assistant Chief Iles and his sidekick, Detective Chief Superintendent Colin Harpur, turned up late in the afternoon, when things had started to get a bit relaxed. Ember expected their visit. Iles had uniform on, Harpur a kind of suit. Iles loved this type of nosing, and not just for free drinks. Ember mixed the ACC a port and lemon – 'the old whore's refresher', as Iles called it – and a gin and cider in a half pint glass for Harpur. Iles would come into such a function mainly to terrorize – to terrorize Ralph, the club membership and guests. Iles glared about and set a shadow over everything. He put a look on his face which said he'd make sure half the people here would be in jail by New Year. No, he did not have to put that look on his face, especially now. It seemed built-in. Protocol would not allow Iles to attend the actual funeral of rubbish like Claud, however much the

ACC might have longed to chortle there, but he could come to the Monty knees-up afterwards, on some pretext.

Ralph had heard Honorée did not go to the funeral either, and she was absent here now. That could mean Ralph's guess about the reasons for Claud's death might be spot on. If he'd been rough with her, she would not want to join in any service or subsequent jollification for him. Ralph had excused himself from the actual funeral, explaining he must set up his club for the after-binge. As Monty proprietor, he did sometimes feel required to attend a member's funeral, particularly for natural causes deaths, and these certainly happened from time to time. But when you'd tried to lose a body permanently in the sea, and it got washed up regardless only a week later, and still damned easily identifiable, you dodged prolonging links with it, whether or not it lay in a floral-tributed box now.

Iles said: 'Ralphy, a sombre interlude.'

'True,' Ember replied. He had to wonder whether Iles blamed him for not ensuring Claud vanished permanently. But Ralph did not actually go into another breakdown panic: victory – a victory over self!

'Harpur and I thought we must look in with commiserations,' Iles said.

'Thank you, Mr Iles,' Ralph said.

'We know you grieve for members who go in such circs,' Iles said.

'Yes,' Ember said. 'These are hard lessons on the uncertainty of life.'

'I'm afraid we're altogether baffled by this one, Ralph,' Iles replied. 'How he got into the sea, why, where he was killed and by whom, and the reasons for what seem to Harpur and me some deliberate nose and cheek mutilations after death. Our inquiries – a blank.'

He was saying, was he, that he would not punish Ralph for the poor disposal? Was he? Or he was saying, was he, that Harpur and he genuinely had no ideas on Claud's death and the subsequent moves of the body? Possible?

'These questions raised by Mr Iles are considerable puzzlers,' Harpur said.

'Indeed yes,' Ember replied.

'Do you think you'll be able to control this bag of slip-shod, rampant derelicts once they've got into their drinking gallop, Ralph?' Iles asked. 'Might you need some CS disabling gas or horseback police?'

'They have to sedate their sorrows,' Ralph said. 'I can sympathize with that. He was incredibly dear to such a range of folk.'

Iles said, still gazing about the bar: 'Pardon me, Ralph, I appreciate how much you cherish the Monty, and have visions for its new role, but, I must tell you, I don't think I've ever known a place able to attract so many of life's degenerates, old lags and out-and-outers at one time.'

'How are Honorée's feet?' Ember replied.

'It was Col who suggested the visit,' Iles said. 'He worries about safety when there's a huge and dubious gathering like this, and liquored up. Harpur *is* a worrier, you know – a stickler for regulations. I've told him I, too, see potential trouble, but that Ralph W. Ember probably knows damn well how to run a Bacardi wake. Harpur still insisted on the call.'

'A formality,' Harpur said.

'Could you show us, for instance, the emergency exit, Ralph?' Iles said. 'This could be important if, say, a fracas occurred, followed by a stampede of low life drunks later on. Strangely, the lower the low life – and it couldn't be lower than this lot – the lower the low lives, the more people possessed of those low lives seem keen to hang on to them.'

'Mr Iles always fears fracas,' Harpur said.

'Ralph and Manse Shale ensure we don't have fracas on the streets,' Iles replied. 'And one is grateful. One is *very* grateful to you, Ralph. Very.'

'Thank you, Mr Iles.'

'That understanding between us must certainly continue,' Iles said. '*Will* certainly continue.'

'Thank you, Mr Iles.' So, everything was OK, was it? Was it? Ralph led them through the crowd to the emergency door. People stood back for Iles, cowering a bit, even though in such a souped-up, 'Farewell then Claud, you jerk,' state, most of them. Ralph pushed at the release bar on the emergency door, which opened beautifully. He personally oiled the mechanism fortnightly while observing his basic main-

150

tenance programme in dungarees. He must get new ones. The three of them went out into the car park.

'And a fine night light above the doors,' Iles said.

This might be the insignia-ed lout boasting he could confidentially pass Ralph a corpse even in the brightest section of the car park. Was Iles here to thank him, but also to indicate that Ralph would be forever vulnerable, whatever safeguards he put in place? Normality again, thank God. 'The light is to aid members in the wholly unlikely event that my club had to be evacuated,' Ember replied, 'but also to illuminate the car park through all hours of darkness so that no intruders, prowlers, vandals or any other contemptibly lawless elements can use the ground for villainy.'

'"Contemptibly lawless elements." They're always about, aren't they, Ralph, and always we must resist them, and resist again?' Iles said. 'But, no, I shouldn't think they'd have much chance for their outrageous schemes here. To me, Col, things at the Monty look perfect. Agreed?' He turned to Ember. 'Exemplary as ever, Ralph.'

'Thank you, Mr Iles,' Ember said. 'I trust your wife and daughter are well.'

# Emergency Services

He was in a car, crouched forward, his face on the steering wheel, arms hanging down, fully relaxed, navy off-the-peg suit with 1999 style lapels, gold signet ring on the right little finger, lumpy wristlet watch of genuine base metal, black slip-ons, leather not plastic.

This death was meant to be public. It gave a warning. Witnesses, gossip, rumour would make the scene even tastier and more terrifying than it actually was. It's known as 'word of mouth', and there would be a lot of words and a lot of mouths and plentiful ears. This method of death – the display factor – made me think it could be the punishment killing of an informant. Was he on show to prove that grasses got butchered, and so discourage others? The police might hold back details of a murder's worst details, and that would be true of any murder, not just the slaughter of a grass. But word of mouth tells everything.

Few grasses live rich. Even rich grasses don't always go lavish, with big properties and wild cars and Acapulco holidays, because it might get folk asking where the cash comes from. This lad was dead in a ten-year-old car on the little slab of driveway that fronted the thirties semi he shared with a so-called common-law wife on this tired-looking, open-plan private estate. Open-plan means no hedges between house and street, and if you've got a sleeping man, or dead man, in a car on the drive, neighbours see him. He's a topic, something for the jungle drums.

Besides that, the car locks had been Superglued. When the common-law wife came out first thing on her way to work and saw him, she could not open any door and ran to a neighbour for help. He did some prodding with a screw-driver, trying to free a route for the key. Other neighbours gathered. One of these brought a hammer. He smashed the passenger window, wanting some distance from the man inside so splinters wouldn't injure him, if he could have been injured. People like to believe the least awful explanation for grim-looking events, and, of course, they could not see at that stage what had happened to his face. He was lying on it.

I heard later about these early moments from the wife and several neighbours. Nobody 999'd at once. They thought they could handle things themselves. Hammer man put it down and reached through where the passenger window had been. He gripped the figure at the wheel with two hands on his shoulders, then drew him gently back in his seat. Now they had a full view of the face and knew he must be dead, not drunk or asleep.

Then a woman did say she would call emergency services. I gather Mrs Elgan, the wife, at first objected. Living in this household, she must have absorbed the philosophy that even the worst troubles got sorted with no reference to the police. In any case, Mrs Elgan might have had someone else she wanted to ring, before the medics and the rest of us turned up. That is, if she knew more about the death than she told. Perhaps she did ring someone else. Possibly this could be discovered from telephone records. But the lady neighbour felt she had a duty, went home and put in the call which brought me here.

Such a death would not normally be handled by anyone of my rank. But this call came at seven twenty a.m., a time when few senior detectives are around headquarters. I live near the scene, and the Control Room decided to get me there as stopgap while the leadership was notified. They'd report they had dug Detective Constable Helen Baring out of bed and told her to preserve the evidence, beat back crowds, notebook some names, ask a few of the simpler questions, establish identities, as starters.

I've been doing that since I arrived, such as how and when did Clifford Elgan come to be in the car? His wife seemed half traumatized, natural after such a discovery. And, also naturally, she would be upset just by having to talk to me, the police. She did not weep, but her mind seemed to stagger

153

and drift. She slipped into long silences and, when I repeated a question, would stare at me as if she never heard it before, and never saw me before. Eventually, she said Clifford had been away on what she called business and was not expected home until this evening. I did ask what kind of business, but she went traumatized again for a while. Perhaps she did not know. Perhaps she considered the question beside the point and uppity – he was dead and not much else mattered, did it? Did it?

Clifford had not taken the car for his business trip, because she needed it, and the Citroën stood on the drive empty the last time she looked – mid-evening yesterday. If this was true, Clifford had been brought to the vehicle, presumably already dead and defaced, some time between her last recollection of it and when she came out this morning at around seven a.m. She had a half-day job in a petrol station and was about to set off when she saw Clifford down on the wheel and found the doors immovable.

Our conversation took place alongside the car. She did not want to leave Clifford and neither did I. Evidence must be preserved. Clifford was now sitting back instead of forward, but that and the smashed window seemed the only changes. I told Mrs Elgan to go into the house and rest. She wouldn't. I don't think I went too hard at the interview, though I did feel once or twice during those pauses that she might pass out. She was thin-faced, pale with large grey-green eyes, and would probably not have looked strong even before all this – busty but frail. She made me think of an Out Patients' waiting room.

'So, who's he crossed?' I said.

'Crossed?'

'Did he do whispers?'

Again she failed to answer but bent down and pushed her head in through the broken window, as if wanting closeness. She was crouched over, restricted in movement by the frame of the window. I had to study her from outside the car through the windscreen. She remained totally still, rigid, tearless as far as I could tell, staring at Clifford Elgan, thinking God knew what. I could not discover it, neither in her body nor her face. She did not reach out to touch him. Perhaps they had never been very physical with each other.

The senior team, led by Peter Arad, head of CID, arrived and I had to turn away from Mrs Elgan and give a run-down. I kept it short, with no mention of my feeling that Cliff Elgan might have been a grass. Evidence? These big-boy detectives had probably seen a hundred murdered bodies in their time and heard a thousand witnesses float their accounts of what had happened. They'd interpret for themselves.

'Thanks, Helen,' Arad said when I finished. He was, or had been, the youngest detective superintendent in any British police force, and would still be well under forty. No question he would make Chief somewhere very soon – the kind of non-stop advancement I had in mind for myself.

'My condolences, Mrs Elgan,' Arad said, bending alongside her at the car window, his face near her shoulder. 'We all feel for you, believe me.'

'Of course I believe you,' she replied, her voice big enough and hard enough for me to hear, although I had moved back, proper for my rank.

As a matter of fact, it suddenly seemed a useful spot. 'Name's Harvane,' a man near me muttered. He stared at the car. 'I want to talk.' He was around twenty-five, thin to very thin, newish jeans, oldish grey sweater, no coat, rubbish trainers, rough teeth, rough close haircut, fair, very calm, dull eyed, slightly stooped, no athlete.

'Mr Arad's in charge,' I said. 'Or there's Chief Inspector Mossmont.'

'Do you mind – I'd prefer not going to the top?'

'Well, I'm definitely not the top,' I said. 'You're a neighbour?'

'No. I'll be in touch.'

'How? If you try through headquarters, people there will want to know what it's about, and put you on to Mr Arad, or Bruce Mossmont.'

'I'll be in touch.'

'I'll give you my home address. My name's—'

'I have them.'

'How? I'm not in the phone book.'

'I'll be in touch. Harvane, Ivor. Ivor Harold Harvane. Me.'

He edged through a group of spectators, walked behind Mrs Elgan and Peter Arad towards the street and away.

Police operate within a very precisely arranged system of duties, ranks and rules. If you want to progress, and, as I've said, I do, you can clearly see the steps towards the summit, and you know the kind of approved behaviour that will see you right. But, if you can handle it, there may also be room for a little secret effort outside the regulations. I should have mentioned to Peter Arad this man Harvane and his offer. I didn't, and not only because Harvane had said he wanted me, had somehow picked me out. Although there is the system's way of succeeding in the police, there can be additional ways, also. I aimed at a nice combination. On its own, the system's way could be a bit slow. You had to jolly it up.

He walked away. Harvane, Ivor Harold, walked away? If that was really his name. No, for God's sake, I could not let it happen. He knew something, did he? Of course he knew something. How would he be here otherwise, spot on time for the body-find? He said he was no neighbour. He had something he would not disclose to Peter Arad or Mossmont or any of the other main men, only to me, myself in person, at some non-declared date. Perhaps. Very perhaps.

I pushed my way out through the little crowd of gawpers and walked. He was a good stretch ahead by now, on a long, suburban street, with a few parked cars and the odd environmental tree, no real cover. The best gumshoe in the world would have had trouble staying unobserved. I did not want to stay unobserved. I wanted Harvane to turn, see me, feel pleased at the urgency of my interest and wait, then agree to come to some reasonably confidential place and spill. Harvane did turn his head once and I gave a small wave, nothing to draw attention, except his. He must have seen it, but kept going at the same pace or faster. Those down-grade trainers flashed like washed-out flags. Signalling what, though?

He came to a junction and went left. As far as I could remember, it was Torl Street, another long exposed stretch leading to the main Bonville Road. I started to run, transformed myself into a real manic sight, but not one that Arad and the others would spot, I hoped. They should be heads-down, busying. When I reached the junction, though, and stared along Torl Street, Harvane was still visible and walking. It looked as if he might have had a run himself, and faster than mine. The distance between us seemed much greater. I kept after him, walking again. It had become a kind of game, with its own mad rules. You did not run while the other could see. In any case, I was tired now.

A car moving down the road seemed to slow alongside him and keep pace. It looked like one of the bigger Audis, dark green. I saw him glance at it, then glance again, but he did not stop or make any move towards the vehicle. Perhaps someone in it was speaking to him. The Audi accelerated slightly and I thought it would leave him. Just an innocent exchange of greetings? But, then, not far ahead of Harvane, it suddenly pulled into the kerb and stopped. He glanced back again, as if to check I was still behind him. This time I did not wave. Harvane would not want the link between us known, if one existed. He walked on. Perhaps he would be ashamed to falter. A couple of men left the car, nimble, committed men, one from the rear, one from the passenger seat, and stood waiting for him on the pavement, again possibly talking, possibly threatening – tensed looking, anyway, though nothing in their hands.

They were white, one squat, wearing a light-coloured suit and a flat hat or beret, near middle-aged, the other younger – twenties – in shirt and trousers, no jacket, longish brown hair. I wanted to run and by now might have been able to find some breath for it, but didn't. I feared it would do him no good with these two if they noticed me hurrying. I kept walking, same pace, like someone on her way to work. Perhaps I was.

He paused when he reached the two men, and almost certainly now they had a conversation. The voices must have stayed low or I would have picked up some sound. It could have been an amiable encounter of friends in the street, with a bit of chit-chat. They were very close to him, really friendly, or not friendly at all, and in a couple of moments the three moved towards the Audi. I could see no force used and still no weapon. The older man opened the rear door and climbed in first, while the other one stood with Harvane. This was the way you put a prisoner into the back seat, so there would be someone blocking the far door, to stop him jumping out the other side. Then Harvane entered the Audi and the younger man closed the door and took the passenger seat. I was still more than a hundred yards from them when the car moved off fast and I could not make out the registration. But definitely an Audi and definitely dark green.

It must be half-term and some children aged about eleven and twelve were playing in and out of a couple of front gardens near where the car had waited. When I reached the spot I said: 'Did you see the men who got into the car just here? Did you hear them say anything.'

'Who are you then, fuzz?' a girl replied. She did not look at me and continued to fence with one of the boys, both of them using long sticks. 'We don't hear nothing, we don't see nothing, never.'

'A man might be in trouble,' I said.

'We don't hear nothing, we don't see nothing, never,' the boy replied.

I felt a fierce, awkward kind of responsibility for Harvane. He had come to talk to me, his choice. He had walked away, his choice. Yet I could not escape the notion that I had brought this on him, whatever it was. Fingered him by following. And the indifference of these children, if you could call it only that – more like drilled-in bloody-mindedness – this attitude of theirs seemed to stick the responsibility for Harvane even harder on me. It was as though these kids stood for that notorious general public wish to look away, when to look might bring danger and pain.

Eventually, I spotted a taxi and flagged it down. 'Into Bonville Road and keep an eye for a dark green Audi,' I said.

'What sort of job is this? You police?'

'A dark green Audi.'

'I don't want nothing with damage. This car's nearly new.'

'Just find it, then you can quit. Anway, we're probably too late, unless there's a jam.'

There was no jam and no sight of the Audi in Bonville Road or in a side streets trawl. 'There,' I said. 'Not a scratch.

I'll recommend an OBE for public-spiritedness.' I told him to drive me back to the Bonville Road junction and walked to the Elgan house. I'd have to give some tale if anyone asked where I'd been. Harvane was still mine, only mine, even if I could not find him and might never see him again.

Later in the day, I was able to talk to Mrs Elgan alone. 'They're going to frame me for it, aren't they, aren't they?' she said. It was part whisper, part hiss, almost a squeal of pain, and yet almost, too, a flat, hopeless observation, as if she would not have expected anything else. 'Oh, so damn clever – cop clever. Dump him on my doorstep.'

'Who dumped him?'

'God, the questions they hammer away at.' She made a decent shot at Mossmont's take-me-as-I-am Midlands accent: '"But surely you must have heard something if Clifford's body was put there during the night, Mrs Elgan. Probably another vehicle to bring the body. Oh, certainly. So, doors closing." Mossmont has a way of saying the word.'

'Which?'

'Body. He's great at getting the lifelessness.'

I could imagine Mossmont's tall, heavily-made frame leaning forward as he put the question, dark hair hanging down over his forehead.

'There were a couple of seconds when I thought he was going to frisk me for a knife or gun,' Mrs Elgan said.

Do you know knives and guns, Mrs Elgan? Would he have found one or the other? But it was a thought only, not words. She put those wide grey-green eyes on me, full of sadness and fight: 'You've hatched it between all of you?' she said. '"Get Iris Elgan." You're at a nothing rank, so they can pressure you. Where two or three are gathered together, there is dirty work in the midst of them. Two or three police.'

So, she had wit and an education – could adapt a New Testament text on the hoof. 'I've been away from the house,' I said. 'I wouldn't know what they were going to ask.' True. When I arrived back here from the taxi, Arad and Bruce Mossmont had been outside, near the car, watching the photographer do his angles. They were still in the garden now. An ambulance stood at the end of the drive waiting to take Elgan to the morgue. I would have stayed near the two senior officers, in case they had something for me to do, and in the hope they would think I'd been around the house and garden all the time. But Mrs Elgan had suddenly and very briefly appeared at a window and beckoned me inside to the spruce little sitting room.

'Am I a heavy sleeper? That's one of their questions,' she said. 'This is arranged. You – you're part of the team. You'd know. You've all got yourselves to look after.'

'What's that mean, Mrs Elgan?'

'You know. They'd know.'

'No, I don't understand.'

'Maybe.' Her voice crackled with disbelief or contempt, or both, or both plus other hate features. I could feel her editing what she wanted to say, in case I was part of some pre-planned police deal and would pass it on and up.

'I think it could have been done quietly enough, so as not to disturb you,' I said.

'Oh, thanks, thank you very much' – sarcasm, yes, but behind the edge of it I thought there might be a fragment of doubtful, hopeful gratitude. 'So tell them that, will you? Or would it mean trouble for you?'

'Why trouble? I'm entitled to say what I—'

'I loved him, you know,' Mrs Elgan said.

'Well, certainly.'

'Really loved him. Not just shacked-up and the fitted carpets and crockery and all that. Loved. He could be a bit of a towering pipsqueak, yes, and forever getting nowhere, waiting for the big chance he would never reach, because he wasn't built for big chances. He knew it. Cliff had a lot of first-class humility. I told him once we should look at his stars in the paper and he said he didn't think he had any. "I've got a birthday, but no stars," he said. Yes, when you'd been Cliff Elgan all your life you got used to insignificance. He was mine, though. He had warmth and kindness. He could even be fun. I wanted him. He could look good. Dignified. He could.' She glanced out of the window towards the car and Clifford's mutilated face, as though nobody would believe now he could have ever looked good, or be fun. 'So how could I wish him dead?'

'I'm sure Mr Arad and Bruce Mossmont don't—'

'I don't think they'd say I, myself, killed him. Just they'll make me part of some conspiracy. But how could I? How, when I loved him? What woman has her man carved, even a man like Cliff?' It was as near as I had seen her get to weeping, and still not very near – more as though she thought she ought to weep, to match the circumstances and the memory of his starlessness. 'They'll make out it's some sex thing – me two-timing him – me and someone, getting rid of Cliff because he was in the way. There was a film – *The Postman Always Rings Twice*. Like that. Murder the husband. It suits them to see it like this. Or to say they see it like this. Did they cut up the husband's face in *The Postman Always Rings Twice*, for God's sake?'

'They'll want the truth, that's all, Mrs Elgan.'

She gasped, as if the simplicity of this had winded her, simplicity in all its meanings. 'Oh, absolutely,' she said.

'I'm sure of it.'

'And I'm afraid you might be,' Iris Elgan replied.

We were opposite each other, myself on a handsome black, leather, fat-armed Chesterfield, perhaps Edwardian and re-covered, and Mrs Elgan in a small armchair, also black, and possibly also old and nicely done up. Who had the taste, Clifford or Iris? She sat hunched forward, staring hard at me most of the time, obviously trying to read my eyes, searching for signs of betrayal. Did she imagine we had some sort of alliance because we were women, and because we had spoken together before Arad and the others arrived? It seemed she possessed no friends among the neighbours who had gathered and, instead, at her time of suffering, turned to me. It did not mean she would speak only the truth, or say everything she knew or suspected. She wanted the womanly bond, but must know as well as I did that I would remain mainly cop, with cop loyalties, cop tasks. This was twice today I had been picked out for special contact.

She had on what I took to be the clothes she would wear to work, grey, tailored trousers and a dark red cotton blouse, red button earrings, perhaps garnets, black half-heel shoes. It was an outfit proclaiming competence. She had an unlit cigarette in her fingers and played with it skilfully like a magician, making it somersault back and forth across her hand. Dexterity, wittiness, the Bible, self-control.

'You said Clifford had been on a business trip. What business?' I asked.

'Various. Oh, yes, various business activities.'

'Buying and selling?' I said.

'That sort of thing.'

'Buying and selling what?'

'As it came.' She spoke wearily, as if suspecting I knew Clifford's commercial specialities from police scuttlebutt and was only asking as a formality, or to annoy and humiliate her.

'Legit?'

'What did you say?' This was that mixture of whisper and hiss or snarl again.

'Legit?'

'You don't care what you ask, do you?' Iris Elgan replied. 'Same style as Mossmont? Your questions are oppressive. I could complain.'

'Sorry. Legit?'

'Oh, I see. Who do I complain to – Mossmont? Of course legit. Would I stay with him if not?'

'Would you?'

She stopped acrobatting the cigarette and lit it. A performance. The cigarette was lifted very slowly to her mouth and the lighter applied with a sweep of her right arm, then held to the tobacco longer than was needed, like torching Joan of Arc. Martyrdom. The corny drama made me wonder if she knew Bette Davis films as well as *The Postman*. She did not speak for a while. I had the crazy impression she wanted a cloud of smoke in front of her face because she was embarrassed by her next words. 'I can't make out how much you know,' she said eventually. 'Perhaps after all you're too low rank to be let in on much.'

'Sounds like me.'

She did another long gaze at my face, another search for signs. I don't think she cared much for what she saw. She gave a tiny shrug, drew mightily on the cigarette again, but did not say anything.

'I wondered if he did some part-time work,' I said.

162

'Me, *I* do part-time. You're getting things mixed.'

'As an informant,' I replied.

'Yes, I know what you meant,' she said.

'Possibly putting him in peril. And then the disfiguring.'

'Yes, I'd heard informants get peril,' she replied.

'Oh? Where?'

'Where what?'

'Where did you hear it?'

She smiled. 'No magic. I read the papers, don't I? Northern Ireland. Informants get killed.'

'And nearer home.'

'I expect so,' she said. 'It's a loathsome trade, isn't it?'

'Is it?'

'I suppose you people depend on grassing. But you know it's disgusting, just the same.'

'I was looking at the Chesterfield and the other things in this room. Beautiful,' I replied.

'You're asking where the money came from.'

'Oh, you've got the part-time job, and then there was Clifford's business efforts.'

'Right,' she said.

'So now and then Clifford did show a profit, even if the big break didn't come?'

'Here are your chieftains,' she replied. 'Get dutiful.' Peter Arad and Mossmont came into the sitting room. Iris Elgan stood up. 'Are you taking Cliff now? I'd like to travel with him.'

Mossmont said: 'Well, I—'

'Of course,' Arad said. 'I'll have a car bring you back.'


I could discover nothing in any of the usual sources about Harvane, Ivor Harold. He had no criminal record, or not under that name. The records cross-referenced aliases and our computer produced no Harvane among those, either. Anxiety pushed me hard and then harder. I might have witnessed an abduction, and God knew what the abduction would lead to. I went through all the recent incident summaries at headquarters looking for reports that might show Harvane had been found somewhere. None. By 'found' I meant found dead and perhaps disfigured, naturally. For a

163

while I played around with the names he had given, Harvane, Ivor Harold, in case they were a jumble of letters which, re-ordered, spoke his true identity. People did this sometimes when devising an alias, as if nervy at completely disowning their usual self. After all, the self is all we have, isn't it? Vary it, disguise it, but don't ever let it go. But I had no luck with Harvane, Ivor Harold's letters rejigged. Roland Hove-Rhavair did not seem a likely anagram answer.

Still very scared for him, at night I tried a drift around some of the drug-dealing bars and clubs, hoping the car pick-up had been only a bit of comradeship, and that Harvane was by now back to usual territory, perhaps with his two pals or more. Someone else must have been driving the Audi. I assumed this would be Harvane's kind of scene because of his looks and clothes and, above all, because of how Iris Elgan spoke of Clifford's career. When people referred briskly to 'business' but could not specify what sort, it often meant drugs. They pinched the respectable term from *Godfather 2*. If Clifford Elgan had been dealing in this field, and Harvane, Ivor Harold was connected with him strongly enough to be drawn to his lying in state, it seemed a decent guess he knew the trafficking game, too.

There were three likely pubs, two clubs and an idyllic pinball sanctuary. I did my slow tour – drank a bit, watched a lot, extricated myself twice from some nice, unslavering but determined chat-ups, and saw neither Harvane nor the men who had waited alongside the Audi. Of course, those two had been at a distance, and the older one under a hat, so no hair colour or scalp quality on view, but I thought I would recognize them. Nobody fitted.

Also of course, I had to realise I might be identified as possible cop immediately I entered the first club, El Dump. Anyone they didn't know, under sixty and not on sticks, they would regard as possible cop. Phone alerts would go out from El Dump to all the other probable calling points and anyone who felt at all dubious would disappear. People who had forced a man into an Audi might reasonably feel they could be regarded as dubious, especially if what I feared had happened to Harvane had happened. I might not be too safe myself in these special pleasure nests and the surrounding streets and lanes. The fact I was a woman wouldn't make the hardest of these people any kinder. They were into equality of the sexes years before official legislation, and killed impartially. It would have been stupid to ask customers or staff if they knew someone called Ivor Harold Harvane, and not just because this was probably not his name.

In the Zola, Zola club and feeling at the end of my alphabet, I decided that really the only route I had to Harvane went via Mrs Elgan. He had been at her house and seemed to know Clifford, or at least *about* Clifford. Perhaps he knew her, too. It was just after eleven p.m. and I thought I would drive up to the house and, if lights still showed, I'd call in. If not, I would visit tomorrow. She might be friendly, seeing me alone – girl to girl again.

As I prepared to leave, a very cheerful grandfather grappled with me, keen I should stay and help make his night a time to remember and cherish, against his looming future in the Eventide Home. He wore an excellent flame-coloured toupé, with leather dude-ranch trousers, holstered belt and long-tasselled waistcoat. He had snorted, swallowed or mainlined something energizing which furled his lips back like minor breakers on a beach, and probably cut his charm. I didn't know, because I'd never seen his lips non-furled. I gave him an elbow in the chest, definitely not hard enough to break even old ribs. From kindness I spoke quickly and intimately to him of a raincheck as he fell towards spilled drink pools, his false hair brilliantly secure.

The Citroën had been taken in for examination and nothing stood on the drive now at the Elgan house. I drove past. Two ground floor rooms were still lit behind the curtains, and the stairs and landing light also seemed to be on, reaching weakly through an open door into one of the bedrooms. I parked a hundred yards on and began to walk back. Maybe Iris Elgan had seen and recognized Harvane among the crowd around the Citroën and would be able to describe his role in things, perhaps even honestly.

I was about three houses away when I saw a sudden extra bar of light shine out and realized the Elgan front door had been opened. I could have done with a hedge or two then, but this was an open-plan estate, not designed to give cover.

At once I stepped into a neighbouring front garden and lay face down on the lawn like a soldier under fire. If I held my head up a few inches I could watch the path from the Elgan house to the street. Nobody appeared on it, though, going to or from the house. A small porch shielded the actual door from my sight, and possibly Iris Elgan was standing in the hallway, about to leave. For where, so late? Or perhaps she expected someone.

I lay still for another couple of minutes and then grew impatient – one of my more attractive failings. I carefully picked myself up and stepped very slowly out from the front garden and back on to the pavement. I calculated that from there I should be able to look around the side of the porch and see the open door. If she spotted me, no disaster. She might know I was around, anyway. Even if not, I had come to call on her, hadn't I, and so here I was? After a couple of steps, I paused. Now, I had a straight view to the door. As I'd thought, it was ajar and I could make out Iris in the hallway, apparently gazing ahead, not towards me. She had on a dressing gown, blue and long. She would not be going out.

I crouched a little and gazed myself. Mrs Elgan's head and features were not completely clear to me because the light came from behind her, but I saw suddenly she had begun to weep, though, without any sound, without any move-ment in her face, except where the tears rolled. I realized then that she was staring not down the illuminated path but at the shadowed spot on the driveway where the Citroën had stood and where Clifford was found. Sorrow could some-times take a while to strike in full. Perhaps only at this moment had she begun to feel the loss. But I thought it more likely she regarded crying as a private expression, not to be given in to when the pigs were on the property, staring, nosing, niggling.

Had she really loved Cliff, then, and missed him unbear-ably now, longed for him, even though he had been that ramshackle dreamer and pipsqueak? Perhaps her love was big enough to embrace pipsqueaks and transform one of them into a prized, desired partner. Love could do such things. I had a rush of delicacy and decided I could not barge in on

Iris tonight with my questions and disclosures and eternally false mateymess, not even for the sake of Harvane's safety. Now, I dreaded that she would discover me spying on her sly mourning, or whatever it was, and I pulled back to the neighbour's front garden. I folded down again. Lawn as career aid. For possibly two or three seconds then, while flat and breathing only the wholesome smell of domesticated soil, I, too, wept. Contemptible. It must be the shock and sadness in seeing her apparently break like that after the earlier control.

I soon put a stop to this sobbing, though – and did more. I came back to my cynical thought, my cop thought, my dominant kind of thought. Had she seen me, knew I was watching, and staged a performance? Did she think Arad and/or Mossmont suspected she was involved in the death, for sexual motives? Her show of affection and grief was to counter that? I felt half ashamed of the idea, but could not get rid of it. I often feel half ashamed of my ideas, and stay with them all the same.

I lay watchful for about another five minutes. The light on to her path suddenly began to shrink as she slowly closed the door. I heard the catch engage, and soon after the sound of a bolt pushed across. I went back to my car. When I drove past the house, it was dark downstairs but a bedroom light had been switched on and curtains there drawn. I hoped she had been able to unload a fraction of her agony in her confidential vigil, or whatever it was, and that she would sleep.

At home, I slept myself – not by myself, though it might just as well have been. I am living and loving these days and nights with one of the only lads I would want to be living and loving with these days and nights, but whose patience with the requirements of my job can run out now and then. Now, for instance. I suppose it's understandable. But I did not want to understand it. Why the hell should I? He had come off shift at eleven o'clock and was watching a political programme on television, waiting for me to return. And now I'd returned. So, Tim, get welcoming. Or maybe not. I told him about my little profitless expedition around the clubs, pubs and other bright centres. He asked who had ordered this and I said it was something I'd thought up myself – always the best kind of detective assignment. He frowned. Although Tim is a police officer himself, and knows how an investigation can drift into all sorts of different settings at all sorts of times, it doesn't mean he has to like everything I do. He detests some of the things I do. I saw he did not think much of my solo excursions into those spots tonight. His caring is well meant, and can be a holy drag.

I'd brushed myself down, as I thought, pretty thoroughly after the lawn contact, but there were some stains and dampish patches on my jacket and tights and I saw him give me a long, all-over look. In fact, I started to tell him about the late trip up to the Elgan house, would have given him the whole me-as-garden-gnome saga, but he turned away, said he was going to bed. I could not be bothered sticking with it as a topic. If he did not want to listen, OK. That was Tim-like for this sort of mood. So, I'd been out around the town. So, I looked a bit messed about. What the hell did he think I'd been doing? Whatever it was – that phrase was busy tonight – whatever it was, he could go on thinking it, or not thinking it but sleeping on it.

When I went into the bedroom he looked blotto. I undressed and crawled in; no body contact, though. You'll know the bit about needing one's space, or *not* needing it, and really needing something else, but having to act as if space and space only is what one must have. There had been other occasions like this. They passed. By morning he would prob-ably have come round to seeing – seeing again – that in my sort of work, done in my sort of way, there could be unusual episodes. Sometimes, I thought it might be a mistake for two cops to live together.

At just after seven a.m. the phone rang. Tim answered on the bedside set, then pushed the receiver at me. I was still hardly awake but took it. 'Helen Baring,' I said.

'The boyfriend answered? I know about him. Tim, is it? Also fuzz?'

'Are you Ivor Harold Harvane?' I asked.

'Something like that. Look, drop it will you? Drop the personal efforts on this thing.'

'You were going to talk to me.'

'I *am* talking to you. Drop it.'

'Are you being—? You're being told to say this? I saw you when those two – Where are they? They're listening? Should I say that? Well, I've said it. Have you been – are you hurt?'

'Let your masters deal with it their way,' he replied. 'Better for your prospects, anyway.'

'Which prospects?'

'Promotion. Life. Generally. And then poking around all those places last night. It's not – it's not convenient.'

'Who says?' I thought I caught for a second the sound of breathing that might not be his. 'You on a mobile? Someone's close? Or on an extension? Or more than one? Should I say that? Well, I've said it.'

'So, drop it?' he said. 'Please. Now, please.' He sounded abject, terrified. He rang off. I did 1471, of course, and, of course, no trace.

'A contact,' I told Tim. 'Someone who could have been useful. I worry about him.' But Tim was asleep again, or pretending to be. Yes, his attitude continued understandable, perhaps – someone disrupting our rest and privacy and our chance to make up for the war stances of last night. 'He could be in a damn tough situation, Tim.' I was gabbling a bit, longing for a response, longing for Tim to share my excitement.

He slept on, or seemed to. So stuff him, as it were. Only as it were.

Next day, I had a visitor at the nick. At first, I did not recognize him, partly because of the strangeness of his outfit. No, not the strangeness – the non-strangeness. Partly, too, it was the huge bouquet of roses he held and which obscured the lower half of his face. He was magnificently dressed now in a double breasted navy-to-black suit with a heavy chalk pinstripe.

'They're lovely,' I said. 'But—'

'But I shouldn't? Oh, indeed I should. My behaviour – last night outrageous. Indeed, near abusive.'

Then I knew. His complexion should have given me the signal, also – that writ-like pallor and dryness lit up here and there by jam-packed clusters of vermilion broken veins.

We were talking in the foyer. Francis Nelmes, on Reception, watched and smirked. He had rung up and left a message on my tape to say a gentleman 'with generous floral tribute' was waiting to see Detective Constable Baring, and could I come down as soon as I was free? The tape gave the time and forty minutes had gone before I heard it. I was tied up in a meeting on the Elgan case run by Peter Arad.

Now, I said: 'Of course, Zola, Zola. How did you—?'

'Find you? I wanted to deliver these in person. I waited.'

'And my name,' I said. 'You have that.'

His voice became very purposeful, intimate. The change was astonishing. For these couple of seconds he ceased to be the rather goofy, beautifully mannered tailor's triumph with three dozen roses, and became formidable. You could see how he might have earned his way to a suit like that, as well as to the expensive bronco clobber last night and a hurricane-proof wig. Who did he do his earning with, though?

'Could we get out of this building briefly?' he said.

'A coffee shop across the road.' I took the flowers up to the Ladies and stood them in a washbasin. Then I went down the emergency stairs and left the building at the side. We sat with espressos at a table away from the window. 'Your name and workplace were handed to me,' he said. 'Didn't feel at ease about that. Why I'm here. Soon after you'd gone last night people at Zola, Zola came looking for you. There'd been some phoning, perhaps, from another club. And I think the manager must have told them you and I had – had had our moment of spectacular contact. They came over and asked me where the lady cop had gone – their phrase, "the lady cop" – and wanted to know if I had been acquainted with Detective Constable Helen Baring for very long. They were civil enough, but I had the impression of seriousness. A lot of it. I was not so far gone that I failed to note what went on. Never am that far gone, however it might look. At Zola, Zola, and in fact, at all the clubs and pubs thereabouts one would be foolish to swamp one's wits altogether. These can be harsh realms. So, I tend to exaggerate, play a role as a merry old has-been in quaint clothes and on a super high. This way, I remain safe – accepted and safe. So far.' He took a small, self-congratulatory sip from his cup. 'I felt I owed you something, you see.'

'The roses. Really not necessary.'

'Roses and what one might call insights.' He nodded a couple of times. 'You know of the death of Clifford Elgan? And the disgusting shiv work on his features? But of course you do! Aren't you a detective?'

'How do *you* know about it?'

'The media, of course. How could one *not* know?'

'Have the media said anything about the face carving?' I asked.

'There have been changes,' he replied.

'What kind of changes? Changes tied up with what happened to Elgan?'

'Business changes.'

'You mean business as in—?'

'The special powdery meaning of business, yes,' he replied. 'I have to consider how such changes might – Well, they could have some bearing on me personally.'

'In case you can't get your stuff regularly?' I said.

'Elgan was probably caught up in these changes, you see,' he replied. 'I hear things. I'm supposed to be rich and late-life-roistering and harmless, so I do hear things. Antennae. I take these random bits I hear and see and try to spot a pattern, you know. Plus there's a wife or partner, isn't there? A "Mrs" Elgan. She's attractive?'

'Do you mean like *The Postman Always Rings Twice*?'

'Ah, literature.' He nodded a couple of times again. 'Oh, Siverall, my name. Angus. Look, everyone knows how the drugs game is run here, of course. I wouldn't presume to tell you.' Then he did. 'There's Careful Stan, obviously, the biggest and most settled firm. I think those boys who came looking for you at Zola might have been Careful Stan's.'

'How many of them?'

He called for more coffees. 'And then, as well as Stan, there are those lesser though aspiring teams led respectively by the abnormally handsome Edgar Luff-Stile – oh, do watch yourself there, Helen – and by Hubert Marven, or Coinop, as Hubert is amusingly known.'

'You said changes.'

'How would it be, Helen, if Edgar Luff-Stile and Coinop decided they could no longer compete with Careful Stan on their own, but that in alliance they might be strong enough to finish him and take over his business?'

'Edgar and Hubert Marven hate each other, distrust each other.'

'Possibly. But suppose they hate and distrust Stan more? They see he's so big that any time he wishes he could eat up either. Perhaps one of them's had a tip that this is just what Stan means to do. He will annihilate Edgar or Coinop first, then swallow the pathetic, lonely survivor. Suddenly, Stan would be in that blissful state of monopoly craved by all dedicated business folk, and Stan is extremely dedicated. Luff-Stile and Coinop might feel they have to strike now or suffer.' Fresh coffees came. He drank all his at once. 'I should go. It's exposed here.' He sat on, all the same.

I said: 'And Elgan is, was . . .'

'Did Elgan have negotiating skills?'

'Buying and selling,' I replied.

'The fixer?'

'Arranging the treaty between Edgar and Coinop?' I wanted to ask whether it was only his old, roistering antennae that suggested this to him, or whether he had some real weighable information and, if so, from where. He lived inside one of these firms? Why was he spilling so much? Only as recompense for his half-baked leching at the Zola, Zola? Really? I kept silent, though.

'Elgan the intermediary,' he said. 'I never met him, but I gather he could have made a fair go-between – suitably smarmy and subtle. That kind of work might turn him into a target.'

So, not a grass, but a gifted middleman – an actual entrepreneur. 'You're saying Careful killed him? Or had him killed? And how does the common-law wife fit into it, then?'

'Or Edgar or Coinop thought he might be selling one or other of them short. You've heard of shoot the messenger?' He stood up. 'One loathes to be melodramatic, but may I suggest we do not leave together?'

'You think Careful Stan could be lurking out there? Or Edgar? Or Coinop?'

'Or we might be seen by someone significant in your building.'

I gasped. 'What are you saying now, for God's sake? Who? Mr Arad? Bruce Mossmont? Who significant? Significant how?'

'Oh, three, by the way,' he answered, ready to make his way out between the tables.

'Three what?'

'You asked how many men came asking about you in Zola, Zola.'

I was hooked by the answer. And scared. 'What did they look like? One thin, long hair – brown? Twenty-five or so? One of the others middle-aged, squat? Hat?' The two I'd seen when Harvane joined the Audi.

'Look like? Like they worked for Careful Stan. Or conceivably Edgar or Coinop.'

Of course, I realized the roses could be part of a scheme to get to me and unload ideas on behalf of a boss. Which boss? But who would want to influence someone as low caste as D.C. Helen Baring? Which boss would have a quaint bit of work like Angus on his staff? Seemingly quaint.

I drove to the Elgan house again. Orders. At the case conference that delayed my meeting with Angus it had been decided I should handle this side of the inquiries, because, as Bruce Mossmont said, I seemed to have established 'a nice warm relationship with Iris Elgan'. He would say what suited him, and this suited him, for reasons I couldn't sort out yet. I've had nicer and warmer relationships with a revolving door than the one with Iris Elgan. Mossmont suggested I should look hard for any sexual aspect, and, once I'd seen Mrs Elgan, he and Peter Arad wanted me to go on to interview the owner of the garage where she did her part-time job. 'See if you detect anything more than employer-employee, Helen,' Mossmont said. They obviously wondered whether the house and car and clothes and body and face that Clifford could provide would be enough to hold her, even before what had happened to his body and face.

I was not sure I saw the reasoning. Couldn't Iris simply have walked out on Cliff, if she wanted to upgrade? Was it necessary to have him killed and carved? Mossmont would probably suggest the carving must be a ploy to deceive us, and make this death look like the display retribution for an informer. Honestly? I doubted whether Clifford would turn out to have big riches or an insurance policy. There wasn't the sort of sex-plus-money motive for a death that drove *The Postman*, or that other run of the same tale, *Double Indemnity*.

Arad or Bruce Mossmont or both would probably go and look at what they now considered the more likely sides of this case themselves, because, of course, they as always wanted the personal *gloire* of an arrest. These were two ambitious, capable, contriving officers. Perhaps they had picked up some of the rumours about Clifford and the drugs firms that Angus gave me and intended to look there. Had I been handed the least promising sub-categories of the case, even though Arad and Mossmont had seemed to believe at the outset – yes, seemed – seemed to believe this case a sex tale, with violence?

There was another visitor at the Elgan house when I arrived. I recognized Edgar Luff-Stile, though only from dossier pictures. He must be around Iris Elgan's own age – say thirty-two, or three – good looking in a blonde, bony, Nordic way, about six foot tall, slim-to-thin, expensively dressed in a beige silk lightweight suit, and what could be a handmade shirt. He stood behind her in the hallway of the house when Iris opened the door. 'Oh,' I said, 'should I come back later? I hadn't realized you would have company.'

'A call to express heartfelt grief,' he said. 'Clifford – so prized by all who knew him, so sweet natured and comradely. How could this have happened?' He shook that long, elegant head eloquently, gently. Iris Elgan introduced us and said I'd been the first officer at the death. 'It must have been terrible for you,' he said. He shook my hand with huge gravity.

'Now you are here for what?' she asked me.

'Oh, such terrible events take much effort from the police, Iris. I imagine Helen – may I? – was not able to talk fully with you yesterday out of respect for your shock, indeed trauma.'

'I wanted to see you are all right, Mrs Elgan,' I said.

174

'Dig, dig,' she replied. 'And eventually bury me.'

'Grand to see you have friends who'll call by and offer support,' I said.

'Look, you've heard of Edgar, have you?' Iris replied. She waved a hand towards him, as though he were some sort of sample.

'Heard of me! Why should she have heard of me, Iris?' He tutted genially for a time and with what might be a show of nerves, smoothed down one smooth lapel of his gorgeous jacket.

'But you're not Drugs Squad, are you?' Iris asked me. 'So perhaps you really haven't heard of Edgar.'

'Oh, thank you very much,' Luff-Stile said with quite a worthwhile laugh. 'Iris jokes. It's so good to see her sense of humour is intact. Very often Clifford has spoken to me about it, said how it helped him through many a crisis.'

'I expect you know what she wants to ask you, Edgar.'

'Do I?' He sounded amazed. We were in the pleasant sitting room now, and I'd taken a place on the Chesterfield. The other two occupied armchairs, Luff-Stile with his legs stretched far out, but still seeming quite tense. It suited him, made him seem like a young worried statesman.

'I said you and Clifford knew each other through business, Ed,' Iris Elgan replied. 'She'd like to know what kind of business.'

'Oh, various,' Luff-Stile said.

'I mentioned "various" to Helen when she asked me yesterday about Clifford's career.'

'Buying and selling,' Luff-Stile said. 'I'd bump into Clifford during all sorts of negotiations. Oh, yes. And he was always gentlemanly, even when we might be rivals in a possible deal.'

I listened, watched, sniffed for sex, as eagerly as Arad and Bruce Mossmont would wish. I did not spot any private glances. It might be a very chic performance, possibly even in the same class as Iris Elgan's weepie session on the doorstep last night. Today, she seemed almost jaunty, brassy, rather than tearful. Perhaps she was on something good. Luff-Stile might have brought it, from stock.

'She thinks what she's been told to think, Edgar. Her

leaders want to believe I did it, perhaps with a special, interested friend as accomplice, such as you or someone else.'

'Did you engage Clifford occasionally to do special assignments for you, Mr Luff-Stile?' I replied.

'Now, who have you been talking to?' Iris Elgan replied. 'This one's no pushover, Ed.'

'Special assignments?' he asked, thin eyebrows high through puzzlement, or just high.

'Negotiating,' I said.

'I have staff for that.'

'A major project, really special, needing deep aptitudes,' I said.

'It's hard to think of such a task. What would you have in mind?' he said.

'Do either of you know someone called Harvane?' I replied. 'Though possibly an alias.'

'Ivor Harold flits about the business world,' he said. 'Capacity unclear.'

'He was up here yesterday, wasn't he?' Iris Elgan said. 'Didn't you walk off after him, Helen?'

'And do you know what's happened to him?' I said.

'Has something happened to him?' she asked.

'Ivor Harold follows an in-and-out sort of career.' Luff-Stile said.

'In and out of where?' I asked.

'Crises,' he replied.

'But what was his connection with Clifford?' I said. What was Luff-Stile's connection with Clifford, come to that? But I was more likely to get an answer about Harvane. Was I? 'Why would he have been here so soon?'

'Clifford commanded the affection of all sorts,' Luff-Stile replied. 'It was a boon to have met him. I'm sure Ivor Harold Harvane, or whoever he is today, would share that response.'

'Did you lose him, Helen?' Mrs Elgan replied. 'Ivor can be elusive. He spoke to you outside here, did he – promised something, side-of-the-mouth stuff? Ivor's strong on promises. And did you tell Chief Inspector Mossmont?'

'Mr Mossmont?' I said.

'He'd know Ivor,' she replied.

'Bruce Mossmont – very much in touch, I hear,' Luff-Stile said.

'I expect Ivor's all right,' Mrs Elgan said. 'I don't get told much now, shut up here since what happened to Clifford.'

'Unforgivable, that mode of death,' Luff-Stile stated.

I left them then. They came to the door to watch me go, like a couple. 'Where now?' he asked.

'Oh, she'll be off to see Gordon Toban, my splendid employer,' Iris Elgan said.

Sitting in the car, I tried to work out what I had learned with her and Luff-Stile. Somewhere between nothing and next to nothing. I had not really discovered why he was with her today. Lovers? If so, did that make the garage owner irrelevant? Employer, nothing more? But even if Iris and Luff-Stile had an affair going, it would not mean they conspired to kill Clifford. In some ways, that thought seemed preposterous and cruel. After all, Iris's tears last night could have been genuine. Likewise Luff-Stile's testimonials to him just now. And what did the business link with Luff-Stile amount to? Angus claimed it had been close. Or was Luff-Stile's story of merely bumping into Clifford now and then in business situations accurate? And the business? No real mystery.

If there had been two-timing of Edgar Luff-Stile by Clifford, and then terrible retaliation by Luff-Stile as Angus hinted, would Edgar be up there now, ministering to Iris, supposing that's all he was at? He stayed after I left, and this surprised me. Didn't he care it might look as though he stepped in there with Iris very fast after Cliff's death? Perhaps this showed the relationship with her amounted only to caring friendship. Yes? Did I want it to be like that, want it to be like that for reasons not altogether connected to the case? *Listen, detective,* I told myself, *does this detective detect a touch of sexual interest from you in that beige-suited, Viking-like bit of criminality?*

No other car was parked close to the Elgan house. Had he left his somewhere near but unnoticeable, the way I did previously? If so, what did this say about the relationship? But perhaps he came by taxi. I should have asked. Yes, I should have asked for two reasons, one of them not proper or much to do with police work, and therefore stronger.

I decided to go home and then call on Toban, the garage owner, after lunch. Tim was working nights and would probably be out of bed by now, almost one p.m. I felt I needed to see him, talk to him, refix him on my sexual map after that session of happy mental wander-lust outside the Elgan house. Tim had nuisance aspects, dud aspects, but at least he did not trade drugs and perhaps kill in the way of the trade, or in the way of love, or a mixture. God, though, it must be thrilling to be killed for. *Stop that, you abominable cheapie. You're a police officer.*

There was another reason for wanting to see Tim. He played soccer in one of the police sides. So did two lads from the Drugs Squad. Esprit de corps in the footie team was as powerful, even more powerful, than the one binding Drugs Squad members. I thought Tim and I could lunch out at Robo's, the pub used by the Squad, and its sort of un-official headquarters. We might run into the sporting buddies, perhaps guide them towards a little chat about Edgar Luff-Stile and Clifford.

'Why Robo's?' Tim said, when I suggested it.

'You like it there. Camaraderie.' He stared at me for a while – probably guessed there was something up. But he did not say so. Most times, Tim remained sensitive and considerate. He would never get anywhere in the police.

The Elgan case looked as if it should be on the plate of two separate, sealed-off, detective teams – the murder experts, naturally – what Americans call Homicide. But also the Drugs Squad. Both groups would be terrified of getting left behind. Both groups would be careful about what they told the other, if anything. This was policing at its purist and most unbroth-erly.

Only one of Tim's pals was at Robo's, Derek Fonde, tubby, balding at twenty-eight, dreamy-looking behind heavy rimmed spectacles, but not dreamy. We ate Lancashire hotpot at a corner table and discussed defensive plans, soccer defen-sive plans, that is, and how to transform them instantly into sweeping counter-attack. I'd sat through enough of these discussions to absorb some lingo and basic ideas, so I could chip in now and then. These lads expected that. They would not have understood indifference. When the ball talk seemed exhausted I said: 'Guess what, Derek! By a slab of good fortune I'm on the Clifford Elgan case.' It was a bit blatant, but twenty minutes had disappeared in the tactics conversation. I needed to get on.

'A tough one, I hear,' Derek said. I watched his schoolboy face, trying to read whether the name was familiar to him, and I knew Tim watched me watching. In fact, I expected fine, professional blankness from Derek, but he leaned forward over the dishes and said quietly: 'What sort of stuff are you finding?'

Perhaps, after all, he wanted as much out of me as I hoped for from him. He might even think Tim had brought me here to say what I knew – enlisting his girl friend to help a dear footballing mate. I almost giggled. The whole idea of the meeting had been upended, had it?

'Was he pushing?' I asked. 'In one of the firms? Plus possibly doing some boardroom manoeuvres?'

'Boardroom?' Derek replied.

'You two, you answer questions with questions,' Tim said. He thought everything could be cut and dried, simple, like chasing vandals. In a way it was nice in him, undevious. Sometimes you had to get devious, though.

Derek said: 'Helen, do you come across a man called Harvane, twenties, or possibly an alias, Bale or Porter-Knight?'

'Harvane?' I asked.

'Ivor Harold, when he's using Harvane.'

'Was he connected with Cliff?'

'These people – they drop out of sight,' he replied and touched his spectacles with one hand, as if trying for better focus on missing people.

'Connected how?' I asked. 'He's in the frame for doing Elgan? Who's been ripping off who?'

'Arad and Mossmont running this case personally, I gather,' Derek answered. 'Bruce Mossmont really hands-on?'

'You think that's strange? Why?'

'Plus Arad himself. This is truly heavy.' Derek mopped at

some hotpot with a piece of bread. There would be nothing more about Peter Arad or Bruce Mossmont.

'I've run across a man called Angus Siverall,' I said.

'Oh, yes, a user. Age shall not wither him, but crack or H might.'

'Are you sure that's all – a user?' I replied.

'How do you mean? Believe nothing he says, obviously. Late-life searcher for experience. Full of shit, all meanings. But Harvane,' he said. 'I'd really like to talk to that one.'

'There has to be a possibility, Cliff was doing something with Edgar Luff-Stile,' I said. 'Hasn't there? Or with Coinop or even Careful Stan.'

'These names! Don't they come up all the time, though?' Derek said.

'Do they?' I replied. I wanted to ask whether he thought Luff-Stile might have done Cliff Elgan. Derek would not have answered, naturally. In any case, I found I couldn't put the question. Luff-Stile was so lovely, so clean-looking in his silk suit, I'd hate to slur him like that, at least in public. I did not find it easy to say anything that could suggest Luff-Stile was in league with Iris – not because of the filthy deceit and brutality this meant, but because it would hurt to talk as if the two of them made a pair. My mind might say they were. I jibbed at speaking the thought though, in case that increased the likelihood. And in case Derek confirmed it. No thanks.

Derek stood up but didn't go at once. He bent down as if wanting more privacy. The bar was crowded. I recognised some faces from around headquarters, probably Derek's colleagues in the Squad. He slanted his body slightly so as to make sure they heard nothing. 'Everyone has to think about the long-term,' he muttered.

'Oh, for sure,' I said.

'The pension will be all very fine, yes, but . . . I can understand anyone who thinks a good bit about the future.'

'Who do you mean?'

'We see people like Luff-Stile in his damn suits and Coinop and Stan likewise, don't we? The Saabs and Mercedes and BMWs. They seem to harvest what they want, no effort or messing. I can understand the point of view that asks, "Am I supposed to just watch them pile it up?"'

'You're supposed to stop them, aren't you?' Tim asked. 'Between you, you and Helen. People in your sort of jobs.'

'*Who* asks "Am I supposed to just watch them pile it up," Derek?' I asked.

'Well, look out for Harvane, would you?' he said. 'Or the aliases. This has been worthwhile.'

'Have we got time to go home?' Tim said as soon as Derek left.

I knew he meant time to go to bed. 'I should hope so.' Important to remind myself where I belonged.

Tim said: 'I thought you did really well with him. Telling him nothing. Lots of seemingly bright talk, but non-stop stalling. How the hell do we ever catch anyone when people like you two spend your time blocking each other?'

'I do love love in the afternoon,' I replied.

Later, driving out towards the garage where Iris Elgan did her part time job, I decided I might have a tail. But perhaps I was getting nervy. Possibly the case had begun to unsettle me – all that undisclosed information and rumour niggling deep inside, and staying inside.

It was not far to the garage, not really long enough to be sure another car stuck with mine, and yet I had the feeling it kept me in sight. If so, this must be someone capable – someone who made sure at least one vehicle lay between us for most of the time, at least one but not more than two, or following became tricky. Possibly the driver had been trained. How could that be? I did not know the car, a dark Vectra, and it stayed too far back for me to manage a good look at the driver. I thought maybe the middle-aged man from that pair who picked up Harvane in the street. It might be only that Harvane and those two obsessed me, and I rushed to identify one or other of them, even though this was not the Audi. I'd have preferred it to be Harvane. I longed to know he was all right. But I had the impression of squatness, even bulk, which did not suit for him. If it was the middle-aged man, he lacked his hat now and there seemed to be a lot of dark hair, some of it down over his forehead and making things difficult. He appeared to be alone. Where would he have learned police-style driving?

And when I put that question to myself, I had the notion for a few seconds that the driver might be not the Audi man but my colleague and superior, Bruce Mossmont. He had that same kind of physical solidity and a lot of dark hair. Mossmont was not middle-aged, of course, and too tall to be described as squat. I managed only an intermittent view, though, and had to guess the driver's height.

I did what we are taught to do and turned off into a very minor street, then slowed to see if the Vectra came, too. Traffic here was negligible, and when he showed I would have a good sight of it and the driver. He did not show. If he had training, he would know this ancient ploy. Bruce Mossmont would certainly know it. I went on, did three sides of a rectangle via other small streets and came back on to the main road. A minute later I spotted the Vectra behind again, still with a vehicle shielding it from me, still doing nothing to get any nearer.

I remembered the other textbook drill and suddenly pulled into the side and stopped, so the car would have to pass and I could get a decent look, including one at the registration. But the Vectra's driver must have been alert for this one, too. He, also, pulled in and stopped – a good way behind me. When the traffic thinned for a moment, the Vectra U-turned and quickly went out of sight. I could have turned myself, perhaps – done that classic tailing gambit and become the pursuer not the pursued. I considered it, still longed to discover whatever I could about Harvane, and especially where he was and in what condition. But the traffic did not break again for three or four minutes, and by then the Vectra would probably be unfindable. Would certainly be unfind-able, because the driver was sure to guess I might come after him and do a swift series of disappearance drills around back streets.

I went on towards the garage, still watching the mirror, but did not see the Vectra. Perhaps the point of tailing had gone for him, once he realized he was spotted. I felt certain now it had been a tail, though not at all certain about the driver. Someone wanted to know my programme, but did not want me to know he wanted to know my programme. Mossmont already knew my programme, though, didn't he?

So, if it were someone else in the Vectra, he might hope to use for himself the list of people I visited. Perhaps the Vectra had been with me when I went to see Iris Elgan this morning. Was I properly watchful on that trip, or later? They could have followed Tim and me to Robo's and then picked me up again outside the flat. Damn worrying, damn promising. The Vectra might still lead somewhere if I could find it again. Possibly the driver would return to near the flat as a way of fixing on to me afresh.

Obviously, I had become important. Great. It was due. A different car might be substituted in any new attempt to tail me – the Audi, perhaps. I must not tell Tim about the possibility. He'd insist on trying to confront the driver. Too head-on, too wooden-top. I definitely would not, could not, tell him that I wondered whether the driver was Chief Inspector Mossmont in a hired car. What would this suggest about Mossmont, and especially the fact that he feared identification? It would mean, wouldn't it, he had some sort of secret connection to the case and needed to be sure I did only those inquiries he told me to make? Anything else might disturb a subtle, delicate system. What sort of secret connection? It could only be a dubious one, couldn't it? A corrupt one? Tim would not be able to cope with such a terrible, destructive idea. Dear, uncomplex Tim. He was good for me, but not in work things.

At the garage, I saw at once that any sort of love link between Iris and the owner was improbable. Unkind? Gordon Toban would be a fair way into his sixties, very frail-looking, big-nosed, big-chinned, watery-eyed, not suave. His appearance irritated me. It meant that if a sexual motive existed in this case, Iris Elgan would more likely share it with Edgar Luff-Stile. I felt another stupid rush of jealous resentment. I fancied a possible murderer, for God's sake, and one I might have to bring in, along with his accomplice, Iris Elgan.

'I certainly do not take offence at your coming to talk to me about the death of Mr Elgan,' Toban said. 'I'd be entitled to, but I don't.' He put those runny eyes on me, amiably enough – by which I mean I would not want any more amiability from them, thanks, and certainly nothing more than amiability. Would Iris Elgan have felt the same? He was in a formerly very good suit but one that seemed to have done plenty of garage time, its sheen gone, the lapels as wide as swan wings. He said: 'Some people these days, following all the police scandals, which we don't need to enumerate now – some people, even people in decent commercial and professional positions, like, say, one's self, these people have come to regard the police as ... well, yes, I have to say it, as enemies – "middle-class alien- ation", I believe it's called. Yet I feel they are hasty and wrong. Despite all the admitted terrible failures of the police, I think the obligation to help officers such as yourself is still powerful, still valid. Or where, we have got to ask, is civilization as we know it?'

'Quite,' I said, though I felt I should reply in sentences as fruity and tumbledown as his.

He touched his nose, a sort of inventorying movement. But, yes, it was still very much there. 'Is it fair to judge a whole organization of men and women by its weakest members? Hardly,' he said. Seated at his desk, he struck it a light, glancing knuckle blow, meant to declare a change of subject. 'And then again, some people would detest a fellow like Iris's husband. So-called husband. A one-time snitch, as I believe it's termed.' He seemed suddenly to go for rougher phrasing. 'You probably know his role. Or fink is another description. There are folk who cannot forgive this, and I don't mean only those criminals who felt betrayed by him. Finking – regarded as odious by even respectable, blameless figures. But narrow, ill-bloody-logical.'

'Did you know Clifford Elgan yourself?'

He had a think about this briefly. 'Iris genuinely saw much in him, and that sufficed for me, regardless. He was strug- gling towards something. I admired him for that, given his terrible drawbacks. Yes, admired, despite some of the methods he favoured.'

'Which?' We were talking in Toban's long office, panelled in pale plastic wood above the garage forecourt. Vertical strip blinds on three large windows allowed us a view through the gaps down on to the forecourt and then the road. I watched for the Vectra – felt the driver was talented enough or well-

184

informed enough to locate me here. But it did not arrive. Toban had a big voice for such a ragbag physique and face. As garage owners went, he must be up there among the hundred most rhetorical. 'What sort of thing does Mrs Elgan do for you?' I asked.

'Do for me?'

'Her work.'

'Iris has real ability with figures and admin generally. Iris knows as much about the innards of this business as I do myself.'

'Is that all right with you?'

'What lies behind a question like that?' He struck the desk again, but a more powerful whack. Probably he had employees he could frighten with such little, mock-violent acts. 'I've explained already that I am basically a supporter of the police even in the present climate, and yet you still come along with a question like that, suggesting I feared the crafty power over my business Iris might have built for herself, perhaps in concert with her so-called husband. And thus you suggest an involvement in the death.'

Thus! Right. 'Not at all,' I cried, 'let me assure you. I—'

'Is the implication that Iris could have passed on information about this business to her finking so-called husband and that he retailed it to either business rivals or the likes of you?'

'Are there matters you would not want given out concerning the business, then?'

'Certainly one must be careful about releasing confidential business matters. Almost any information can be twisted to make something else, can't it? I don't need to tell a police officer that. The adjusted notebooks. You've heard of them, I expect.'

'Did you feel Iris might have, say, pillow-talked material about your business to Clifford, who sold it on?'

He seemed especially hurt when I spoke of Iris and Cliff close on adjoining pillows. Perhaps a tremor of jealousy. I am an expert. Was I wrong and there *had* been something extra going between him and Mrs Elgan? Still? 'Absolutely not,' he said. 'Not the least fear Iris would pass confidentialities to Clifford. Iris is, and always has been – indeed, always will be, I am sure – always has been a marvellous asset to this company.' Toban leaned forward at his desk, to see more easily through the strip blinds. 'Now, here's someone calling who will no doubt set up even more poisonous notions in your police mind – though I stress again that I am in general one who regards the police with approval reaching almost to affection.'

'Thanks.' I looked where he was looking and wondered if I would see the Vectra. No, this was one of the biggest silver Mercedes. It had parked away from the petrol pumps. I thought I recognized the man who climbed out, perhaps from the media, possibly, again, from dossier pictures. 'Coinop?' I asked.

'These unkind, vulgar nicknames,' Toban said. 'I prefer to refer to him as Mr Hubert Marven. A truly gifted businessman.'

Did Toban know the *kind* of business? Was he involved? According to what I'd been told, the firm where Coinop had his true success might want merger with Edgar Luff-Stile's outfit, to combat Careful Stan. Perhaps Angus guessed right and they had been using Cliff as broker.

'We are proud to look after his cars and so on,' Toban said.

'Nice.' Which and so ons? But I did not ask this, not yet.

'Oh, I know of the gossip,' Toban said.

'There's gossip?'

'Don't make out you haven't heard. A cop, yet you haven't picked up these slanders? But they are only that, grubby slanders.'

The desk intercom sounded and Toban answered, said to show Mr Marven up. 'Would Iris Elgan have dealt with Marven's account, and so on?' I asked.

'What does that mean?'

'What?'

'"And so on." There's an intolerable smear in those words.'

'I'm sorry. I thought you'd used them first.'

'I'm sure Hubert Marven won't be in the least put out to encounter you with me. Why should he be?' Toban replied.

'In his work Hubert meets all sorts, including very possibly high officers in your Service.'

'Which?' I asked.

The door opened. 'Well, here we are, here we are,' Toban replied with a delighted laugh, and left his desk to greet Coinop as he entered the office. He wore a very rural-looking sports jacket and tan trousers. The pattern in the jacket had the slightly excessive vividness that could characterize real quality or crap – reds and greens, mainly, but also touches of yellow. I did not really doubt that Coinop's jacket was quality, grand quality, virtually ducal. An obese duke. He and Toban went through a magnificently thorough hand-shake in the middle of the room, something suggesting a huge effort by each to trust the other, though unsuccessfully, of course. 'We have a detective with us, Hubert.'

He glanced at me, the podgy neck swinging his heavy, wide head easily around, like moving a lockgate. 'I thought so. The clothes. The garden shears hair-do. You haven't got to stay, have you kid? So, on your way.' His voice was light, vigorous, full of the truest loathing.

'I've told her, Hubert, you would not feel affront – that like me you are tolerant of police, even with all we know about them.'

Coinop changed the glance into a stare. His hair did not get to the top of the scalp any longer, but bunched reddish and thick just over his ears. 'About Clifford? What happened to Clifford, definitely right out of order.'

'Absolutely,' Toban said.

'You won't never hear me say the crud had it coming,' Coinop replied.

'I'm sure Detective Constable Baring would not expect that, Hubert.'

Coinop still had the glare on me. 'I never seen you before, did I? You the Squad?'

'This is a murder, Mr Marven,' I said.

'That right?' Coinop replied. 'Well, well, well, is that right?'

Toban had a small laugh.

'So, you trying to put it on to Gordon?' Coinop asked. 'Look, sleuth, do you think someone placed so nice and tidy like Gordon would ever get himself dirtied by a slaughter of some nothing like Cliff?'

'Thank you, Hubert,' Toban said.

'We're doing a lot of visits,' I replied.

'So, you trying to put it on to Gordon?'

'Did you know Clifford well, Mr Marven?' I replied.

'I never seen you before,' Coinop said. 'What right you got to ask questions, kid, just coming out with them that way? You got any notion in the least how things work?'

'Which things?' I replied.

'Generally. You asking questions alone?' Coinop said. 'Do your chiefs know you're out by yourself?'

'Are you friendly with them?' I said.

He frowned for a time. Then he spoke like a revelation, breathless, contemptuous, his huge chest bucking: 'You suggesting some mesh? You trying to put it on me? On *me*?'

'We're doing a lot of visits. We're talking to everyone who was in touch with Clifford.'

'You swallowed that rubbish talk about Cliff trying to con me – some join-up plan with Edgar?'

'It's rubbish, is it?'

'Would I join with Edgar?' Coinop said.

'I don't know.'

'No, you don't, do you? What she here for, Gord?'

'Iris.'

'Iris?' Coinop would be thirty-six or seven, between fat and gross, white, un-nimble, his heavy hands well-jewelled. 'You think Iris would do her own man in his own car on his own drive?'

'We're not certain he was actually killed there,' I replied.

'What *are* you actually certain about, kid?' His voice minced.

'I don't understand the relationship between you and Mr Toban,' I replied.

'Relationship?' Coinop asked.

'The business connection.'

'I got cars, don't I? Gordon's a garage. He knows Mercs. Got two hisself.'

'It's like a network,' I replied. 'You, Mr Toban, Iris, Clifford.'

Coinop thought some more. And then there was what looked like the biggest change yet. His voice went even edgier. 'Did you call her up, Gordon – get her here to talk to me like this?'

'I didn't know she was coming, believe me, Hubert.'

'Well, I don't know about that,' Coinop said.

'What?' Toban asked.

Coinop had stayed standing, his superb jacket done up around the slob frame on all three buttons, as if for protection. Toban was back at his desk. Coinop waddled over there with quite a bit of majesty and sat on a straight-backed chair in front of him, acres of his behind hanging to each side. 'What I don't know about is if I believe you. You trying to push something off of you on to me, Gordon, the old drill? She got you all tied up, yes, so you think, Stick it on to Hubert instead.'

'Hubert, I swear—'

'You and Gordon fixing this one between you, kid? Trying to fix this one between you. Don't you know how things work here?'

'You've asked me that.'

'Don't you know how things work here?'

'Where?'

'Don't come the dumbo with me, you dumbo,' Coinop replied. 'You think you can get an arrangement with someone like Gordon and between you you see off Hubert Marven? Hubert Marven personal. That's mad. That's cheek.'

'Of course it is, Hubert,' Toban said.

'I could pick up a phone and you'd be nowhere,' Coinop told me.

'Calling who?' I replied.

'Calling never mind who,' he said.

'Good, Hubert,' Toban said. 'Don't kowtow to her.'

'So, just take care of yourself, Gordon,' Coinop replied.

I loved this sudden gap between them, Coinop's suspicion and rage. They might be genuine. I said: 'Was Mr Toban doing something with Iris Elgan – something deep, not just account books?'

But they were into a possible private battle now. 'Hubert, please, please, you mistake things,' Toban said.

189

'You're turning into a real disappointment, Gord.'

'An accident she was here,' Toban cried. 'There was no intention to put you on a plate for her. Oh, detective, tell him this or—'

I said: 'Was Mr Toban doing something with Iris Elgan – something deep, not just account books? What is this garage? What is it a cover for? But whatever it is, you're in it, aren't you, Coinop? You're not going to tell me.'

'I've instructed her not to call you that, Hubert,' Toban said. 'So crude and presumptuous.'

'As I see it, this was to be an emergency session between you two,' I said. 'I strayed in. Sorry. Maybe Gordon – Gordon, the high-fly Chamber of Commerce man – Gordon is supposed to advise you on how the join-up with Edgar Luff-Stile should be done, now Clifford's skills are not around. Or maybe how to get out of it. Possibly you've done your firm real harm by killing Cliffy, Coinop, no matter how much he was fooling you. That's if you did kill him, obviously.'

'Kid, you want me to tell you what I notice?' Coinop replied.

'About what?' I asked.

'What I notice is the way you say his name.'

'Who?' I said. 'Cliff?'

'No. You say it full of sex,' Coinop answered.

'I thought that, too,' Toban said.

'Whose name?' I asked, but pretty sure of the answer.

'It's happening all the damn time,' Coinop said. 'Them suits. The blondness. The sick slimness. That way he talks – the sliminess. The women really go for him. Even cop women. Maybe especially cop women.'

'Oh, I'd definitely think so, Hubert,' Toban said. His eyes seemed to grow more clouded, as if mourning a loss.

'You gets a knee tremble everytime you thinks of him, don't you, detective?' Coinop asked. 'Your clothes and that haircut – but you still pray he'll notice you, don't you?'

'Who?' I said.

'Edgar, of course,' Toban replied.

'Edgar Luff-Stile?' I asked, with the widest laugh I could lay on. 'Oh, really!' Did I get a knee-tremble every time?

No. Only now and then.

'Which is why you come and try to put it on me,' Coinop said. 'Or on Gordon. You'd love to frame me. Or Gordon. How police operate. Women police.'

'You're telling me Edgar Luff-Stile did Clifford?' I replied.

'There it is,' Coinop said. 'Again.'

'What?'

'The way you say him, killer or not,' Coinop replied. 'So loving, so full of . . . well, of dirty passion and protection. You're taking care of him, aren't you?'

'I picked that up, too,' Toban said. 'She's looking for fall-guys, so her glossy favourite gets no aggro. You and I, we're mere victims, Hubert.'

Coinop's huge face gleamed with big anger. 'I won't take it,' he shouted. 'I got friends.'

'What kind of friends?' I asked.

He waved down towards the Mercedes. 'I got position, I got readies. Women – they see a bit of extra weight here and there in my type, and they treat me like offal. All the time it's happening. I show them the Mercedes or the BMW but I know they're still looking at the slight body thickening here and there, and making their decisions, their damn choices.'

'Inhuman, Hubert,' Toban remarked. 'Short-sighted of them.'

'Yes, both, both,' Coinop said. He sobbed twice. His head fell forward, like someone waiting for the axe. It would have to be a big axe and a first class blow and a strong basket under. 'While they turn away to someone like Luff-Stile. Iris the same. Is this what life is about, then – looks, suits, rotten glamour? I got to say I think there's more than that to it.'

'Like what?' I asked. 'Like building a drugs cartel? How are you going to work with Luff-Stile if you think he's a killer and hate his looks and his suits?'

'But *you* don't hate them, do you?' Coinop replied.

'Is the hate because you decided Edgar and Cliff were trying to rip you off some way, Coinop?' I said. 'The merger's dead – as dead as Cliff? This conference with Gordon was officially to bury it?'

191

'Haven't I protested about you calling him Coinop on my premises?' Toban replied. 'Intolerably flippant.'

And then, of course, of bloody course, the Vectra was behind me again when I drove away from my meeting with those two hearty charmers, behind me as it had been behind me earlier, two vehicles back, almost unnoticeable but not unnoticeable if you qui vived for such things. The driver I could still not make out properly, but I found myself muttering to myself 'Mossmont' and 'Why, why Mossmont?' The idea scared me – scared me far more than if I'd been able to decide definitely the tail was the middle-aged mystery lad at the Harvane street pick-up. But I could not. I struggled for glimpses in the mirror during those moments when the Vectra became a bit more visible. And I decided that the driver's upper body might not, in fact, be the upper body of a short and bulky type, but of someone tall and well-built, someone more like Mossmont.

There was one other anti-surveillance dodge I could try. Enter a roundabout as if to take one of the exits ahead, but then accelerate right the way around and, if you're lucky, you find yourself nicely behind the tail. True, it would be another of those manoeuvres second nature to any police-trained driver. Mossmont might not fall for it. If it *was* Mossmont. Why would a police officer tail another police officer, unless the tail believed the target officer corrupt, or unless the tail had his own corrupt and secret links, and worried they might get disturbed? He'd want to be sure I went where I'd been told to go, and only there. Perhaps he'd heard of my other, private discoveries on this case, or what I thought were private.

The scenario terrified me, not just because I could be in danger the way Clifford Elgan had been in danger. It grew wider than that – sort of philosophical, and almost religious. Big, big ideas? Maybe. They might be true, all the same. If Mossmont were corrupt it meant even the most gifted people in the Service could be soiled and spoiled by temptation. The whole law and order system appeared rotten. Money – dirty money – could win. To me that looked like decline and fall.

I drove on to the Barracks Yard roundabout and signalled I would be taking the second left exit. I let the indicator blink its false message until automatically cancelled and then belted around to the right. I kept going, touched fifty and got some wheel squeal on the turns, and came off where I'd started. And it worked. It worked? The Vectra lay ahead, its driver probably baffled because he no longer had me in sight, and prevented by other vehicles from bringing his car around to search. I had exactly the sort of position he kept earlier, two cars between him and me. Was it the back of Mossmont's head?

Perhaps he would be content to have me in this position so he could lead to somewhere he regarded as suitable for . . . suitable for whatever he had in mind. No denying, I suffered dread. Just the same, I dogged the Vectra, sweat on my paws and elsewhere, chest pains, though probably not a heart attack, yet. Nothing in the training covered the black subtleties of snooping on a boss.

Mossmont led towards the edge of the city. He did not seem to check the mirror much. He must feel sure I'd stick. This apparent casualness brought my doubts back. Was it really Mossmont after all? He would have been taught to get the maximum from his mirror. The suburbs faded and we were on a flat coastal road running between a mixture of fields and a developing industrial estate with its bright-coloured, repulsively angular, metal framed, grant-aided, economic-miracle new factories. After a few more miles he turned off on to a narrower road that must lead right down to the sea. It was remote here. He would know I'd follow. I found the Vectra parked at the end of this road. Bruce Mossmont had left the car and climbed the earthwork seawall. He watched while I drew in, then beckoned me to join him. Nearby stood a small, brick, windowless building with one locked door. It would be a sewage control point for the outfall pipe I saw stretching out across mudflats once I joined Mossmont. 'Some spot,' I said.

We placed ourselves between the building and the sea, so as not to be outlined on the seawall. The cars below were hidden unless anyone came right down the side road. Like a lovers' meeting, and not like.

'I wanted to be sure you were safe,' he said. 'It's important you stay with what you are ordered to do, only that.'

'I did,' I said. 'Visit Toban.'

'I feel you might be into other aspects of the case. It's dangerous.'

'Am I being warned off?'

'You're being asked to stay within certain defined limits. *Asked*.'

I said: 'That seems a normal sort of instruction for a superior to give a subordinate. Couldn't it have been said at headquarters? We needed this rigmarole?'

'I saw you leave the Elgan house for some reason on the day the body was found.' He waited but I did not explain. 'A character called Harvane there? Sometimes called Harvane. And then contact with that old, know-all, know-nothing junkie, Angus Siverall. Flowers and so on.' He waited but I did not explain. 'Not good areas for you to drift into.' Mossman was round-faced, blue-eyed, frank-looking, somehow boyish in appearance, and not at all frank or boyish. He would never have made his rank at this age if so. Did he mean I should stay out of private arrangements he had somewhere? I thought of Coinop's threat to get on the phone to a friend if I turned into real trouble. Perhaps Coinop hadn't needed to get on the phone.

'Coinop was at the garage,' I said.

'Yes.'

'You knew he would be there?'

'I saw him arrive in his second-string Mercedes.'

'You did turn up at the garage then, eventually?'

'I wanted to be sure you were safe.'

'How could you do that if you disappeared?'

'I didn't disappear for long,' Mossmont said. 'I saw you go in to see Toban. You failed to spot me then, that's all.'

'But I was watching for you.'

'Of course you were. You missed me.'

'I don't believe it.'

'You have some tailing skills, Helen. Not the lot.' Mossmont began to descend the earthwork wall towards his car. 'So, stay within the limits. I'll tell you exactly what you should look at. Don't stray. I can't be around non-stop to guard you.'

194

'From?'

'I'd like to. Impossible.'

'You know the Mercedes. Do you know Coinop?' I had to yell the questions. He was down near his car.

Mossmont waved – a single, brisk movement, did a three-point in the Vectra and left up the side road.

In bed with Tim, I felt a special brilliant joy in him tonight. Well, of course, there should always be a special brilliant joy about sex. There isn't, though, is there? Or there hadn't always between Tim and me, lately, at any rate. Would I fantasize about some elegant derelict like Edgar Luff-Stile otherwise? Well, possibly. Life does offer a bucketful of prospects and it can seem mean not to respond. Tonight, though, it seemed as if Tim and I were closer than we had ever been, even closer than at the beginning all those months ago, closer all ways, not just the bodily ways, though these were wonderfully right, too. I could have said I was happy, but I never do say that. It challenges all the circling, flying, stalking, creeping, ganging evils to move in.

When we talked afterwards, still close, I thought I could see what had happened, what had transformed things. In fact there was a touch of farce to it, because football had helped. Yes, the eternal and eternally irksome footie! Just the same, a marvel had come about. *Don't knock it, Helen.* This would last, I knew. I could tell Tim suddenly sensed he understood me better. He had nipped past most of those barriers my sort of work built around me. The fact was that, after a while, detective work begins to impose a new personality, a changed self on almost everyone who goes into it. If it does not, you can probably still handle the job, but it will be *only* a job, not what it ought to be, a mission, an apostleship to that fractured, doddery concept, law and order. And if it does transform you, you begin to find relationships outside the mysterious trade guild very difficult. Maybe that's the reason things had slipped with Tim and me.

But, all at once, he had somehow found a way to help him deal with that. Thank God he still wanted to. I loved him for it. 'I saw Derek Fonde at soccer practice today,' he said.

'Ah, how's the Drugs Squad?'

'Strange. That is, I don't know about the Squad, but Derek was strange. He obviously wanted to talk.'

'About the rich art of throwing in from touch?'

'About Drugs Squad business.'

'What? Yes, strange.' I tried to stay relaxed and comfortable against Tim's body, but knew I had tensed. I thought back to that lunch in Robo's with Derek, and to his usual uptightness and secrecy behind the dozy-looking face. There'd been a revolution?

'I think he wanted me to pass on to you what he said.'

I stayed put and spoke into the patch of skin on Tim's back between his shoulders, where my mouth happened to be – spoke as if sleepily, as if casually. 'Which things would those be then, the ones he thought you'd tell me? Crumbs from the know-all's table?'

'I don't think he knows all and he knows he doesn't know all. But what he does know scares him. And it scares me, appalls me, Helen. If I believe it. Not sure.' Tim sat up. He, obviously, couldn't play at offhandedness any longer. The blissful sex seemed in a different era. He was a mix of excitement, fright, solemnity. I lay there, pretending to composure for a little while longer. 'Why scared?' I asked.

'Remember Derek asked you about the man with the aliases?'

'Harvane? Also known as Bale and Porter-Knight, according to Derek,' I said.

'Of course, he phoned you. Before that, you saw him disappear, didn't you?' Tim asked. 'It's a buzz he's picked up since we met at Robo's.'

'A buzz is a quarter of a quarter of a tenth of a rumour.'

'*Did* you see him disappear, Helen? Derek thinks it's terrific if you did – shows you were ahead. He believes you know more than anyone. I said, of course you did, that's the way you are, always in front.' He bent and kissed me on the side of my neck. It was nice. I sat up. This is what I meant just now – Tim seemed to want to understand my kind of

196

work, suddenly could appreciate it. Empathy, by God. I kissed him back, on an eyelid.

'What buzz?' I asked.

'Some kids in Torl Street saw Harvane get into an Audi, I gather. And then they spoke to you. Or didn't. One of the kids lives near Derek. Talks to him now and then – for money, I suppose. Do you remember the kids?'

Insolent, negative, malevolent little twerps. Or negative to me. They had wanted money for talky-talkies, had they? 'These kids knew Harvane?'

'He's a pusher, isn't he?' Tim replied. 'I expect a lot of kids know him.'

'Where is he?' I asked.

'There was Harvane and two other men in Torl Street, I gather. Derek had names.' Tim left the bed and went naked to his uniform which hung on the wardrobe door. I hated that – silver buttons gleaming in the electric light like self-righteousness. He produced a piece of paper from his tunic pocket and read. 'Oscar Gershom, Dean Haniel. Not note-booked, you'll notice. I'm learning your ways, Helen.' He rejoined me in bed. 'They're pushers, too. Derek knows them all. So did the kids. Driver unidentified, though.'

I took the paper from him, memorized the two names, then gave it back. He tore it up. 'What did they do to Harvane? Or is that where Derek's knowledge stops? He thinks I can find him? Oh, Tim, Harvane could be in a woodland grave somewhere, or on the sea bottom with a sinker. Those two—'

'Ah, you thought abduction.' Tim asked. 'No. They're all pals. The three of them got out of town. Stayed out of town, according to Derek. Scared because of what happened to Elgan. Perhaps they worked like him – between the firms. Dicey.'

'How does Derek know this? More buzz?'

Tim laughed. He obviously did not want to be pushed into anger tonight. 'Some buzz, some deduction, I think. The three dropped out of sight. They were missed around the usual pushing grounds. Derek noticed, asked here and there. They certainly worked sometimes for Careful Stan. I expect you knew. Big upheavals going on among the firms. You probably know that, too.'

'I'd heard about the last bit.'

'They thought they'd get caught in the middle. Like Elgan.'

If Derek and Tim were right and those three stayed out of town, Angus Siverall had invented the trio who supposedly told him about me in Zola, Zola. Perhaps Angus wanted to conceal how he knew about me. Or, possibly they were three different men. Angus had said only that they looked as if they worked for Careful Stan. Speculation? He could be all wrong and they might have come from anywhere. From anyone. So, conceivably, Bruce Mossman was right and I did need protection.

'But Harvane was going to talk to me,' I said.

'Derek knew that.'

'He's in touch with Harvane now?'

Tim raised his hands to indicate ignorance or guess: 'Maybe. Or it—'

'Or it could be more buzz.'

'Something like that.' Tim paused, rubbed a hand across his mouth, almost as though wanting to stop what he had to say next. 'Harvane had apparently been told by Careful Stan to contact you and brief you. You only.'

'Does Stan know me?'

'Stan knows all he needs to know, apparently.'

'What's that mean?' I asked.

Again Tim paused. He rushed the next words: 'This was to brief you about a supposed corrupt cop, someone at the top, who worked, works, for one of the rival drugs gangs – Coinop or the other one. Do you know it?'

I made out I had to do some thinking to recall the name. 'Edgar Luff-Stile's outfit?'

'Right. Stan wanted it exposed that there was a high-place crooked cop, because obviously it could hurt his business if one of the other syndicates had HQ help.'

'So, he sends someone to talk to a low-place Detective Constable? Come on, Tim.'

He looked hurt, as if slighted. 'He sends someone to talk to a detective who lives with a uniformed cop famous for his simple-minded integrity and all those other standard issue virtues. Stan reckoned you'd tell me and I would be sure to whistleblow. Wouldn't be able to prevent myself.'

'My God,' I said.

'It might have worked. Harvane meant to do it for him. He'd told you he'd be in contact, hadn't he? But his two pals apparently panicked after Elgan's death, thought nothing safe any longer and persuaded him to get out with them. That's what you saw happening on Torl Street, persuasion, not force, and in his own interests. They were terrified they might also be on someone's list for what they knew.'

It was possible. 'And the corrupt cop?' I said. 'We believe this?'

'I don't know. Derek believes it. Maybe he lives in that kind of climate.'

I remembered Derek's words about the inadequacy of the police pension. Had he been hinting at the need to build a store while there was time?

'But me, I don't know,' Tim repeated.

He would not want to believe it, of course. Tim needed to have faith in the leadership or he felt lost. I waited and then said with all the matter-of-factness I could: 'Derek named Mossmont, did he? I wondered myself. He's been spying.'

Tim shook his head. I thought at first it was from Tim-type sadness that someone like Mossmont could slide so far. But then I saw he meant I had things wrong. Oh, God!

'No,' Tim replied, 'Harvane wouldn't have said Mossmont.' His voice almost faded out. For a second it was as if he really could not speak what had to come next. Then he muttered: 'Higher.'

I found I was whispering myself now. 'We're talking about Peter Arad?'

'It's anarchy, Helen.'

'This is based on yet more buzz? Only that?'

'Derek says unquestionably Arad.'

'But evidence?'

'That's the point – he thinks you might have it or could get it,' Tim said.

'No, I haven't got it. How could I? I don't even believe it.'

'But you could get it, couldn't you, Helen? Of course you

could.' There was another of those understanding kisses on my neck, understanding and admiring.

'Perhaps I could, but I won't.' Of course I could. Of course I'd try. Of course I'd keep quiet about it. The habit of furtiveness doesn't just turn and run. 'It's rubbish,' I told Tim, 'not even buzz quality.'

I considered tailing one or other of them, Arad or Mossmont. Despite Tim and Derek, I had not given up all my notions on Mossmont. But if I did try it, I'd probably stalk Arad first. Hadn't I done enough of that with Mossmont, for the time being anyway? And then . . . then Derek's information, if you could call it information. Perhaps the whole notion was stupid. What did I really have against either boss? I had buzz, some of it only hearsay buzz. Now and then my instincts screamed that neither of them could be involved, and told me to think of Harvane as the killer, or Angus Siverall, or glamorous Edgar – and, if Edgar, Iris Elgan might also be part of it.

My instincts looked a bit of a jumble. More than a bit – a jumble all the way through. My thoughts on Harvane seemed a mess. I worried for his safety, but suspected him of a contemptible killing. Angus I wondered about because . . . well, possibly only because I understood hardly anything to do with him, could not explain his role and his knowingness, and therefore assumed, in best police fashion, he must be sinister. Edgar I was wowed by in that silly, dangerous, hormonal-romantic way, but I could also see why it might be part of his business plan to finish Clifford, if Clifford had played dirty. Everything I heard about Clifford said he might have. Iris Elgan I wanted to be innocent and devastated with sorrow, but I couldn't altogether believe it, and my view of her stayed idiotically darkened anyway, because she might be having Edgar Luff-Stile.

Toban? Coinop? Possibles. But I found they were only on the edge of my suspicions, though I wondered why. More instinct? Normally, I'm someone who trusts my non-logical, subconscious urges. They are not bad. However, on this case I had too many, each contradicting the rest. Impossible to sort out one strong line.

And so back to Arad, or Bruce Mossmont. More tailing, by car and on foot? More risk of being rumbled by people who knew a barrelful more about tailing than myself? Yes, daunting. But I don't let myself get daunted, do I? So I decided to have a go at it and drove out to Arad's house in the evening. If Derek had known about the priority I gave the Superintendent, he would have felt flattered. Derek picks up gossip, I try to turn it into evidence. Derek hints at what Tim called anarchy in the law and order brass, and I'm the one who nips out to discover as fact that, yes, this is how things are – to discover as fact that we're all into total break-up.

If Arad emerged I would get behind him, supposing I could. It might be easier here than from headquarters in the centre. Disaster for ever should he spot me. It was something you did not do, spy on a Detective Chief, Mossmont or Arad. Office talk said Peter Arad lived alone after divorce in a big, detached, high-suburbia place, perhaps five bedrooms, with gardens on two sides and an Edwardian-style conservatory. Apparently his wife had custody of their child.

I did as I'd done at the Elgan house and left my car a distance away, though not so far this time. If Arad motored out I'd need to get to it fast. The drive wound around to the house through tall bushes and some trees and I could not see from the road whether Arad's Rover was parked up nearer the property. Ironwork gates to the street stood open, so if he did come out by car he could be very swiftly away. A metal plaque on one of the gates gave the name Tarragona. Someone had been on holiday or a honeymoon. Through the foliage on my walk past I saw lights shining in several rooms downstairs, none above.

I walked on. I would not be able to patrol like this too often. In such an area, people on foot at night were rare. Homeowners here might feel jumpy about a stranger persistently eyeing up the neighbourhood, maybe short-listing for break-ins. It was a leafy spot and not very well lit, and I tried to keep in close to the hedges when I could. But there were stretches of ground where I'd be very visible. I turned and started back. Stupid to leave Arad's house unwatched for long. He could stroll out and disappear. If he drove I would at least hear the car.

And, approaching Tarragona, I thought for a second that, in fact, Arad *had* come out and was walking away from me. I corrected the impression at once. This was a shorter, slighter man than Arad. Like me, he seemed to stay hard against the hedges when possible, wanted to merge with them, get some cover from them. He had on a long, dark overcoat and some sort of close-fitting woollen hat, also dark, pulled down half over his ears. Did he come from Arad's house? I must identify this figure quickly, in case he had a vehicle nearby.

There was a side road and I took this at a run, and then the first to the right. I reckoned I would have circled a block and might meet him coming towards me. Of course, Arad's house lay out of sight while I did my circuit and he could leave unseen. How had priorities moved like this? Why had the long overcoat suddenly become so crucial?

I'd calculated OK, and when I finished my dash I saw the man head-on. I still did not know why I'd made him important. Even less so now. 'Angus?' I said. 'Angus Siverall? Yet another chic outfit?'

'Ah,' he replied. 'the girl detective. My dear, I thought I might see you here.'

'Why?'

He shrugged. Nothing else. The overcoat moved sweetly up and down with his shoulders and all the time kept beautifully curved contact around the nape of his neck. This was some garment – a triumph of material, cut, and superb indistinctness when set against a shadowy hedge at night.

'You're still interested in Mr Arad?' I asked.

'And now you're interested, too.'

'You trawl, do you? Have you called in on him?'

'I was passing by. I don't know him. Would I be likely to call in?'

'I don't know,' I replied.

'And you? Will you call on him? Or is this just another of your lurks?'

'Why your interest here?' I replied.

'I wonder about him,' he said. 'Connections.'

'With what, with whom?'

'Quite. Whom. I adore grammar.'

'So would you follow him?' I said.

'Would you?'

'Tell me, Angus, was it just a spontaneous grope in the Zola, Zola, or did you plan it, so you could get contact with me?'

'Contact with you is what I disgracefully tried for at the club, my dear. I hope I've convinced you of my shame and regrets.'

'Not sexual contact. Business. You've got some role? Did you follow me out here? Do you work for someone?'

'And in a way you're right, Helen,' he said.

'You do work for someone? For Edgar? Coinop?'

'Role. I need to get near the actuality now and then – need to watch people in the clubs or need to come out here and see Mr Arad's home, breathe the bourgeois air he breathes in his off-duty times. It's my hobby as an elderly gent – to be in touch, to know what's called "the scene", I think. When you're old, you want to see all you can of life and hang on to it, the way death-bed folk cling to the blankets as they go.'

'This is total bollocks, isn't it?' I said.

'Good that we meet once more,' he replied. 'We share a wavelength.' He raised a nicely gloved hand, turned away and began to walk quickly out of Arad's road, hugging the line of the front hedges still, occasionally seeming to be swallowed by the shadows. He would reappear a long way ahead, a shadow himself, that thin, blurred, vigorous figure, briefly under one of the street lights before fading out again. Where was his car? Why had he parked far off – like myself? Did he need to breathe so much of the district's bourgeois air just for the sake of general interest – a hobby, really an old chap's curiosity?

It worried me, the clever, dark rightness of his clothes and his crafty approach to the house. He obviously didn't want his vehicle associated with this road by residents. Why? What had happened? Had *anything* happened, or was he only doing what he said, collecting atmospherics to put solidity into his amateur, old fart's fascination with 'the scene'?

I suddenly felt like an amateur myself – not an old fart amateur, just a dimwit, through-and-through amateur, skulking at the edges of this situation, sneaking around in front of the house, picking up useless, bitty glimpses of it through the hedge and bushes. I must get nearer. True, the house had not been my objective when I first arrived here. I'd intended following Arad, if Arad appeared. He had not appeared. My sole encounter was with Angus, and he changed my aims. I could not escape the thought that he might have been into Tarragona – perhaps only the gardens, perhaps the house itself – possibly to see Arad, possibly only because he wanted a look at the place, for his memory lane scrapbook. Either way, he had done better than myself.

Next time I walked past I looked for gaps in the hedge. I did not want to go in by the open gates. It was too light there, too obvious to neighbours opposite, and in full view if Arad did suddenly come out from the house. I found what seemed a thinning in the growth and forced myself through it, no subtlety or gradualness, just maximum fast push. I was in jeans and a black leather jacket which did their bit to protect me, but I took a couple of digs in the face from short, spiky branches and tore the lobe of my left ear. I emerged to the side of the conservatory, about twenty metres from the house and shielded by hydrangeas. I took a pause and dabbed with a handkerchief at the blood on my ear and running down my neck.

Lights shone in two downstairs rooms, one immediately opposite and one at the front of the house. The room opposite might be the kitchen. Its window was uncurtained and I could see dark wooden wall cupboards up to the ceiling. The light from there reached out towards me. I would be caught in it as soon as I moved from behind the bushes. The compulsion to enter the place suddenly seemed mad. What did I want to do? The question hammered at my mind because I must think how I'd explain if Arad discovered me. I had come in case Arad was sold to a firm – to Stan or Edgar or Coinop – and I hoped to find something that would prove things one way or the other. I would not be telling Arad this, though, if he spotted me.

Should I pick my way back through the hedge and let this loony project die? The investigation had become too big for me, hadn't it? Somehow, the passably sensible plan to tail Arad had been distorted, had turned into foolhardiness. And

I knew what that somehow was, or who it was – Angus Siverall. I had turned him into a competitor, and if competitors appeared I always competed, no matter how crackpot the contest.

I was retreating slowly towards the hedge, tense, crouched, my handkerchief still held to my ear, when I saw very briefly upstairs a ray of light shine on one of the uncurtained bedroom windows, then move hurriedly away before dying. Someone wanted to correct a mistake? The beam should never have reached the window. I did not think it came from a house light – more like hand-held equipment, almost certainly a torch. Had it been swung carelessly? I remained still, between the hydrangeas and the hedge, watching the window. After three or four minutes, that light perhaps came on again. I could not be sure. If so, it was a long way back now and possibly shaded.

Now, another change of purpose. I forgot about withdrawing through the hedge and stepped forward again, this time not even pausing with the hydrangeas as shelter. I skirted the square of light from the kitchen window and reached the side wall of the house. I kept on towards the rear, away from the kitchen light. I could hear nothing, no voices, no television or radio. A door at the back did not seem properly shut and, when I gave it a slight push, I could see why. The lock had been forced, perhaps levered. Angus? Angus really broke into houses, or this house, at least? Why? And, if it had been Angus, who was upstairs in the house now? It could hardly be Peter Arad. Would he be so jumpy about showing a light? I wished I had a torch myself, or anything that might work as a weapon.

I had another of my pathetic, treacherous sessions of hesitation then, and actually thought of ringing up Tim to ask him to go into Tarragona with me. Definitely not a matter of being a woman and weak, was it? Was it? No – a matter of being alone and going into a situation where the hazards were unknown, not their nature or number. Training stressed that if possible, you avoided acting solo when among undefined risks. It applied to both sexes equally, no special, protective terms for women. No . . .

But I refused to call for male help, even when the male

help was Tim. This was my investigation. M. I. N. E. It could not be more personal, more maverick, more outright subversive. I was on the point of slinking in illegally to the head of CID's home, meaning to nail him for corruption and murder. At least, I hoped it would be a slink. Oh, Lord, let it certainly be that, and unresisted. I decided one person could move more quietly than two. Slinking was for one. Me.

I slipped slowly into the house, leaving the damaged door open behind me. The training said, 'Always prepare an exit', and this was one instruction I did follow. It had probably been learned from burglars, so would be well tried. I glanced about. The outer door put me into what seemed a passage-cum-utility room. On the far side, another door, part open, led to the rest of the house. A little light reached here from a hall or corridor. I saw some gardening tools and a pair of big-footed wellington boots, a couple of full plastic sacks closed with cord at the top, perhaps waiting for the refuse collection. There was a long, low freezer, its red On indicator bright in the half dark, and a blue, iron, rusted stepladder. Seed boxes full of soil were spread across the floor. I went gingerly around these and tried to visualize Angus doing the same very recently, the long overcoat almost sweeping all that germination.

A tall, thin, rectangular looking-glass stood against one wall, perhaps meant to be fixed in a bedroom one day and give top-to-toe scrutiny. I was reflected in it now and thought I looked nearly all right. My mouth appeared clamped hard shut through stress and my eyes had almost disappeared because of a concentration frown, but I could not spot actual fright in my face. Perhaps the poor light helped. I didn't stay gazing too long, in case I eventually discovered panic signs. I did experience actual fright, very actual, no question, but it was good it failed to show, surely. I felt aware or nearly aware, of some other vague disquiet that badgered me while I stood before the glass. Thank heaven, it stayed vague, undefined. *Ignore it, Helen, dear. Strangle it, Helen, dear. Escape it, Helen, dear.*

I moved further into the house. What looked like framed certificates hung on the walls, but I did not bother to study them. I stood still and tried to pick up any sounds elsewhere. Now, I could see the foot of the stairs, broad, heavy-banistered, rich-red-carpeted, in keeping with the minor magnificence of the house. I concentrated my listening there, waiting for movements by the torch bearer in one of the first floor rooms. As much as possible I must keep the stairs in sight, or I could be surprised by someone coming down. Someone? It had to be Arad, surely. But why would Arad use a torch in his own home and not the bedroom light? Why would he seem edgy that the beam might shine out?

I reached a sitting room, its door wide open. A couple of table-lamps burned there. The curtains were drawn. The room looked comfortable and clean. Arad probably employed domestic help now his marriage had finished. How had he been able to hold on to the house in the break-up? Did that suggest he settled his wife's share of the assets with cash? Half the value of Tarragona and its contents would be at least £300,000. Arad had had that kind of capital? Where from? The room was respectably furnished with fairly modern stuff, no particular style that I identified, but all the pieces solid-seeming, untatty.

There remained a lot of the downstairs to cover but abruptly I thought, *Leave it, leave it, dozy kiddo, and get up to the bedrooms.* I suspected I was putting off the obvious and urgent through fear. You're never more exposed than on a staircase. You can be done from above or below – especially from above, here. To get up there was necessary, though, and overdue. I turned around and almost took that first step towards the stairs, but my mind gave another dismal lurch – perhaps still trying to keep me from the upper floor.

All at once I realized what had unsettled me so much about the utility room. It was the tall, oblong mirror in the corner. The glint of it, the bevelled edges, its changing pictures, galloped bright and upsetting into my memory now. I'd restricted my contact with it to a swift glance, in case what I saw shattered my spirits. I'd been afraid of looking too long and finding through looking that I looked afraid. And, as I pointed myself towards the first stair now, I realized what it was about the mirror that had threatened to disable me then. It was not just the possibly disheartening picture of myself, but something reflected from behind me. At the time, I had managed to ignore it, shove it down into my deep, messy subconscious, virtually harmless. Yes, virtually.

But in the glass I had naturally seen a part of the utility room, and the part included a freezer, a long, low freezer. In that distant, shut-off pit of the subconscious a word had stirred as I stared briefly at the glass, a word I had managed to suppress and obscure then, before it could properly spell itself out. I had moved on fast, rejected the mirror and all it wanted to reveal – all it wanted to reveal about myself and the surrounds. The word which I so deftly side-stepped, so firmly prohibited, had been 'coffin', of course. The long, low freezer was white, but, this apart, resembled a casket, whether viewed in the glass or direct.

I forgot the stairs now. My legs seemed dodgy and might not manage the climb. That was not why I stopped, though. I felt ashamed – ashamed of whatever had prevented me from recognizing in the utility room a few minutes ago that I should open the freezer and check. Fright had a strength and range which I'd stupidly underestimated. It made me neglectful, sloppy.

After a moment, I forced my legs to work and take me back to the utility room, but this time, because I dreaded entering it, I did loiter for a second and read the framed certificates. I discovered that Peter Arad attained Grade Six in his piano lessons as a boy and Intermediate with Distinction on the flute. A monstrous, saucy thought came. Perhaps I needed it. God, I muttered, what a loss to music if he's corpsed and finger-stiff in the freezer, never able to hit a note again. It was long enough to accommodate Arad with only a little folding of his long, cop legs.

Naturally, he was not in the freezer. It contained two bottles of Plymouth gin, lying there like a conspiracy, nothing else. This was the way connoisseurs did it, so the gin did not warm up chilled tonic or bitters. As I looked at these pretty bottles, it seemed abject that I should have slipped into such an alarmist notion, should have allowed the mere shape of the freezer to power my imagination.

*Helen, dear, you're a laugh, you're a fantasizing child,*

*not much past the horror comic stage and Peter Pan. If it's
not sex fantasy it's death fantasy.*

However, Peter Arad was non-fantasy dead in the other
main downstairs room, this one with a markedly Victorian
or Edwardian motif, except, of course, for the television,
video machine and CD system. He had been shot in the back
of the head, probably by a small calibre pistol. Little mess.
I was bleeding more myself from the torn ear. I'd given up
dabbing at it with the handkerchief and would leave a trail
through the house, right up to the corpse. *Change your initi-
tial from H. to DNA, sweetheart.*

Arad occupied a tall-backed, handsome armchair – an
Edwardian frame but re-covered in some excellent modern
blue, speckled material. He sat sideways on to me, so that
I could see his eyes were open and unmoving, and could
also see where the bullet had entered his skull. I observed
a little scorching. The gun muzzle must have been very
close. This could mean someone not confident with firearms,
unsure of hitting from a distance. But how would the killer
get so near? Arad seemed to have been watching television
when shot, though the set was off now. He wore excellent
black lace-up shoes, suit trousers and a white shirt, the sleeves
of the shirt shortened by metal armbands worn just above
the elbow. Somehow, the brilliant whiteness of the shirt
made him seem especially pathetic, like a prisoner smocked
for execution. And the armbands ate at his dignity. They
looked fussy and crude, as if he couldn't pick clothes to fit
right. Someone in gear too big for him always appeared
pitiable. The armbands suggested manacles.

As soon as I saw Arad I knew he must be dead, yet from
my spot a half step into the room I spoke: 'Sir?' I said,
and waited a while. God, after all the boldness that brought
me here, was I still really only a girlie peasant, sure to
tumble back into curtsy subservience as soon as I met
crisis? 'It's Helen Baring,' I explained to the shirt, armbands
and lace-ups. 'I'd just looked in to see you were all right
. . . but—'

But you're not. I left this last bit unsaid. It did not need
saying. None of it needed saying. Nobody listened. I've
always thought it symbolized everything about the modern

human state when you saw someone sitting mesmerized in front of a dead television screen, as you did occasionally. It was even worse to see someone dead sitting in front of a dead television screen. Wasn't this the ultimate in non-communication – that famed modern sickness?

Oh, God, philosophy. It can strike anywhere. I turned away from Peter Arad and at once began to climb the stairs. This time I kept going, with quite a bit of speed, but also with remarkable quietness, I thought. I was moving in to what seemed like almost complete darkness on the first floor. Only a little of the downstairs lights reached the landing and gave a bit of visibility. I kept my head up, staring towards the bedrooms and bathrooms, looking for any momentary fleck of that other light, the torch beam. But no. Conceivably someone had come down the stairs and left the house while I was in the utility room on my dim ritual, or gazing in at Arad and doing that daft, crawler's monologue. Alternatively, it would be an easy escape for anyone experienced to drop from a bedroom window into the garden.

I would have to be cagey when, finally, I told the tale of the body's discovery – if I ever did tell it. I might have to edit out the beam on the window or there would be questions from senior people about why I did not call for aid. Torch or no, they would want to know how I had come to enter the house without back-up. They would be especially enraged if it appeared we'd had a suspect on the premises who was allowed to leave. Why hadn't I whistled up the firearms people, when a firearm had been used and might still be in play?

I had another option, too – leave the body unreported. Suppose I *did* report it; I would have to explain how I came to be in the house at all. That would mean describing my secret and solo inquiries, starting from the first day and Harvane. Yes, powerful people at headquarters were sure to get ratty. If I stayed silent, the body would still be found by someone else, when Arad failed to turn up at work. But what about the blood trail? My ear still dripped.

I stepped on to the landing and did another pause there. I could make out nine doors. That would probably mean five bedrooms, a couple of bathrooms, a lavatory and perhaps an airing cupboard. Four doors were wide open, three to bedrooms, one to a bathroom. Two others stood ajar and I could not see enough to know what lay beyond them. The rest were shut. I tried to work out which room might be the one where I'd seen the torch shine. I fixed on a part-open door and stepped towards it immediately, but not the whole distance. What you do not do when entering a problem destination of this sort is to go in direct and straight, framing yourself like a free gift, especially if the only light on offer is behind you. There was a loaded pistol in this house, or had been until recently, and someone who knew how to use it, at least at short range. It could be very near me in this room. I stood with my back to the landing wall for a few seconds alongside the gap left by the open door and listened again. And then I bent low and moved very fast around the frame pillar of the door and flattened myself against the bedroom wall on the other side.

I had it right. This was the room. At once the torch shone from somewhere over near the window and held my face in its beam. The light seemed weak now. Perhaps the batteries were fading after whatever duties they had been doing here. But despite the faintness of the ray, I could not see past the glow to who directed it. I remained bent over, wanted to straighten yet found it impossible. Power had gone absent for a moment from my body. This feeble beam could make me as easy a target as if I had stood and posed in the doorway. In any case I thought that if I straightened, if I moved at all, it could look like resistance, even an attack, and the shooting would start.

A woman said: 'Who's with you?'

It was only a second before I recognized the voice. 'Iris? Iris Elgan?'

'Who else is here? There was talking downstairs.'

She had heard my respectful chit-chat to the high-rank dead. 'Other officers,' I said. 'We're going right through the house, as you'd expect. It takes a battalion.'

'I've been sitting in the dark since I heard the sounds, hoping you'd all go away, knowing you wouldn't.'

'Hardly,' I said. My mind sprinted, but mostly it concerned itself with the gun. 'You know shooting?'

'Clifford's pistol. I had it hidden when you lot arrived on the death day.'

'Hidden where?'

'Hidden. I knew how to squeeze a trigger. Arad was asleep in front of the TV. I didn't need to be a markswoman.'

'But are you?'

She was not. Some strength had returned and I began to straighten from my crouch posture against the wall. I don't know whether that did scare Iris, made her think I'd try to rush her, as I'd imagined. Or it could have been simply an accident. At any rate, the gun went off. I heard the bullet crack into the wall yards from me. Yes, the gun and the bullet sounded small, but like a real gun and a genuine bullet, just the same. Instead of straightening I went fast to the floor and lay there. That was training for a gun situation, though not this kind of gun situation, where the person firing could approach and make sure there'd been a hit, and try another shot, if necessary. Getting to ground in a rush like that, I bumped my ear and felt the blood start to run worse.

The ray of the torch swung as Mrs Elgan stood up and she walked swiftly from the other side of the room and came to look down on me under her light. 'You're hit at the side of the head,' she said. 'Same as Arad. More blood, though. You'll die. Like Arad. Your colleagues will come now, but you'll die.' It did not sound triumphant or sorry, just a statement. She was never one to signal feelings. After a few seconds she said: 'So, where are they, this battalion? They'd hear the gun. Why haven't they come running? Do you know what I think? You're here alone. Alone? You talk to yourself?'

Her voice went up a little, but still nothing extreme. I tried to guess at her thoughts. If there were no other police in the house, would she calculate she might get out and disappear? Might she do that second shot to make sure I really did die like Arad and could not talk? This was her kind of killing situation – no distance, no room for mistakes.

So, before she could decide properly whether I was badly hurt and helpless – whether I was dying – I let her know I was not. I swung my legs around hard at hers and got full, destructive contact. She yelped. The torch beam once more yawed out of control and I heard what I took to be the pistol hit the carpet a moment before she crashed down herself. I turned fast on to all fours and stretched out an arm, moving my right hand in wide, frantic arcs, feeling for the weapon. I did not find it. The torch, only just alight now, lay near, and I grabbed at that instead. It was still in her hand but I tugged it with all the ripe power of a gold medal frenzy and tore it from her. Then I used its feeble light to make the arcs I had tried with my hands and almost at once located the pistol. It looked like a 6.35 mm Baby Browning. She could see the gun herself then and reached for it, but I saw a weariness, a slowness about the movement, almost a hopelessness. Perhaps she was dazed. It sounded a heavy collapse when I knocked her legs away. Or perhaps she did not much care any longer. A fraction of her mind might believe the house full of police, despite what she had said. She would doubt she could escape.

I stood with the gun in one hand and the torch in the other. I stepped to near the door, found the switch and turned on the bedroom lights. I placed the torch on the carpet. Going to Mrs Elgan, I held out my free hand to help her get up and sit her on the side of the bed. 'Are you all right?' I asked.

'Do you understand?' she replied, and obviously assumed I did not, and would hate admitting it. She was correct. She seemed about to begin an explanation but then said: 'The bullet in your head. You'd better get help, I suppose.'

'I'm only winged.' I did not want her to think of me as the sort of blunderer who got shot; nor did I want her to feel stupid, useless with a gun. She had enough trouble and humiliation coming. Her pallor was even more striking than when I saw her last, those large eyes brimming with defeat. She wore jeans and a denim jacket over a brilliant amber T-shirt. Sometimes an attempt at casualness went wrong, made people look as if they had given up working out a mode for themselves and instead turned limply to history.

The bed was double and unmade. Two walls of the room contained built-in wardrobes. A small, pretty Edwardian dressing table had a place in the window bay and a large, old fashioned roll-top desk stood against the left wall. It was open and its writing surface covered with papers. Had she been going through that material with the torch? Near the desk, I saw a tall, straight-backed antique chair. This must be where she was sitting with the flashlight and gun when I entered the room.

'No, I don't understand,' I said. Now and then you had to admit failures.

'Who could? Why are you here – in the house?'

'I don't even understand that properly,' I replied. I could do diffidence now and then. It helped make people talk.

'I can't stand the sound of blood dripping from your head like that,' she said.

'It's ruining the carpet.' My handkerchief was sodden and could do no good. I opened a wardrobe, took a folded white shirt from one of the shelves and held it against my ear. 'You think Peter Arad killed Clifford? You've done Arad as revenge.'

'Mainly as revenge.' She gave a sniff, as if insulted. 'A business aspect, too. Revenge is – well, revenge on its own is naff, isn't it? I know he killed Clifford, killed him and the rest of it. I've known from the beginning. But we deal with these things ourselves, don't we, and play dumb till we're ready? I couldn't tell you in case you were part of it and might warn Arad I knew. Could have been dicey for me.'

'Which we?'

'You're never going to understand. You don't know the trade, do you? Cliff was more or less totally contemptible, you see.'

'But you stayed with him, grieved over him, killed for him.'

'I said more or less totally. Only that. It leaves some room for loyalty. Some room for love. If every woman left every man who's more or less contemptible there'd be no couples left. Fine points are important.'

'He was a grass?'

'Well, of course, originally. This was before me. I'd draw the line at shacking up with a grass. Probably. Then he worked with Edgar. Sometimes with Coinop.' She looked towards the door. 'So, you *are* alone. You'll win a coconut for this, won't you? As a grass, he used to whisper to Arad.'

'Yes, I supposed so.' I walked over to the desk and glanced

214

at some of the papers. They seemed to be only household bills and insurance documents.

Iris Elgan said: 'I did a search for evidence that Arad took pay from Edgar or Coinop.'

'But if it was from Edgar—'

'He'd have told me? It's not that kind of arrangement between us.'

'What kind of arrangement is it?' I asked.

'You sound damned interested.'

'My job to be interested.'

'As interested as that?' she replied. 'He *is* gorgeous, isn't he?'

'Is he? I don't think I'd noticed.'

'Not much. He's gorgeous, but he's also cagey and secretive on business things. He'd tell me only a fraction, even if concerned Cliff. But I guessed Clifford had managed to draw Arad into the business. Clifford could be smart. He was really proud of recruiting Arad. It's the kind of thing that can develop from a grassing link, isn't it?'

'Is it?'

'Oh, all the grey area realm. So easy.'

'Is it?'

'You know it is. Cops are ending up in court all the time because of that.'

'And Clifford was—'

'Clifford had to get super-clever and super-subtle, didn't he, because that's how Clifford was – what I mean, more or less contemptible, ultimately. I can tell you about it. It doesn't matter now. Anyway, I expect you've heard.'

'Cliff was go-betweening an alliance between Edgar and Coinop,' I said.

'There you are! I knew you couldn't be as blank as you pretend.'

'I have my contacts, naturally.' Thank God for Angus and his intuitions. Perhaps that's all they were, after all – good and correct but not proving any involvement. His little passion – keeping well-informed about villainy, but no part of it, like reading crime books.

Iris said: 'Clifford was supposed to fix this teaming of Edgar and Hubert, but, of course, Cliff being Cliff, he fed the details of the deal to Careful Stan, so he'd know how to smash the pair. Cliff thought there was a bigger, richer future with Stan than with those other two. He saw them as lightweights, I expect. Perhaps rightly. But also wrong. No rich future showed for him.' She paused, seemed about to weep, as she had seemed that morning when Elgan sat dead in the Citroën. Again she avoided that, though, or reserved it for when she was by herself. She would be by herself quite a bit.

'Arad found out Cliff was two-timing?'

'Arad found out and Cliff found out that he'd found out. Cliff always told me everything. Everything? A lot, at any rate. I think – well, I know Cliff threatened Arad that if he fingered him to Edgar and Coinop, he, that's Cliff, would let the world know about Arad's second job with whoever it was – Coinop, I think. Maybe Edgar. Doesn't matter. And Arad made him quiet, dead quiet, you see, then carved him up to simulate a grass's execution. Maybe Arad had some help. It would be tricky getting Cliff into the Citroën.'

'Help from Mossmont?'

'Mossmont? Why do you say that? Oh, no. From someone in a firm. I think Mossmont suspected Arad had gone over and was stalking him. The rumours said that. Mossmont's pure and a would-be purifier, to date.'

'Yes, that could be right,' I said.

'Help or not, it was Arad who actually did Cliff, no question.'

I found I believed her. Although Arad had moved up so fast, perhaps he thought it not fast enough and felt himself worth more money. You could meet such people in all jobs. He might have looked at the future as Derek Fonde looked at the future that day, and found the pension prospects unthrilling. Even a detective as bright and seemingly wholesome as Arad could get grossly compromised. And, if that happened, his apparent brightness and wholesomeness might make him more ruthless, because he had a superb image to preserve. Remember Lucifer. I thought I saw now how Arad could afford to buy out his wife during their divorce. Perhaps the divorce began from Arad's corruption. Some wives could not tolerate that, if they discovered it. Or things might have been the other way around and Arad went looking for additional money when menaced by the divorce and possible loss of his house.

Harvane could have known some of this, possibly all of this, and would have told me, had we met. Then, though, he and his friends had done a flit. He grew scared and telephoned to say I should quit. They must have feared ripples from my inquiries would find them, even in their hideaway. Somehow I felt vastly comforted that Harvane had no part in the killing – the reverse.

'Why was it so important to see Arad's papers?' I asked her. 'I mean – with the risk of staying in the house?'

'I wanted to find if they spelled out the link with Luff-Stile. Or Coinop. To see it actually in words. Or money figures. Sort of making it official.'

This I did not believe. I wondered if in fact she had planned to continue Clifford's slippery, gainful work, however contemptible she seemed to think it. Seemed, yes. She had a fat quota of ambivalence, this lady. She might have been in search of something official here, as she called it – information to convey to Careful Stan and help him in the eternal crusade for that grail, monopoly. She knew Clifford's career activities so well that she must have been deep into the business herself. But would she do that to Luff-Stile if the connection with him was more than business? Perhaps it wasn't, as she had said. I found I wanted to believe this, longed to believe it. *Cow-fool, Helen.* Nothing would ever come of that for me, would it? Would it? Hadn't I just seen one cop finished by closeness to the wrong folk, and now here I was lusting for a drink at the dregs myself? 'We ought to go,' I said.

'You're the one with the gun. Anyway, yes, before you bleed to death.' She stood up, supporting herself for a moment against the bed with the back of her legs. Then she moved away and seemed reasonably stable.

'I wondered if you knew someone called Angus Siverall,' I said.

'Who? Your contact? Who is he?'

'Well, I wasn't sure. But apparently just what he claimed to be, an inspired onlooker, someone who needed a bit of gutter to keep life meaningful.'

'They're always a nuisance. Many like that. Slumming and its gloss.'

'He didn't do the rear door, did he, before you arrived?'

'Don't you think I could manage such a pitiful little item, and quietly enough not to jar against the TV sound and wake him?'

'Yes, I suppose I do.'

We walked to my car and I took her to headquarters and said what needed to be said, but not a crumb more. Bruce Mossmont sent a party and an ambulance to Arad's house. 'I can't see how you came to be there in the first place, Helen,' he said.

'You're never going to get that out of her,' Iris Elgan replied.

'I made sure you weren't tailing me tonight,' I told Mossmont.

'You're learning fast all the time,' he replied.

'Or perish,' I said.

'My, my.'